Betrayal

Book Two of the Priestess

Melissa Sasina

BETRAYAL
Book Two of the Priestess

First Edition: September 2010 (Original title *Destiny*)
Cover Change First Edition: May 2011
Second Edition: December 2013
ISBN: 1481029673
ISBN-13: 978-1481029674

For Mike, my first test reader and editor.

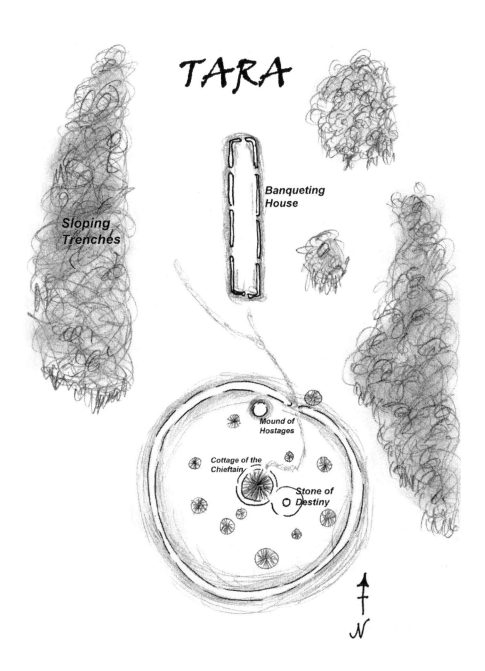

Melissa Sasina

Chapters:

Melissa Sasina

1. MESSANGER'S ARRIVAL

Réalta Dubh narrowed her eyes upon the churning sea before looking off towards where Éire lay in the distance. It had been a little over eleven years since she had last set foot upon Éire's shores. Eleven years since the death of her sister, Tríonna, to a Milidh attack. Since her youth, Réalta had foreseen the coming of the Milidh, had foreseen the bloodshed. When Ith came, praising Éire with grand words of adoration, she knew the time of those visions was drawing dangerously near. In her sister's daughter she had seen great potential, a girl who was destined to become a great High Priestess.

When the Milidh came that fateful night, attacking the village of Tara as a warning to the High Chieftains over Ith's death, Réalta took Tríonna's daughter under her guidance, bringing her to Rúnda and training her in the ways of a priestess.

The girl, Shiovra, showed great determination in her learning, her desire to protect kin and clan immense. Keeping her safely secluded on the isle of Rúnda, Réalta taught Shiovra to the best of her abilities, just as her mentor Líadán had done for her. However, in the end, it would seem that seclusion would drive a rift between them.

Réalta had not foreseen Deidre's death, could not have prevented the words that were spoken by her own son, Daire. Ceallach had warned her that Shiovra remained on Rúnda too long, yet she had not heeded his words. Perhaps if she had, Shiovra would not have left in such a manner. Perhaps she would not have turned her back on her.

Beltaine was approaching steadily and caution would need to be taken to ensure that the alliance with the Milidh clan of Dún Fiáin did not fall apart. If such was to happen, Réalta feared the worst for kin and clan. Peace between the Túath High Chieftains and the sons of Míl was becoming increasingly unstable. She could hear it in the whisper of the wind, feel it in the tremble of the earth. The threat of war loomed like a creature in the night, waiting for an opportune moment to strike.

The sound of approaching footsteps reached her ears, muffled under the noise of the restless sea which crept up the shore to lick at her feet.

"Has there been any sign of my Mother?" Réalta asked without turning.

Ceallach came to stand beside her. "No, but there are tidings about Gráinne," he replied in a low, deep voice. "Ailill has cast her aside as punishment for taking Miach's life."

"Gráinne will not take that lightly. Although she may not act straight away, she will remain a threat to us." Exhaling slowly, Réalta continued, "If her words to Shiovra in Caher Dearg were spoken true, she aims to sink her claws in Tara. Knowing Gráinne's ambitions, she will do everything within her power to achieve thus."

"From the information I have been given, Cúmhéa remains under her command," he informed her. "It is quite possible that Deasún and Árdal are as well, but that has not been confirmed yet."

Réalta nodded. "Tell Kieran to keep his ear to the wind. I want to know every move Gráinne takes before she makes it."

"Will she seek vengeance here?" questioned a younger male voice.

Réalta turned, setting her eyes upon Anlon. The young man had come to Rúnda just before the harshness of winter, seeking safe refuge from his own mother, Gráinne. Réalta understood quite well the concern that weighed heavily in his voice. "Gráinne would not be so foolish as to risk lashing out here," she assured him. "My power may be fading, but I am still strong enough to teach my sister a lesson, and she knows that well."

Anlon turned his attention across the sea before he spoke again, voice low, "What of Tara, then?"

She followed his gaze. "Gráinne lacks the ability to attack Tara as she stands now, even with the village's defenses weakened," she replied firmly, "but that does not mean Gráinne will sit idle for long. When the time comes and she makes her move, I will bring an end to her madness myself."

* ~ * ~ * ~ * ~ *

The passing of the spring equinox brought Beltaine closer and with it warmer winds. Winter had been thankfully quiet, though Mahon knew the calmness could easily be hiding a brewing storm. He did not trust the intentions of the sons of Míl in the least; and Odhrán was no exception. He was loath to accept the Milidh man's presence in the village, but tolerated it due to a promise of alliance that was made previously.

Walking along a well worn path, Mahon paused before a standing stone. Reaching a hand up, he ran his fingers across the surface of the cool rough granite. The Stone of Destiny had spoken, and for none other than one of the Milidh: Odhrán.

Mahon had long protested Odhrán's presence in the village, but his words had gone unheeded with Ainmire and Ceallach. The Milidh man had been sent to watch over and guard his sister Shiovra until the time of her union with the clan of Dún Fiáin arrived. Mahon feared, though, that Odhrán's presence within the village was far from being that simple. More than once he had seen the Milidh man's eyes carefully studying the men who protected the village.

However the Stone of Destiny had spoken for Odhrán. Mahon could not deny he was surprised. From what he had seen of him, the Milidh man was a tactical thinker and would do well to protect the village. Though, in the end, Odhrán had denied the calling of the stone after Ainmire's death and refused to lead the village. Mahon was torn between relief that Odhrán refused to become Tara's chieftain, but also troubled that in his refusal, he was burdened with the task.

Mahon was pulled from his thoughts at the long, low note of a horn across the wind. The sound of the horn was followed by a second and third. The village of Tara had company.

Turning from the Stone of Destiny, Mahon walked back along the path till the main gates of the village came into view. He remained still, watching as a man on horseback was escorted through the gathering villagers and up the hill in which he stood. Crossing his arms, Mahon waited in tense silence.

Mahon's eyes narrowed upon the man as he neared, taking in everything from his clothing to the small dagger at his waist. His suspicions were confirmed as the horse came to a pause a respectful distance away: the man was Milidh.

"Be you Lord Mahon, son of Coughlin and Tríonna, kin to the late Ainmire, and chieftain of Tara?" the man inquired.

Continuing his study him, Mahon nodded. "Aye," he replied with an even tone. "And you would be?"

The man gave a small, respectful bow. "Forgive me, Lord Mahon," he continued. "I hail from Dún Fiáin. Lord Culann and Lady Álainn send me to present a gift upon the Lady Shiovra and bid tidings to her." The man paused, his eyes looking past Mahon as he dipped into another low bow.

Glancing over his shoulder, Mahon saw Odhrán approaching from the main cottage.

Odhrán merely nodded at the man in return.

Mahon turned his attention back to the messenger. "What tidings do you bear for my sister?" he questioned firmly.

"As agreed upon, the union between the Lady Shiovra to Lord Culann's son shall commence on Beltaine," said the man. "I have come to ask the High Priestess to prepare for her return to Dún Fiáin for marriage."

* ~ * ~ * ~ * ~ *

Shiovra's hand continued to falter, the shuttle slipping from her fingers as her work on the loom was forgotten. The sound of a horn on the wind and Odhrán's sudden departure from the main cottage brought a slight feeling of unease to the priestess. Even Daire had set his work aside to stand guard in the doorway, looking out with his hand resting on the sword at his waist. Úna, round with child, looked up from her stitching to glance uncertainly at Shiovra.

"That was not a warning, was it Lady Shiovra?" Úna queried, moving closer to the priestess.

Shiovra shook her head. "Nay," she replied, glancing at Daire.

"It appears as if a messenger has arrived," informed the man from the doorway. "He is speaking with Mahon and Odhrán, but I cannot hear what they say."

Standing slowly, Shiovra approached her cousin. "From where does this messenger hail?"

Daire did not move, replying in an even tone, "I have never seen him before, but he appears to be Milidh."

Shiovra remained silent for a moment. There was no doubt in the priestess' mind that the Milidh messenger had come for her. Her marriage into the clan of Dún Fiáin was undoubtedly drawing near and her thoughts drifted to Odhrán. Shiovra had grown close to him, far closer than she knew she should have for a man who had been sent to watch over and protect her. Upon their initial meeting, she hated and distrusted him. Yet, as she came to know Odhrán better, she found a desire growing within her. She had taken him as a lover, knowing full well that should they be discovered the union of alliance between their villages would be greatly endangered.

"The messenger approaches," informed Daire, pulling Shiovra from her thoughts. He turned from the doorway and ushered her toward the center of the cottage, gesturing for her to take seat beside hearth fire before taking his place to stand beside her.

Sitting down, Shiovra smoothed her clothing and waited with her hands resting on her lap.

Mahon was the first to step into the cottage, followed by the messenger then Odhrán.

Shiovra meet Odhrán's gaze briefly before her eyes drifted over the messenger as he stepped closer, giving her a small bow of respect. He was an older man, with a thick, dark beard and shoulder-length hair adorned with several small braids. Although he had come to them as a messenger, everything about the way the man carried himself spoke that he was in truth a warrior.

"Greetings, Lady Shiovra, I am Bradan of Dún Fiáin," the man said, bowing once more.

The priestess nodded without standing. "*Céad Míle Fáilte,* a hundred thousand welcomes, Bradan of Dún Fiáin," she said kindly. "I hope that you find Tara to your liking."

"Indeed, my lady. Your village is quite beautiful," replied Bradan.

"Will you be staying long?" Shiovra questioned.

"Nay," answered the man. "I shall stay for the evening, but come dawn I must take my leave and return to Dún Fiáin."

Shiovra nodded. "Then we shall be the gracious hosts and make you feel welcome for the night."

"My thanks, Lady Shiovra." Reaching into a large pouch at his waist, Bradan pulled forth a small bundle. "I come bearing a gift from the chieftain of Dún Fiáin and his wife as well as tidings." He held his hands out and offered the bundle to the priestess.

Shiovra took the offered gift with a nod of thanks. Sitting it in her lap, she took a moment to study the soft woolen cloth before unwrapping it to reveal a finely wrought copper bowl bearing an intricate design etched inside the flawless curve.

"The emblem of the clan of Dún Fiáin," the messenger explained. "My lord and lady thought it would be nice to bestow upon you a little of themselves."

She ran her fingers along the smooth lip of the bowl, glancing up to meet his gaze. "I thank you for journeying so far to bring me such a lovely gift," the priestess told Bradan gently. "I am glad that your journey went unhindered. Traveling has become more dangerous with hosts of Fir Bolg and Misshapen Fomorii gathering. I hope that your return to Dún Fiáin continues unhindered."

"My thanks, Lady Shiovra."

"Bradan, what are the tidings in which you bear?" Shiovra asked, though she knew what his reply would be. She could feel Odhrán's eyes upon her, but did not return his gaze and held Bradan's eyes calmly. She would not allow even a trace of her feelings for the Milidh guardian to show, lest Bradan catch wind.

"Your presence is requested in Dún Fiáin," he proclaimed. "Lord Culann desires for you to wed his son on Beltaine."

"If that is his wish," Shiovra replied with a small smile. "I shall make preparations for my departure and honor the promise of union. Come

Beltaine, the clans of Dún Fiáin and Tara shall be united."

* ~ * ~ * ~ * ~ *

Gráinne lounged on a fur covered bench beside a fire, her bright red-auburn hair falling unbound over her shoulders. The neckline of her shift had slipped down, exposing the bare skin to the heat of the hearth fire. Running a finger lazily along the lip of her cup, Gráinne watched the flames dance upon the wood.

"You called for me?" questioned the man kneeling before her.

A smile crossed her lips as her cold green eyes fell upon the man. "Aye," replied Gráinne, shifting to lean toward him and run pale fingers along the old jagged scar adorning his left cheek. "You are one of my best, Cúmhéa, and if you would, I have a favor to ask of you."

"What is that which you desire, my lady?" replied Cúmhéa, turning his face into her touch.

Gráinne's smile twisted maliciously. "I want you to teach a lesson to the High Priestess of Tara." She would not allow Ailill to cast her aside and keep her from getting what she desired; what should be hers. If he interfered, she would deal with him just as she had done to her husband, Miach, with a dagger through the heart. "You have an interest in her, do you not? Such a pretty young thing she is. It would be a pity if something happened to make her *unsuitable* for marriage to the son of Dún Fiáin's chieftain."

A gin played across Cúmhéa's mouth. Catching Gráinne's hand within his own, he brought it to his lips. "I shall do as you desire with great pleasure."

* ~ * ~ * ~ * ~ *

Celebrations were held within the Banqueting Hall honoring the impending union. As chieftain, Mahon had no choice but to preside over the festivities, and so he sat at the head table, deep into a cup of mead. Earnán and Naal sat to his left, speaking to Bradan while on his right sat Shiovra, Daire, and Odhrán. Úna attended, but under the ever watchful eye of Eithne.

A man sat with a bodhrán, a small drum made with goat skin stretched across a wooden frame, bringing forth a lively beat with a double-headed tipper while another spun tales of wonder in the form of song. The people of Tara heartily enjoyed the celebration, partaking in the feast and dancing along to the music.

Shiovra sat quietly, taking slow sips of her honeyed mead as she watched the villagers enjoying themselves. Her gaze drifted to Odhrán more than once and when their eyes met, a grin would play across his lips. Even in the presence of so many, Shiovra could not keep herself from playing such a dangerous game. Several times during the winter months, she lost herself to

Odhrán more and more. As she held his gaze, she could feel heat rising treacherously in her body, aching to be enveloped by him once again.

A hand touched her shoulder.

"Lady Shiovra?"

Starting slightly, she turned to Úna. "Aye?"

"I am weary and believe I shall retire for the night," Úna said. "Could you please keep an eye on Daire for me? Do not let him have too much mead." It was subtle, but there was the slightest trace of laughter to the woman's voice.

Shiovra smiled and glanced at Daire who had gained Odhrán's attention and laughed, taking a drink of his mead. Turning back to Úna, the priestess nodded. "I shall be sure he does not make a fool of himself," she reassured her.

"I thank you, Lady Shiovra," Úna said. Turning away, she disappeared in the throng of celebrating villagers.

Taking a small sip of her mead, Shiovra kept a watchful eye on her cousin as he jested with Odhrán. Though Daire took no notice of Odhrán's occasional glance her way, she was well aware of his gaze. His eyes lingered, sending a rush of heat through her body.

The music suddenly shifted into a slower, somewhat somber song.

Daire sat his drink down and abruptly turned to her. "Come, dance with me, Shiovra," he urged suddenly.

She studied him a moment before nodding and standing.

Daire slipped an arm about Shiovra's waist and led her to where everyone danced, pulling her into the slower and fluid like dance. "Are you sure about this, cousin?" he asked quietly.

She knew the exact meaning to his words. "I will do what I must to ensure the safety of these people and my kin," she replied softly. "Ceallach and Ainmire may have seen this union as a means to gain foot in enemy territory; I see it as an opportunity to gain true peace, even if it is but one Milidh village."

Daire offered her a tight smile and stopped dancing. "Come with me," he told her, gently grabbing her hand. Guiding her outside the Banqueting House, he led her slowly toward to the hill where the village was bathed in the silvery glow of moonlight. "What of Odhrán?" he pressed. "Do you think he will pose a threat to what you intend?"

Shiovra was silent a moment. Odhrán was a man known for carefully guarding his intentions from others, making it difficult to know what he was thinking. She knew her cousin and brother did not trust him, knew that though Daire had come to understand Odhrán a bit more, he remain wary to trust him completely. Such was understandable. Shiovra had distrusted and hated him as well. Odhrán was Milidh and it was the Milidh who had attacked Tara eleven years prior. It was the Milidh who had taken her mother's life.

7

"I do not believe he will," she told him. "Though you may not always agree with his methods, he has not once betrayed this village or his words."

"You trust him?"

"Aye," replied the priestess honestly with a small nod.

Nodding, Daire stretched. "Who am I to question the decisions of my High Priestess?" he asked. Pausing, he turned his face to look up at the stars splayed across a clear night sky. "The day is growing late, you should sleep soon and I should go see to my wife." Reaching a hand up, he gave her shoulder a gentle squeeze. "Sleep well, cousin."

"Aye," She watched him as he continued along the path towards the high fort and stood unmoving for a long while, the wind gently drifting past her as it carried the sounds of merriment. Reaching a hand up, Shiovra tucked a stray lock of red-gold hair behind her ear.

"This is where you disappeared off to."

She turned at the sound of Odhrán's voice, her blue eyes meeting his green tinged brown.

He came to stand beside her, remaining silent for a while before he spoke. "A full moon approaches," he said quietly.

Shiovra nodded, stealing a glance at him from the corner of her eye. "Aye," she replied after a moment of thought.

"As does the time for you to fulfill your promise to the clan of Dún Fiáin," continued Odhrán. The wind rustled his brown hair which brushed just past his shoulders.

The priestess looked up at the star-filled sky. "The chieftain of Dún Fiáin upheld his word and sent warriors to help protect this village. It is time for me to uphold mine."

~~*~*~*

Shiovra was abruptly woken to the soft yet urgent calling of her name. With a soft moan of protest, she opened her eyes and sat up on her elbows. Once her eyes adjusted, her gaze fell upon the anxious face of Daire as he stood at the foot of her bed with the curtain pulled aside, the dim glow of a dying fire surrounding him. "What is it, Daire?" she questioned drowsily.

Daire's hand tightened on the cloth. "Shiovra..." he breathed in a hushed voice. "It is Úna...something is *wrong*. I cannot find Eithne..."

Frowning, Shiovra crawled to the foot of her bed. "I shall tend to Úna," she told him as he moved aside. Looking around the cottage quickly, she could not find the Neimidh woman. "Where is Úna?" she demanded quietly.

"In a cottage nearby," he replied. "We were trying to find Eithne, but the pain grew too great and Úna could go no further."

Grabbing her cloak, Shiovra tossed it over her shoulders. Glancing over to where Odhrán slept, she found him awake and pulling his shoes on.

"I will help Daire search for Eithne," he told her. "You tend to Úna."

Nodding, she slipped her own shoes on. "Which cottage is she in, Daire?"

"The one you used when you first returned to Tara," replied Daire.

Shiovra offered him a weary smile. "Do not fret so," she told him gently, "Focus on finding Eithne."

"Aye."

Pushing open the door, Shiovra stepped out into the darkness of early morning. The wind was strong, carrying the heavy scent of coming rain as it slammed into her. Clutching her cloak tightly closed, Shiovra ran down the path to a small cottage. She could hear Úna's pain ridden moans even before the priestess opened the door.

A small fire burned in the hearth and Úna sat on the bed, hand resting on her swollen belly. The Neimidh woman's face was pale and sweat soaked, her unbound hair matted. Her breathing was heavy and labored.

"Úna."

Úna's eyes snapped up to meet Shiovra's. "Lady Shiovra—" the woman panted before wincing and crying out in pain. "It hurts…"

Shiovra made her way to the low table and poured some water into a bowl. Grabbing the bowl and a small folded cloth, she knelt beside the anguishing woman. "Here now," Shiovra said gently, dipping the cloth into the cool water and wringing it out lightly before dabbing it across the woman's face. "What hurts exactly?"

"Here…it hurts…here…" Úna murmured through staggering breaths, motioning to her lower abdomen. "Like when…I am on my…monthly flux…only worse."

Shiovra nodded, refreshing the cloth in the water and repeating the process. "Does it hurt constantly?" she asked calmly, trying to ease the woman's worry, though she knew this pain was only the begging of what would come to be a very long morning.

Úna shook her head. "No…it comes and goes…"

"You are in labor, Úna," the priestess told her. "Your child desires to be born. What you feel is it's passage."

Úna grimaced once more under another wave of pain. "It is unbearable—"

"Nonetheless you must bear it, Úna. Such it what comes from lying with a man," Shiovra told her sternly. "The pain will pass soon enough and then you will forget all about it. You will have a new life in your arms to worry about." Shiovra reapplied the cool cloth to Úna's face.

The door opened suddenly and a disheveled Eithne rushed into the cottage, quickly joining Shiovra at Úna's side.

"She has gone into labor," Shiovra explained. "The pains come quite frequently."

Eithne nodded. "Move behind Úna and help support her," she ordered. Shiovra obeyed without question.

Grabbing the bench from beside the fire, Eithne sat at Úna's feet. Pulling off the thin blanket, she lifted the maid's shift. A frown crossed her face and she shook her head. "This may take some time…"

$$* \sim * \sim * \sim * \sim *$$

Late morning had come upon the village of Tara and neither Eithne nor Shiovra had stepped from the cottage. Úna's painful cries tore through the wicker door-lintel, sending waves of anxiousness rippling through Daire's body as he paced outside. He had never felt so helpless before and blamed himself for the pains Úna was suffering through. Daire shuddered each time Úna's screams ripped through the air. Even Odhrán, who stood leaning against the cottage with his eyes closed, flinched at the sound.

Rubbing his face, Daire cursed himself tenfold. If he had never lain with Shiovra's handmaid, he would never have placed her in such great pain. However, when the Neimidh woman had shown such great interest in him, he found he was unable to resist.

"Shiovra."

Daire came to an abrupt halt at the sound of Odhrán's voice and turned quickly to the cottage door.

Shiovra stood in the doorway, her hair, once tied back, escaped its binding and clung to her face. "The child is finally coming. Eithne can see the head," Shiovra told him, then hesitated slightly. "This birth is taking its toll upon Úna. I worry with how weak she has become."

Daire remained quiet, unsure of what to say.

Suddenly, the lusty cry of an infant filled the air; the babe had been born. Eithne's voice called out from within the cottage. "Lady Shiovra!"

Daire watched in worry as his cousin disappeared once more into the cottage. Hushed whispers reached his ears under the soft cry of the infant. Daire could do naught but listen as his child's cries were slowly quelled. More whispering followed and Daire strained to hear what was being said to no avail. Turning to Odhrán, he asked, "What do you think is happening in there?"

Odhrán remained silent.

A scream ripped through the air once more.

Without hesitation Daire made for the door, only to be restrained by Odhrán's firm hand on his shoulder. Meeting Odhrán's gaze, the Milidh man only shook his head in reply.

Úna screamed again.

Daire's entire body tensed and he clutched his hands, worrying that something had gone terribly wrong.

"Daire."

His eyes snapped to the door.

Shiovra stood in the doorway, running the back of her hand across her forehead. "You have a daughter, Daire," she announced. "The child does well." Shiovra paused as another cry from Úna tore through the air. "There is another."

For a moment, Daire found he was unable to comprehend her words. "Another...?"

"Twins," the priestess told him. "Úna bears you twins."

Daire felt as if the time had come to a crashing halt. He had prepared himself to face having one child to take care of, one small life that would depend on him, but two? His mind could hardly grasp to concept of being a father of twins.

It was not long before Eithne called out to Shiovra.

"Pardon me." Having said thus, the priestess turned and disappeared once more into the cottage, leaving him to stand outside completely and utterly dumbfounded.

"Twins..." he breathed, walking away from the cottage door. "Twins...?" Slumping down to the ground, he paid little heed to the damp, cold grass beneath him. Running a hand through his unkempt hair, Daire laughed lightly. "I was terrified at becoming the father of one child...and now I am the father of two..."

~~*~*~*

Shiovra looked down at Úna in concern. The Neimidh woman was completely exhausted and the second child's head had only begun to show; her breathing shallow, haggard, and her normally sun kissed skin even paler than the priestess'. With Úna's quickly deteriorating state, Shiovra was greatly apprehensive that the woman would not survive the morning. "I do not believe she will be able to handle much more," Shiovra breathed.

"Still she must," Eithne replied simply. "This other babe must come out soon, or Úna's life will be forfeit. The child *will* kill her if she does not deliver soon. She has already lost far too much blood." Holding Úna's legs steady, she demanded, "Push, Úna, push!"

Úna screamed in pure pain, body trembling and convulsing beneath Shiovra's steadying hands.

"Be strong, Úna, for your children," Shiovra whispered encouragingly.

The woman whimpered in response.

"You need to push harder," ordered Eithne.

Tears streaming down her face, Úna shook her head. "I...I cannot—"

"Do it!"

"But I—"

Eithne frowned, demanding in a harsh voice, "Be strong, woman, and push!"

Squeezing her eyes shut, Úna struggled to push one final time. As the child slipped from her body, she collapsed back against Shiovra, her breathing harsh.

While Eithne tended to the child, Shiovra lay Úna back on the bed. Dipping a cloth into water, she applied it to the woman's dangerously pale face. "You did well, Úna," she told her with a tight smile in a vain attempt to reassure her. "Daire will be proud. You should rest now."

"What...is my...second child?" Úna breathed in question.

"A boy," Eithne replied. "You have a girl and a boy." She smiled warmly. "What shall you call them?"

"Fíona and Bran."

* ~ * ~ * ~ * ~ *

The approach of evening covered Tara with an array of brilliant colors as Daire made his way towards the Sloping Trenches. After the birth of their children, Úna had fallen into a deep, fever induced sleep. Though Eithne reassured him that his wife would recover, he could see great concern in her eyes. Looking down at Úna's weakened state as she slept, Daire thoroughly cursed his wanton desires. Had he never taken the Neimidh woman to bed, she would have never succumbed to such pain. Running his hands through his hair, Daire swore loudly.

"Úna's fever has lowered."

Shiovra's voice startled him and Daire turned.

The priestess approached him with a cloak wrapped tightly around her shoulders. "Eithne will keep watch over her throughout the night," she continued. "The twins look healthy and are sleeping for now." Shiovra paused beside him, watching the setting sun. When she spoke again, her tone was hard, "I will be departing for Dún Fiáin come morning. If you wish to come, you must speak with Úna first. You will not leave this village if she does not wish you to do so."

He nodded. "Aye."

"Daire, I will not lie to you," Shiovra began. "Carrying your children, giving birth to them, has left Úna very weak. I do not believe she will ever completely recover."

Rubbing the back of his neck, Daire exhaled and slumped down to the ground. "Will she continue to suffer because of me?" he asked, voice tight.

"Úna will not see it as suffering. She *loves* you," the priestess told him. "The best you can do for her is not to blame yourself. By remaining strong you will lend her some of your strength."

Daire nodded.

Shiovra touched his shoulder gently. "Return to the village soon," she ordered. "You need your rest too."

"Aye."

Turning, she walked away, her footsteps muffled in the damp grass.

Daire continued to watch the sun sink lower on the horizon, slowly disappearing behind the hills. When the darkness of night began to blanket the sky, he heard rustling behind him. Glancing over his shoulder, he found Odhrán approaching.

"Shiovra said she will be leaving come morning," began Daire, looking back at the sky. "She holds a strength I will never understand. For the sake of this village and peace she will wed into a clan we have long considered an enemy, to a man she has yet to meet."

Odhrán remained silent.

"You have proven more than once that you will do anything to protect my cousin," he continued. "Though you have threatened her, challenged her, you never went back on your vow to protect her. You have risked your life, gotten wounded, all for a woman you had never met." Daire glanced up at the man. "You have gained her trust as well as my own."

"Still quite possibly a foolish choice," affirmed Odhrán with a grin twisting his lips.

Daire could not help the small chuckle that escaped him. "You have said that before," he replied, smile fading from his lips. "Tell me...after Shiovra is wed to the chieftain's son, will you still be at her side to protect her?"

"She is my priestess and I her guardian," the Milidh man told him. "That will *never* change, no matter who she is wed to."

2. DEPARTURE

Shiovra Ní Coughlin, High Priestess of Tara, was once more leaving the village she called home to journey to that of an enemy clan. Standing in the doorway of the main cottage, she looked down the hill at the rest of the village, at the people who looked to her for strength in dire times. When Tara had been attacked because of her, Shiovra had gone to the Milidh village of Dún Fiáin without hesitation to seek their aid. It was a risk she had been willing to take for the sake of protecting Tara.

Culann, chieftain of Dún Fiáin could have refused her request for aid, could have forced her to wed his son at that time in return, but he had not. Ten warriors were sent to Tara to aid in the village's defense. However Culann's words remained strong in her thoughts as if he had only just spoken them:

There will be war between the Milidh and Túath clans. There is no avoiding it. Knowing this, will you still continue with the union to my son?

Culann's words held great truth, of that there was no doubt in her mind. Though the sons of Míl maintained an air of peace with the High Chieftain's of Éire, Shiovra felt that is all that it was: an air. The peace they held was nothing more than an intricate stratagem to gain a sense of ease. Cracks had begun to form in an already unstable wall and the smallest of breezes would send it tumbling down violently. When that time came, Éire would become bathed in the blood of battle. Shiovra knew that time drew dangerously near and so she would continue to do all that she could to protect the people of Tara, even if it came to them losing their home.

The soft sound of footsteps caught Shiovra's attention. Looking up, she found Mahon walking up the path toward her, wearing the clan tartan. To see her brother wearing the clan tartan was indeed a rare occasion usually reserved for festivals and important meetings with allying villages. As for Shiovra herself, the last time she remembered wearing the clan tartan was when she was a child.

Mahon offered her a small smile and asked, "Might we speak inside?"

Shiovra nodded and followed him into the cottage.

"I know I cannot stop you from leaving," he began as he approached a small box sitting along one side of the cottage, close to his own bed. "But I can, at least, send you off properly." Reaching into the box, he pulled out a small, carefully wrapped bundle and handed it to Shiovra. "She would have wanted you to have them."

Accepting it, Shiovra moved to sit on a bench as she opened it. The outer cloth was rough and worn, but inside lay something that nearly brought the threat of tears to her eyes: a gold torc along with several bracelets, arm bands, and anklets resting upon a neatly folded tartan. "Mahon…" Her words fell short as her throat tightened.

"Wear them with pride, just as mother once did," Mahon instructed. "You are of the Túath clan, the daughter of Tríonna and Coughlin. You are a Tara's High Priestess."

Shiovra remained silent, brushing away a stray tear as it escaped to roll down her cheek.

Mahon touched her shoulder gently, leaning down. "You are the strength of this village. Be sure to show the Milidh village that," he told her with a smile. Straightening, Mahon walked to the door and paused. "I will be waiting at the main gates. Once you have finished preparing, meet me there." Having said thus, he left to the cottage.

Shiovra watched him leave, before glancing down at the gift he had given her. The woolen tartan was soft beneath her fingers. She could see that Mahon had taken great care in its safe keeping. Wrapping it back up, Shiovra walked to the table where her traveling bag lay and tucked it on top of the beautiful shift that Eithne had made her. Making sure her pack was closed securely, the priestess walked from the cottage and down the path.

Mahon did not wait at the gates alone. He was joined by Odhrán, Meara, and Eiladyr while Naal and Earnán approached, leading four steeds. Shiovra noticed that Daire was nowhere to be seen. As she neared, Odhrán stepped forward and took her pack, securing it to one of the horses.

"I am entrusting my sister's safety and life with you," Mahon told Odhrán in a firm tone. "Do I have your word that you will not fail in your duties as her guardian?"

"Aye," replied Odhrán simply as he checked the horse's reins.

"She will not be leaving without me," came Daire's voice. He was followed closely by Eithne, who appeared completely exhausted. Daire met Shiovra's gaze and offered her a tight smile. "Úna woke early this morning. She insisted that I go with you."

"I will watch over her carefully," Eithne assured the priestess. "Though she is still weary, her skin has regained color and she is eating well."

Shiovra nodded. "Please send word immediately should she fall ill once more or her weakness lingers." She ordered.

"Aye," replied Eithne.

Odhrán turned to Shiovra. "It is time to depart."

Nodding, the priestess allowed the Milidh man to assist her in mounting the horse while he himself took firm hold of the reins. Shiovra glanced at Mahon, offering him a warm smile. "Merry Part, brother."

"Merry Part, sister," he replied. "May you return safely. All of you."

Once Meara, Eiladyr, and Daire had mounted, Odhrán followed suit and climbed astride behind Shiovra.

The Priestess remained still as the man reached his arms around her and flicked the reins before giving the horse a slight kick. She could not deny the apprehensive feeling tugging at the back of her mind as the steed cantered from the village gates and turned southward.

Odhrán pressed against her back, bringing his mouth to her ear. His voice was low when he spoke, "I will never leave your side, no matter what. You are my priestess and I your guardian."

Shiovra nodded, but his gentle words did little to dismiss the malevolent whispers carried by the wind; a storm was brewing.

$$* \sim * \sim * \sim * \sim *$$

The companions continued steadily until nightfall before stopping to make camp. The breeze was gentle and warm while a bright moon hung in a clear, star filled sky. Setting camp among the trees, Eiladyr gathered wood for a small fire while Meara and Shiovra tethered the horses. Taking his bow, Daire disappeared into the trees to hunt for their meal.

"How long do you believe it will take to reach Dún Fiáin," Meara asked as she came to stand beside the priestess.

"A week if we keep at a steady pace," Odhrán said, stepping from the shadows of the trees and into the moonlight.

The Neimidh woman nodded, pulling a blanket from her pack and laying it on the soft turf. "We will not be resting at Ráth Faolchú, then?"

"The union is to take place on Beltaine. The priestess' departure from Tara was already delayed, we cannot risk delaying it any further by stopping at Ráth Faolchú," replied Odhrán bluntly as he ran his fingers along the tethers, double checking that they were secure.

Shiovra saw mild disappointment cross Meara's face, yet the woman said nothing as she continued to lay out her bedding for the night. Glancing at Odhrán, she found his eyes on her. Holding his gaze for a moment, she turned to focus on her own bedding.

It was not long before Eiladyr returned. He had not gathered much, but it would be enough to keep them warm for the night. Crouching down, Eiladyr made a small pile of dried leaves then set branches as kindling. Holding his hand out, a small flame flickered to life above his palm. Bending, Eiladyr brought his hand to his face and blew lightly on the flame. It shifted, reaching out for the dried leaves before nestling among them. Small at first, the flame grew in intensity, spreading till the leaves were consumed and the kindling burned. Grinning, Eiladyr added larger branches to the fire and continued to nurture the flames.

A branch snapped loudly as Daire returned holding a hare by the ears. "It is all I could find," he said in a despondent tone.

"It will be enough," Meara told him, taking the hare.

Shiovra sat down on her blankets and turned her back to the fire, unwilling to watch as the Neimidh woman prepared the hare for cooking. The feeling of unease continued to tug at the back of her mind.

Odhrán moved to sit beside her, propping an elbow casually on his knee.

"Culann's words were spoken true. There *will* be war between the Túath and Milidh clans. It hangs heavy in the air, the scent of a coming storm," Shiovra said after a moment of silence. She glanced over at the Milidh man as he sat beside her, looking off into the darkness of the trees surrounding them. "When the battle is upon us, what will you do?"

"Survive," he replied simply, eyes remaining on the woods.

The priestess was quiet for a long while, listening to the gentle cracking and popping of the fire as it mingled with the rustle of leaves and sweet song of crickets. "The man I am to wed," she began, breaking the silence, "can I trust his intentions? Can I trust that when blood is shed that he will not turn on me and the alliance we have forged?"

Odhrán met her gaze. "He will honor his word of alliance and protect you, just as I have." Standing, he touched her shoulder. "We still have a long way to go. You should eat and rest."

* ~ * ~ * ~ * ~ *

Ceallach Neáll rode hard, pushing his mount to the limits. However, even as he entered the boarders of Tara, he knew that he was already too late. Horns sounded on the wind as he urged his worn steed through the gates and up the hill to the main cottage. "Mahon!" he shouted, pulling his steed to a halt and quickly dismounting. "Mahon!"

Without question the guards stepped aside and allowed his passage.

Ceallach shoved the wicker-work door open as he strode into the cottage. "Mahon!"

A curtain along the far wall pushed and Mahon clambered from his bed. "What is it so early in the morning?" he asked, running a hand through his disheveled hair. When his eyes met Ceallach's, a frown crossed his face. "Ceallach?"

"Has she gone already?" asked Ceallach.

Mahon's frown deepened. "She?" he asked.

"Your sister! Where is Shiovra?!" Ceallach demanded, impatient with Mahon's response.

"Gone. She set out for Dún Fiáin yesterday morning to fulfill her promise of marriage to the chieftain's son," he replied. "Why?"

Ceallach cursed under his breath, turning away and hastening from the cottage. "I must reach the priestess' side before…" he began, voice trailing off as he climbed stride his steed once more.

Mahon grabbed hold of the horse's bridle. "What is going on, Ceallach Neáll?" he demanded. "You *will* tell me. Has Dún Fiáin betrayed us?"

"No," Ceallach replied in a hard tone. "Gráinne has made a move against Shiovra and it is of utmost importance that I reach her in time or your sister may suffer greatly at the hands of the Hound of Mide." He looked down at Mahon. "Pray to the Dagda that I reach her in time."

* ~ * ~ * ~ * ~ *

With the first graying of dawn, the campfire was snuffed and the horses prepared to continue their journey. Sleep had not come easily for the priestess, leaving her weary and sore, but she made no complaint when the time had come to move. In silence she gathered her blankets and placed them back into her pack before mounting her horse.

She rode in silence as Odhrán lead the way, reins in hand and sword at side. The Milidh man's eyes never left the trees surrounding them, constantly searching for movement. Even though the woods were quiet, Odhrán did not neglect his watch.

Her eyes drifted to the serpentine woad marking on his wrist; a symbol Milidh druids bore. Druids were the keepers of knowledge, passers of judgment, and council to the sons of Míl. Odhrán did not speak of his marking and she did not press him to tell her. However Shiovra could not help but wonder just what the Milidh man she had chosen to trust was keeping from her.

As midday approached, the silence that had settled over them was finally broken. Eiladyr began to sing, soft and hesitant, in a low tenor voice. The melody was simple, yet carried a sorrowful and lonely note to it as it mingled with the gentle rustle of leaves and cry of birds.

Shiovra watched Eiladyr as he sang, his eyes focused on the path before them. His words, though she could not understand them, flowed smoothly like a tranquil stream.

When Eiladyr finished his song, he cleared his throat and offered the priestess a small smile. "Do you remember how I said that not all my brothers were bad?" he asked abruptly in his heavily accented voice, his words spoken mellifluously. "That I had one brother who would drink with me?"

"Aye," replied Shiovra, nodding.

"I would find him sitting along the borders of our village singing that song. He said mother used to sing it us when we were very young, though I do not remember." Eiladyr laughed, rubbing the back of his neck. "He was much better at it than me."

"We should stop and rest," Odhrán interrupted, tugging at the reins and pulling Shiovra's steed to a halt. He offered his hand to Shiovra, helping her down from the horse. "I will scout the area. Eiladyr, you tend to the horses."

The man nodded, dismounting.

"I can hear a stream nearby," Meara said, pulling her water-skin from her pack. "We should replenish our water while we have the chance."

The priestess glanced at Odhrán and he nodded in turn. "I will help," she told Meara. Gathering some water-skins, Shiovra followed the Neimidh woman through the trees.

The stream was not hard to find and fairly close. If need be, they could call out and easily be heard by the others. Sunlight drifted down through the leaves, illuminating the depths of the crystalline water as it tumbled over stones smoothed by time.

Crouching down, Shiovra reached a hand out and let the cool water caress her fingers.

Meara sat on the grass beside her, laying her spear at her side. She was quiet for a long while as she filled some water-skins. "For all I have done and seen, I do not think I would have the courage to do what you are doing," she began, breaking the silence. "For the sake of alliance, for the safety of your people, you are going to wed one who has been considered a hated enemy."

Shiovra nodded. "Long have I loathed the Milidh for taking my mother from me, for killing so many in malicious retribution for Ith's death," she told the Neimidh woman. "I even detested Odhrán. He stepped unwelcomed into my life, threatened me, challenged me...yet he risked his life for me, received wounds because of me, and offered something I was wary to return: his trust." Pausing, Shiovra cupped some water in her hand and let it trickle slowly back into the stream. "Through him I have learned that not all the Milidh are the same."

The Neimidh woman was silent a moment, then asked in a low voice, "And now? Do you trust him?"

"Aye." Shiovra dipped a water-skin into the stream and filled it. "I was hesitant at first, fearful that he placed a ruse on me, but no longer."

"Odhrán is a valuable ally." Filling her last water-skin, Meara grabbed her spear and rose to her feet. "Dún Fiáin did well to send him as your guardian."

The priestess remained silent. More than once she had coupled with Odhrán, more than once she risked being discovered. Each time they coupled she put the alliance in danger. And yet, she could not turn him away and willingly fell headlong into dangerous desires.

"We should return," said Meara, eyes focused on the trees surrounding them.

Pulled from her thoughts, Shiovra secured her last water-skin and stood. When they rejoined the others, Odhrán stood waiting with two bowls in his hands.

"Eat," he told her, holding out the bowls while Daire took the water-skins. "We still have a long way to go before we make camp for the night."

* ~ * ~ * ~ * ~ *

Ceallach continued to press his steed hard. At first, the path the priestess and her guardians had taken was easy to track, but the further from Tara he rode, the harder it became to find traces of their movement. Dark clouds gathered as evening began to approach while the scent of rain hung heavily in the air. Ceallach cursed under his breath. A rainstorm would slow his progress down greatly, possibly placing even more distance between him and the priestess.

Though he did not doubt the ability of the priestess' guardians, the Hound of Mide had earned his name for a reason. Cúmhéa was the cruelest of the Huntsmen. Tracking his prey mercilessly, he would corner them and play with them before brutally taking their lives. The priestess would be no exception. Cúmhéa would hunt her, separating her from her protectors by whatever means necessary. It is what the Huntsman would do after her capture that sent Ceallach's blood boiling. Cúmhéa was a man who not only took pleasure in the hunt, but in women as well.

Hands tight on the reins of his steed, Ceallach urged the steed faster. Even as heavy grey clouds consumed the light of day and rain began to softly, slowly patter down, the Fomorii man did not falter. Pleading silently to Dana and the Dagda, great mother and father of all the Túatha Dé Danann, Ceallach pressed onward.

* ~ * ~ * ~ * ~ *

With the coming of night, rain moved in quickly, forcing the companions to seek shelter beneath a large capstone situated upon three standing stones. It was just large enough to shelter them from the immediate rainfall, but did little against what was blown in by the howling wind. A struggling fire had been built in the center of their makeshift shelter and the companions gathered around it quietly.

Shiovra sat looking into the fire, her thoughts as turbulent as the weather. She would have to handle her actions in Dún Fiáin very carefully. She could not risk what had passed between her and Odhrán coming to light. Each day brought her closer to the Milidh village and the promised union. Each day was a constant reminder that Odhrán was her guardian warrior and she his priestess. Their coupling should have never happened and Shiovra knew all too well the risk she placed on a union Tara desperately needed.

Her eyes drifted to Odhrán and she found the Milidh man watching her. When they had met, Shiovra had never imagined that she would ever trust him, let alone find that she loved him. And now, with the union approaching, she refused to give him up. Odhrán had sworn to remain at her side, sworn that she would remain his no matter what, and not once did the priestess doubt his words.

Tearing her gaze away, Shiovra rose to her feet and moved to lean against one of the standing stones. Looking out into the rain, she questioned her own decisions. She had yet to meet the son of Dún Fiáin's chieftain and even if Odhrán said the man would honor the promise of alliance, she still feared it was all nothing more than a tactical ploy. Sending warriors to help guard Tara could as well have been a ruse to further gain their trust. Regardless of what was to come, Shiovra would take any risk necessary to keep her people safe.

Sighing, the priestess took a step out into the rain and titled her head up, letting the cold liquid run down her face and wet her clothing.

"Come back, you will fall ill."

Shiovra glanced over her shoulder at Daire.

"I will be fine," she reassured her cousin, looking up at the black sky. Taking a step further into the rain, she began to walk slowly away from their meager camp. Shiovra could hear Daire's questioning voice muffled under the howl of the wind and thundering rain yet she paid him no heed as she continued to walk toward a small cluster of trees a short distance away. Once under the cover of the trees, she shivered lightly under the chill of the wind on her wet clothing. Taking a deep breath, she savored the rich, earthy smell that always came with rainfall.

The rain fell harder, sending fat drops down through the leaves above her head.

Sitting down, Shiovra pulled her knees to her chest and wrapped her arms around them. She could see the campfire flickering in the distance, but she knew they could not see her in the rain filled darkness. Resting her cheek on her knees, she closed her eyes.

She started suddenly as a pair of warm arms wrapped around her. Flinching, the priestess snapped her head up to find Odhrán.

"You should not have come alone," he told her in a firm tone.

Shiovra held his gaze for a long moment before letting her eyes drift slowly down to his lips. She remembered vividly what his kiss felt like and how much she enjoyed it. Of how his touch could be like a path of fire traced across her skin. Biting her lips, Shiovra realized her thoughts were treading on dangerous grounds.

Reaching a hand up, she ran thumb along his bottom lip, the skin wet from the rain. The heat of his hands and arms penetrated the coldness of her soaked clothing delightfully. Unconsciously, she leaned closer to him, the desire to feel the heat of his body growing. Shiovra knew she should not; knew she should have never welcomed his touch and should have pushed him away. But she had not and now her body moved of its own accord, pulling closer to his enthralling warmth.

Eyes lingering on his lips, Shiovra's hand slipped to the nape of his neck as she brought her mouth to his; hesitantly at first before quickly losing herself. Though they had coupled more than once, Odhrán had always been the one to initiate any intimacy between them, even the most chaste of kisses.

Pressing closer against him, Shiovra wrapped her arms around his neck, digging a hand deeply into his hair.

Odhrán shifted, pulling her onto his lap so that her legs straddled his.

Her heart raced. Their companions were not far off and they could easily be discovered at any moment, putting the alliance into further risk. However all worries were quickly forgotten as Odhrán's hands glided over her body, burning through the cold, wet fabric. A soft moan escaped her lips and he deepened the kiss. Her entire body reacted to his slightest of touches. Shiovra neatly gasped when Odhrán's hands found the flesh of her thighs, working up the lengths of her skirts.

His hands continued to push up under the sodden cloth, grazing across her hips, sides, and up to cup her breasts.

The contrast of cold rain and the heat of his hands sent a shiver down Shiovra's spine. Moaning softly, she titled her head back.

Odhrán brought his mouth to her neck while his hands began to kneed the tender flesh of her breasts.

Shiovra felt her body tighten in response.

"Show me more, priestess," he breathed in her ear, nipping at her ear lobe. "How much are you willing to risk?"

She could hear the need in his tone and it only fueled her own. It was a dangerous game they continued to play, but Shiovra cared less. Shifting, she roughly pushed his tunic out of the way and unlaced his breaches. Slowly easing her body onto his, Shiovra joined him in a hungry pace.

Rocking against him, she could only stifle her soft cries in his hair as she savored the wonderful sensations that flooded her body each time they coupled.

Odhrán held onto her firmly, his breathing as quick and rough as her own.

"Odhrán…" she whispered as her body became more sensitive to where they were joined.

The Milidh man tightened his hold.

"Odhrán…" repeated Shiovra.

His movements became more demanding, rougher.

The heat flooding Shiovra's body was becoming unbearable.

Odhrán's hands left paths of fire along her skin. Shifting her clothing up further, he brought his mouth to her breast.

Shiovra gasped, her body arching in response. The intensity she felt grew in enormous strength until all the priestess could do was cling to him as her body pulsed with release. Gasping for breath, she trembled and her body fell still against him.

Moving his mouth back to her neck, Odhrán's hands found her hips and eased her back into a steady pace. "More," he ordered.

Regaining control of her body, Shiovra continued rocking, meeting each demanding thrust with her own.

A grunt passed his lips and he tensed, spilling himself within her.

Shiovra remained still for a short while, her breathing and the beating of her heart calming. Reluctantly lifting her body from his, she straightened her clothing.

Odhrán caught her hand in his own, trailing his lips along her palm and wrist. "You take a great risk with me, priestess," he told her, a small smile tugging at the corners of his lips. "One I enjoy very much." Keeping hold of her hand, he stepped out from under the trees. The smile faded from his lips as he said, "We need to return to camp before suspicions grow."

* ~ * ~ * ~ * ~ *

Four days of travel had brought the companions steadily closer to Dún Fiáin, leaving but a day and a half till they reached the Milidh village. There was no hesitation when they passed the borders of Ráth Faolchú, yet the unvoiced desire to tarry there hung heavily in the air. Leaving the hidden village behind, they crossed the open meadows quietly and unhindered.

By midday, they rode once more into woods, the trees growing thicker very quickly. Clustering closer together, Daire and Meara took the lead with Shiovra and Odhrán following while Eiladyr took up the rear.

The woods were oddly quiet. There was no sweet song of birds, only the creak and moan of the trees and branches in the wind. They had not gone far in before a thick fog began to creep its way through the trees, rolling and stretching. A chill followed the fog, weaving around them as wisps reached out.

Shiovra's eyes narrowed on the shifting fog, a slight chill running through her body. She could feel eyes on her, watching, waiting. Hands tightening on the reins, she searched the shadows for any movement. Beside her, Odhrán shifted closer, his hand moving to rest on the hilt of his sword.

"I feel it as well," he said in a hushed tone, knowing well the thoughts that coursed through her mind.

The priestess glanced at Meara and Daire, noticing they continued on with ease. "What should we do?" she asked under her breath.

The Milidh man's reply was simple, "Keep moving."

Falling silent, Shiovra continued her watch on the shifting fog and shadows. She would catch a subtle movement in the corner of her eye, but it would quickly vanish. Glancing at Daire and Meara she saw that they were slowly, but surely, being consumed by the fog, though they had not gotten further away. A quick look back at Eiladyr proved the same. It would not be long before even he would vanish from her sight.

The priestess' hands tightened on the reins. She regretted not having noticed it sooner. "Fomorii..." she breathed, tone hard.

"Aye," Odhrán replied in a low voice. "They are watching us, moving closer."

"I have lost sight of Daire and Meara," whispered Shiovra.

Reaching a hand up and taking hold of the horse's bridle, Odhrán suddenly urged it to a halt.

She looked down at him in question.

Odhrán brought a finger to his lips as he looked around them, eyes narrowed on the thick milky fog churning like a wild sea all around them.

Closing her eyes, the priestess listened intently, trying to find any sounds that could betray the Fomorii's movements. At first she was met with stifling silence, but then she heard it, a faint rustle to their left. Eyes snapping open, she turned to the sound sharply, her actions immediately catching Odhrán's attention.

The Milidh man began to move, but he was not quick enough.

A spear cut through the fog like a dagger to land in the ground before the horse's hooves with a loud thud.

Frightened, the steed reared up, nearly toppling Shiovra from its back. She kept her grip tight on the reins as the horse came back down on its forelegs and began to gallop off, away from their set path. Tugging hard on the reins, she tried in vain to stop the frightened animal but to no avail. Glancing over her shoulder, she saw Odhrán running after her.

He reached out for her, voice muffled as he shouted her name. Soon the fog engulfed him as well, blocking him from her sight.

"Odhrán!" she called out. "Odhrán!"

Only the sound of silence greeted her.

Shiovra struggled to gain control over her steed.

Another spear whistled past her ear, the slight breeze it created rustling her hair.

Glancing over her shoulder she could only see the dim shadows of the trees in the ever thickening fog. Turning back forward, Shiovra only had a moment to register the low branch of a tree before it collided with her. Caught off guard, the reigns were torn from her hands and she tumbled from the steed to land roughly on the ground, the air knocked from her lungs.

Shiovra lay upon the soft turf for a moment, unable to move and struggling to gain a full breath. She sat up painfully, every part of her body throbbing and aching. Looking around, she found she was alone and fear crept its way through her body.

The priestess tried to stand, muffling a cry of pain as it laced from her ankle and up her leg. Upon closer inspection, she found a small bruise already forming, but nothing appeared to be broken, only sprained. Rising unsteadily to her feet, she placed as most of her weight on her uninjured ankle.

"Odhrán!" she called out, hoping that the Milidh man would be able to hear her voice.

Deafening silence surrounded her. Even the sound of the steed's hooves upon the ground had already faded away.

But she was not alone.

Before her a shadow moved within the fog, slowly moving closer.

"We meet once more, High Priestess of Tara."

3. MERCILESS ENCOUNTERS

Daire's concerns began with the fog. Something about it troubled him immensely. He had noticed, upon looking behind himself, that it was becoming much harder to keep an eye on the rest of their party. Pulling his steed to a halt, he and Meara waited for the others to catch up. And when Eiladyr, who had taken the rear, reached them, alone, Daire's fears were confirmed.

"They were between us, how could they have simply vanished?" muttered Eiladyr, rubbing the back of his neck as he looked at the trees surrounding them.

The dense fog, which had once flooded the woods, was creeping away, receding back the way in which it had come. They were left with calm, sunny woods full of life.

Daire's eyes narrowed darkly on the fog as it moved away. Cursing lividly under his breath, he dismounted and began to string his bow. "I am a fool," he muttered as he secured both ends before grabbing his quiver and tossing it over his shoulder. "We need to find them."

"What is it?" asked Meara, a frown crossing her face.

"Fomorii," he replied shortly as he began to walk back toward the fog. Daire cursed himself thoroughly; he should have known. Fomorii blood ran in his veins and as soon as the fog appeared and the chill crept into his body, he should have shouted warning. Perhaps if he had, Shiovra and Odhrán would not have been separated.

Meara's restraining hand on his arm brought pause to his step. "Daire, wait," she ordered. "We need to think this through. To jump headlong into a Fomorii trap without a plan would be pure folly. We need to figure out how we are going to track them without losing each other in the process. There is no way of knowing how many Fomorii await us in that fog. We need a strategy first."

"Aye, Meara speaks true," Eiladyr said in agreement. "I want find them as much as you, but we cannot simply walk in there without a battle plan."

Exhaling in frustration, Daire nodded.

* ~ * ~ * ~ * ~ *

Shiovra recognized the voice far too well and anger swelled within her. Taking a step back, she winced in pain as she was reminded of her injury. Her eyes did not move from the shadow lingering in the fog ahead of her. Hands tightening on her skirts, Shiovra focused on gathering the energy around her, cursing the Fomorii fog for interfering with her abilities as a priestess. Unable to draw power from the land around her, she would not only have to face the Hound of Mide alone and weaponless, but defenseless as well.

The rolling murkiness of the fog began to part, slowly allowing passage to the shadowed figure. As it neared, it began to take shape until a man emerged.

"What a pleasure to meet again, my beautiful High Priestess," he continued, a wicked grin twisting his lips.

The huntsman was just as she remembered him with a shaggy wolf-gray hair, shifting gold-brown eyes, and a crude scar running along his left cheek. It had been only a year prior that the priestess had fallen into Cúmhéa's clutches as he took her as a prisoner to Méav. In spite of the destruction reeked upon Caher Dearg, Cúmhéa had managed to survive.

She watched him carefully as he drew closer, not daring to look away, yet what she saw in his cold eyes and the thoughts lurking behind them disturbed her greatly.

Cúmhéa continued to advance towards her. "You have caused me much trouble, priestess, you and that Milidh cur of a guardian," he said in a low, dangerous voice. "Gráinne has graciously requested me to teach you a lesson. One that I will take a great amount of *pleasure* in giving."

Disgust filled Shiovra as she could see lust burning in his eyes.

"What do you say, priestess?" pressed Cúmhéa, licking his lips. "Care to have a taste of the Hound of Mide?"

She moved hastily to run past him, but the huntsman was quicker, sidestepping to block her path.

"There will be no chase, priestess. I no longer wish to hunt my prey when I already have you in my teeth," he growled, reaching for her.

"Keep your filthy hands off me," Shiovra snapped in return as she hastily took several painful steps back.

The wicked grin spread wider across Cúmhéa's face.

She knew she needed to get away, to place some distance between her and Cúmhéa, but with her ankle injured as it was she knew chances of escape were slim. True fear began to work its way through her body. "Dana help me…" she whispered under her breath.

He laughed maliciously as he crept closer. "Your plea falls on deaf ears, priestess," chuckled Cúmhéa. "The Túatha Dé Danann cower in Brú na Bóinne with their tails between their legs fearing a dagger in the back from Milidh curs." His eyes drifted across her body. "While we, the rest of the Túath blood, are forced to deal with the Milidh alone."

Shiovra clenched her fists tightly, her nails biting into the tender skin of her palms. Taking a few more steps back she found she had backed herself up against a tree. Her breathing was rough and her heart pounded in her chest.

He stopped before her, leaving hardly a breaths space between them as he brought his hand up slowly.

Shiovra refused to look away, a shudder running through her body as his rough fingers touched her cheek and slowly slid down her neck.

"I will have you," he breathed heatedly, tearing the neckline of her shift to reveal the soft swell of her breasts. Cúmhéa leaned forward, bringing his mouth to her ear. "I will taste every bit of you…"

Her fist snapped up to strike him hard in the lower abdomen. As he doubled over from the strike, reaching for her once more, she hastily ducked out of his grasp. "I said keep your filthy hands off me!" hissed Shiovra.

Cúmhéa leaned against the tree for a moment, his laughter growing stronger. "You will not deny me pleasure, wench!" he growled. Straightening, he turned and began to walk menacingly towards her. "You will give yourself to me even if I have to force you!"

* ~ * ~ * ~ * ~ *

Odhrán ducked behind a tree as an arrow cut through the fog, narrowly missing his head. It was quickly followed by three others which thudded against the trunk, followed by silence. Pressing against the tree, Odhrán pulled his sword from the scabbard and waited. All around him, the fog remained ever shifting, creating shadows everywhere; however he would not let that keep him from finding his priestess. It was time for the hunters to become the hunted.

An arrow cut through the fog to his left.

Odhrán decided his first target. Leaving his cover, he moved swiftly from one tree to another, keeping each footfall as quiet as possible. A shadow began to take shape in the murkiness as Odhrán neared his prey. Slowing his pace, he made a wide arch before drawing closer and coming up behind a Fomorii with a bow.

He had seen the creatures known as Fomorii more than once and the one before him was no exception. Its flesh bore a sickly undertone and was flecked with scales. Thin scraggly, hair covered its head. Webbed hands with sharp claws held the bow with an arrow drawn and ready.

Odhrán only paused a moment to be sure the creature had not noticed his presence. Bringing his sword up, he quickly thrust it into the Fomorii's back. His attack was followed by a nauseating sound. Pulling his sword out, he twisted his arm to strike the creature in the head with the pommel.

The Fomorii fell unconscious to the ground, a pool of blue tinged blood forming beneath it.

Bending down, Odhrán took the bow and slung the quiver over his shoulder before turning to find his next prey. Keeping to the same tactics, he made his way through the fog quietly, ducking behind trees as he scouted the area.

Hushed voices reached his ears.

Following them, Odhrán pulled a dagger from his belt and slowly moved closer till two figures began to take shape. In one swift movement be brought his hand up and let the dagger fly before ducking quickly behind a tree for cover.

A strangled cry filled the air, followed by a thud.

Odhrán held his place and waited.

Not long after an arrow struck the tree.

Odhrán moved in swiftly upon the Fomorii archer.

The creature dropped its bow with a hiss and drew a blade, standing ready for the impending attack.

Odhrán moved swiftly, bringing his sword up to meet the creature's. Letting his blade slide along the Fomorii's, he quickly brought it back in.

Hissing in an indiscernible language, the Fomorii lunged in its next attack.

Odhrán easily dodged, stepping aside.

Growling in irritation, the creature lunged once more at the Milidh man, shifting its stance swiftly.

Odhrán stepped to the right, but not quickly enough as the sword caught him painfully on the side. Cursing, he brought his blade up high in a side swipe, bluntly hitting the Fomorii on the side of the head with the flat of his blade, a resounding crack filling the air.

Blood trickled down the side of the creature's head where the blade nicked the skin. Dazed from the attack, the Fomorii cried out in rage and raised its blade, blindly attacking where Odhrán had been standing.

Waiting for the creature to stumble past, the Milidh man brought his sword down, thrusting it through the creature's back and piercing the heart.

The Fomorii fell suddenly limp, the blade falling from its hand as it crumpled to the ground without a sound.

Odhrán stood still a moment, his breath coming hard. The wound at his side protested greatly and blood began to stain his tunic. He knew it needed to tend to, but locating the priestess came first.

Cleaning his sword off on his cloak, Odhrán grabbed the discarded bow and cut the string. Should there be more lurking in the fog, he did not want another weapon used against him. Straightening, he walked over to the Fomorii he felled with his dagger and retrieved it from the creature's throat. Cleaning it on his cloak, he returned it to his belt. Once more, Odhrán cut the Fomorii's bowstring. Gathering a few more arrows for his quiver, Odhrán took a moment to catch his breath.

The priestess could not have gotten far. And though the fog was meant to separate them, it would not keep him from retrieving what was his. Tearing a strip of cloth from his cloak, he took a brief pause to wrap it around his wound before stepping once more into the thick, rolling fog.

* ~ * ~ * ~ * ~ *

Thrice over Daire entered the fog only to find he was back where he started. Taking his frustration out a nearby tree, he cursed loudly. In spite of the Fomorii blood flowing in his veins, in spite of his abilities as the guardian of air, Daire could do nothing to dissipate the fog. Running his hands through his hair, he felt useless. His cousin, his *priestess*, was missing and he could do nothing.

"I do not understand…" muttered Eiladyr, rubbing the back of his neck as he glared at the thick murkiness. "Each time we enter the fog, we get turned around and end up back here. It does not make sense."

"Fomorii fog is meant to keep us out," Daire told him.

"What are we supposed to do then?" demanded Eiladyr. "How can we find them if we cannot even get anywhere but here?!"

"Is there not anything we, as guardians, can do?" asked Meara, her voice calmer than the man's.

Daire shook his head. "Our power is useless on Fomorii tricks," he said bitterly. "No matter what we try, it will be futile against this fog. We cannot know what is going on in there, but there is no doubt in my mind that whoever is in there, whoever is doing this, they are after Shiovra."

"Daire," Meara hissed in a hushed tone.

Glancing at the Neimidh woman, he saw her bring a finger to her lips. Frowning, he looked at the trees surrounding them and listened.

The sound of hoof beats reached his ears, faint but quickly growing in intensity.

Grabbing his bow, Daire reached back and grabbed an arrow, holding it

30

ready. Beside him Meara and Eiladyr stood ready with their own weapons, ready for whatever came at then.

They did not wait long before a man on horseback came riding up to them, his pale white hair and ice-blue eyes standing out against the dark color of his cloak and steed.

Daire lowered his bow as his eyes fell upon his father.

Ceallach Neáll pulled his steed to a halt. Looking at each of the companions, his eyes narrowed upon his Daire. "Where are they?" he demanded. "Where are Shiovra and Odhrán?"

"In there," replied Daire shortly, gesturing to the fog. "We have tried going after them several times, but no matter what we end up back here. We are useless against this Fomorii trick."

Ceallach studied the fog with an impassive face. "The three of you remain here," he ordered. "I am going after them. Such tricks cannot stop me when I am Fomorii myself." He glanced at Daire. "Though you are only half my blood, with some training, you can manipulate it as well. For now, I must reach the priestess. The Hound of Mide lurks in these woods." Turning towards the fog, Ceallach urged his horse forward.

Daire cursed under his breath. Cúmhéa was the worst of the huntsmen; dangerous, malicious, and relentless. Daire could only hope that Odhrán had not gotten separated from Shiovra as well. "And what should we do?" he shouted after his father. "Just sit idle twiddling our thumbs?!"

The Fomorii man paused for a moment, glancing at him over his shoulder. "Wait here. I *will* find them and return."

Daire could only stand watch as the fog quickly consumed his father. When a hand came to rest gently on his shoulder, her looked over to see Meara.

"He will find them, we have to believe he will," she told him gently. "Let us make camp and wait."

Fists tight, Daire nodded.

* ~ * ~ * ~ * ~ *

Shiovra hastily backed away from Cúmhéa, her ankle throbbing painfully in protest to each step she took. Stumbling over a root, she fell back against a tree. Panic rushed through her as Cúmhéa quickly closed the distance between them.

"That was very foolish of you, priestess," growled the man. His eyes grazed over her chest, bringing his hand up to hook a finger where he had torn the neckline of her shift. "I was going to be *gentle* with you, but no more." Cúmhéa chuckled lightly as he tugged down, ripping the fabric further. "Now you will *suffer*." He crushed his body violently against her own as he ran his hands along her sides.

Shiovra flinched, her breathing rough. The feeling of his body pressed intimately against hers filled her with utter revulsion. "Get off me..." she breathed, turning her head away quickly when he brought his face close to her own. Though fear gripped her, anger boiled within her and threatened to break free.

Laughter swelled from the man. "What was that?" he asked, tone amused.

"I said get off me!" she shouted, bringing her hands up and, in a surge of strength, pushed as hard as she could. As the man stumbled back, Shiovra brought her foot up and kicked him.

Falling to the ground, the smile faded from Cúmhéa's lips. Furry burned wild in his eyes and he growled like a wolf. "You little wench!" Cúmhéa spat in rage, slowly climbing back to his feet. He made to charge at her, before howling in pain as an arrow whistled through the air and embedded into his leg. The priestess momentarily forgotten, Cúmhéa spun to face the attacker.

From the depths of the fog filled shadows emerged a man with a bow. He walked slowly towards them, pulling another arrow from his quiver and knocking it ready.

Clutching her shift closed where it was torn, Shiovra watched the man approaching as carefully as Cúmhéa. His dark auburn hair reached to his shoulders and had been pulled back for the most part. However it was his features that brought a frown to the priestess' brow. The man's resemblance to Eiladyr was so strong there was no doubt in Shiovra's mind that they were kin.

"Sod off, Morgan," snarled Cúmhéa.

"I will not allow you to force yourself on this woman," the man countered, voice heavily accented.

Cúmhéa took a step forward. "I have my orders," he said darkly. "The priestess is *my* prey to deal with."

Morgan shifted his footing and aimed the arrow for Cúmhéa's uninjured leg. "How unfortunate for you that Gráinne has fallen from command," said Morgan with an undertone of amusement. "I will not allow you to taint the priestess nor take her life. Ailill demands the priestess alive and alive she shall be."

"She is *my* prey!" Cúmhéa growled, taking another staggering step forward.

Morgan quickly lowered the bow and released the arrow to embed deeply in the ground at Cúmhéa's feet. Just as swiftly, he readied another arrow and took aim for the huntsman's heart, "Another step and it will be your life," he warned. "Go, flee to Gráinne. Tell her that should she seek to take this woman's life again, she will have to deal with *me*."

Growling in frustration, Cúmhéa ripped the arrow from his leg and tossed it at Morgan's feet before turning and running off.

Shiovra looked at Morgan for a moment before taking a cautious step away from the tree. His eyes snapped to her immediately and she froze. The man may have saved her, but by his own words he served Ailill, a man who wanted her captured to further gain his own power. "Will you be taking me to Caillte, then?"

He was silent for a moment and then said, "No."

An odd mixture of surprise and confusion filled the priestess.

"My orders are to watch you, to study you," Morgan told her matter-of-factly, returning his arrow to the quiver. "Until I receive orders for your capture, you will not be my captive." Setting his quiver and bow aside, he began to remove his outer tunic. "Here," he said, handing it to her.

Shiovra watched him with a cautious gaze, unmoving.

"To cover yourself."

Hesitantly, she took the tunic.

Returning his quiver to his shoulder, Morgan picked up his bow. "Do not misunderstand me, priestess," he said with a mischievous grin. "I have my orders, but if we meet again, I will take you to Caillte." Turning, Morgan walked away, disappearing into the thinning fog.

Shiovra looked down at the tunic, then at her own ruined shift. Cúmhéa had torn it quite severely, revealing her breasts. Cursing the huntsman, she pulled Morgan's tunic over her head. Looking around at the woods surrounding her, she realized that she didn't know which direction she had come from. Biting her lip, Shiovra limped from tree to tree, using them for support.

She had not gone far before she heard the soft gurgling of water nearby. Following the sound, she found her steed standing docilely beside a small stream. Shiovra reached her hand out and gave the horse a pat on the neck, before checking it over for any possible injuries. With her steed she would be able to find her companions with much greater ease.

Keeling down beside the stream, Shiovra dipped her hands into the cool water, washing them off before cupping some to drink. She did not take her eyes off the woods surrounding her, wary of another possible attack. Though the man named Morgan had stopped Cúmhéa, she was most certain he continued to linger nearby.

A branch snapped to her right, quickly followed by another.

Lurching to her feet, Shiovra spun toward the sound.

Odhrán leaned against a tree, bloodied hand holding his side. His tunic was stained crimson, as was the makeshift bandage circling him. "Shiovra…" he breathed before collapsing to the ground, dropping an oddly crafted bow and quiver in the process.

"Odhrán!" she cried out, limping over to him. Searching the man over carefully, she was relieved to find he still breathed, though his wound looked angry. She needed to clean and dress the wound lest it become worse. He had already lost too much blood. Tearing strips from the lengths of her shift, she returned to the stream. Wetting a few, she hurried back to Odhrán's side and pulled him up into a sitting position with great difficulty, removing his tunic. Carefully cleaning the wound, Shiovra took note of how deep the injury was and cursed not having the proper herbs to treat it with. Grabbing dry strips, she bound the wound tightly.

The Milidh man only groaned softly in response.

Shiovra paused, her eyes drifting to the blue woad marking covering the entirety of his back. She had seen it before, the twin winged serpents intricately intertwined, each consuming the tail of the other. Reaching a hand out, she traced a line with her finger. Shiovra had only seen the marking one other time, even though they had coupled more than once. It was as beautiful as it was fearsome.

Odhrán's soft groan drew her from her thoughts.

Pulling her hand away, she lowered him onto his back as gently as she possible. Taking his blood stained tunic, Shiovra returned to the stream and cleaned it the best she could, removing most of the blood. Wringing it out, she stood and draped it over a tree branch to dry. Turning to her horse, the priestess pulled out the betrothal gift she had received and unwrapped it, filling it with water.

Looking down at the rippling water, a frown crossed her brow as her eyes were drawn to the intricate design etched inside. She had not looked at it too closely when Bradan presented it to her. The pattern twisted and knotted, yet it was what lay in the center of it all that caught her attention: twin winged serpents matching the ones on Odhrán's back.

The emblem of the clan of Dún Fiáin. My lord and lady thought it would be nice to bestow upon you a little of themselves.

Shiovra's hands tightened on the copper bowl as her eyes turned to Odhrán. He had been sent to Tara to guard and protect her, to prove not all Milidh were deceitful. To show that some could be *trusted*. He had become a trusted companion and dutiful protector, risking his life more than once for her. He had awakened dangerous feelings within her and she had given him her heart and body, despite the threat it brought to the alliance. And now she did not even know who he really was. Mixed feelings of uncertainty, betrayal, and anger twisted within her.

Walking to Odhrán's side, she looked down at the man as he lay with his eyes closed. Despite how she felt, he would need further tending to. His face was slightly flushed with a fever and his skin clammy. Kneeling beside him, She tore another strip from her shift and wet it in the bowl, cleaning the dirt and sweat from his face.

The sound of hoof beats reached Shiovra's ears, heavy and quickly growing closer.

Grabbing the bow and quiver, the priestess twisted to face the steed's approach. Testing the string, she grabbed and arrow and pulled it ready. Without knowing if it was enemy or ally who approached and with Odhrán unconscious she would need to act quickly.

The horse burst through the thicket, rearing up as it was pulled to a halt arms length away.

Looking up at the rider she was met with Ceallach Neáll's pale blue eyes. Shiovra breathed a sigh of relief as she lowered the bow. "Ceallach…"

The Fomorii man leap to the ground and crouched down before her, taking her chin in his hand and turning her face from side to side. Dropping his hand, he continued to look her over as if to reassure himself that she was alive and well. "You are uninjured."

"For the most part," Shiovra replied, gesturing to her swollen ankle. "Cúmhéa is a bit worse off." Setting the bow down, her eyes drifted to Odhrán. "Odhrán has been greatly injured. I tended to the wound the best I could, but he grows worse."

Standing, Ceallach dug through his packs, pulling out a small clay jar and fresh bandages, handing them to Shiovra. "Réalta made this," he told her. "It is not much, but it will help until we reach Dún Fiáin."

Discarding the makeshift bandage, Shiovra cleaned the wound once more. Removing the leather tie holding the cap on the clay jar, she dipped her fingers into the salve and applied it as gently as possible to the wound. His skin burned beneath her touch, and it troubled her. Shiovra's eyes never left Odhrán's face as she continued her ministrations.

Though he had challenged her, threatened her, he had never given her a substantial reason not to trust him. That was until she had seen the marking on his back and the engraving in the bowl, leaving Shiovra with one important question she had a feeling she already knew the answer to. After what his clan had done to her village, her *mother*, she had never expected to trust one of the Milidh. Time and time again Odhrán had proven himself a loyal guardian and strong protector, not only of herself, but of kin and village. He had gained her trust, however now she feared the possibility of it all having been nothing more than an intricate tactical ploy.

"Shiovra."

Shiovra continued to rub salve onto the wound, only faintly registering Ceallach's calling of her name. When the Fomorii man's hand came to rest gently on her own, stilling her ministrations, she started and looked over at him.

"Troubled thoughts have lead to rough treatment," he told her quietly, nodding his head to the wound before removing his hand.

The priestess looked down, hastily pulling her hand away. Lost in her own troubled thoughts, she had angered the wound further.

"If you would like to speak of what troubles you, we can," Ceallach said, "but first we must bind the wound. I will hold him steady while you bind it."

Shiovra nodded silently.

Ceallach pulled Odhrán up, holding him still so that she could wrap the bandages around the man, tightly binding the wound. "Where is his tunic?" asked Ceallach.

Standing, the priestess retrieved the shirt. It had not had much time to dry, but it was better than wearing one covered in blood and dirt. Handing it to Ceallach, she watched as the Fomorii man carefully put it on Odhrán, avoiding the wound with ease.

"We need to get him on the horse," ordered Ceallach, slinging one of Odhrán's arms over his shoulder and standing with a grunt. "The others are waiting for us."

Quickly moving to Odhrán's other side, she grabbed the unconscious man's arm and helped Ceallach carry him to the horse. After minor difficulty, they managed to hoist Odhrán onto her horse, securing him with leather thongs.

Grabbing the reins of both horses, Ceallach gestured for her to walk with him. "Was it Cúmhéa who wounded Odhrán so?" he asked after a prolonged silence.

Shiovra shook her head. "No," she replied softly. "He was greatly injured when he found me. Cúmhéa was already gone."

Ceallach was silent for a moment. "Then Cúmhéa did come for you?"

"Aye." A shudder crept through her spine at the mere memory. "He would have…he—" Shiovra felt her throat tighten. "I hurt my ankle falling from the horse and Cúmhéa found me. He tried to—force himself on me—and injured as I was, unable to use my power with the Fomorii fog, he would have succeeded too." She took a deep breath, calming herself. "Had it not been for a man called Morgan, Cúmhéa would have gotten his dark lustful desires."

"Morgan?" murmured the Fomorii man in thought. "I do not know that name. Did he say anything to you?"

Shiovra nodded, relating all that Morgan had said and done. When she finished, she glanced at Ceallach.

A dark frown was written clearly across the man's normally stoical face. "Caillte…"

～～*～*～*

Daire paced beside the fire, bow in hand. He had finally relented and set up camp as nightfall approached, nevertheless it did little to diminish the restless feeling pulling at him. Ceallach had ordered them to remain there, but when the fog had lifted and his father had yet to return, Daire found he could not simply sit back and wait. Even the serene sounds of the woods at night could not calm his worries.

"He has been gone too long," muttered Eiladyr from his left. "That Fomorii fog…we have no way of knowing what lurked within, of how many misshapen Fomorii crept through the blinding murkiness. There is no doubt this was a trap and our priestess was the prey. And now she has been taken from us and we are supposed to just sit here and wait?" The man stood and kicked at the fire, sending flames reaching high briefly under the swell of his power and anger. "She could be hurt or captured! And what of Odhrán? He went missing too! We need to go search for them!"

"Eiladyr speaks true," Meara's calm voice reached Daire's ears.

He glanced at the Neimidh woman as she stood with the horses. "No," Daire said after momentary hesitation. "While I agree that we should search for them, we need to remain here. I have to trust that my father will find them…"

Eiladyr sat down heavily without further protest, grumbling under his breath in a language Daire could not understand.

Silence settled once more over their camp, leaving only the gentle sound of crickets and night birds.

The wind shifted through the trees, whispering softly.

Daire paused, looking carefully at the trees surrounding him. He was nearly certain he heard hushed voices.

A branch cracked behind him.

Spinning, Daire quickly strung his bow and grabbed an arrow from his quiver. His actions drew the attention of Eiladyr and Meara, who in turn took hold of their own weapons. Readying an arrow, Daire narrowed his eyes on the trees, waiting.

Another crack of a branch and the snort of a horse reached his ears before Ceallach and Shiovra emerged from the shadows and into the fire light, followed by their steeds.

Daire had never been so relieved to see his father, however his elation was quickly replaced with concern as he discovered Odhrán draped over Shiovra's steed, heavily injured. Rushing to the horse, he helped Ceallach and Eiladyr untie the Milidh man and lay him down carefully onto the ground.

"What happened?" demanded Daire, looking at Shiovra.

"We were separated from each other and attacked," Shiovra replied, glancing at Odhrán. "I do not know what happened to him exactly. He had already been greatly wounded when he found me."

"What about you?" he pressed.

The priestess limped over to a fallen tree and sat down. "I was attacked by Cúmhéa," she continued, voice heavy with weariness.

Daire listened carefully as his cousin related her tale, from falling off her horse and injuring her ankle, to Cúmhéa's attack and Morgan's appearance, and finally Ceallach finding them.

Crouching down in front of Shiovra, Daire caught her foot in his hand.

He gently poked and prodded at it. Aside from some minor swelling, nothing appeared to be broken. Exhaling with relief, he met Shiovra's eyes and offered her a small smile. "I am glad you did not suffer further," he said.

Eiladyr moved to sit beside the priestess and she turned to face him. "That man Caillte sent to watch you, the one who saved you from Cúmhéa…what did you say his name was?" he questioned.

Daire noticed tightness to Eiladyr's voice and it did not sit well with him. The man who had saved Shiovra, the man who had been sent to watch and study her, was someone that Eiladyr knew.

"Morgan," replied Shiovra.

Mixed emotions crossed Eiladyr's face as he looked away.

Daire's eyes narrowed on him. "You *know* who his is," he said accusingly.

"I do not know for sure…" the man replied.

"Who is Morgan?" demanded Daire.

Eiladyr did not move, looking intently into the fire. When he spoke, his voice was low, "One of my brothers."

4. HIDDEN TRUTH

Shiovra woke to sunlight shifting through the leaves to warm her face. Reluctantly sitting up, she looked around their meager camp. The fire had long burned down, leaving but a few embers faintly glowing in the ash. She found Ceallach walking around their camp, deep in thought. Eiladyr snored softly, his face close to Daire's ear as he lay half out of his bedding. Meara lay curled up near the fire, head buried under her cloak.

Crawling to where Odhrán rested, she reached a hand out and hesitated. If all he had done, all he had said, had indeed been a tactic from the beginning, then she had sorely misplaced her trust. Even so, he had gotten injured once more because of her and at least deserved proper care in return. Touching his forehead with the back of her hand, she was relieved to find the skin cool. Lifting the hem of his tunic, she gently pulled aside the bandage to look at the wound. The redness had faded, but it would take time before it healed completely.

Pulling away, she stood and cleaned up her blankets, shaking away dirt and leaves before folding them and placing them in her pack. Shiovra glanced at Ceallach and found him inspecting the bow and arrows that Odhrán had with him when he found her.

"These are Fomorii make," he told her as she approached, running his fingers along the curve of the bow. "I would not doubt that his wound was from a Fomorii weapon as well." Ceallach sat the bow down and turned to the priestess. "From the thickness of the fog, there had to be at least two of

39

them in the woods."

"I took out three."

Shiovra turned at Odhrán's voice.

The Milidh man stood slowly, grimacing as he straightened. "One managed to catch me with a sword," continued Odhrán, placing his hand across the wound. He looked at Shiovra. "Were you injured?"

She stiffened under the intensity of his gaze. "I am fine."

Odhrán's eyes drifted over her body, finally resting on her feet. "Your ankle begs to differ," he said.

Shiovra did not reply, her hands tightening on the folds of her skirts.

"You are angry with me," Odhrán stated bluntly.

"Aye."

"Then we shall speak of it," he told her.

"Aye, that we shall," agreed Shiovra, turning and walking deeper into the trees. She knew he followed without looking, his footsteps light on the ground behind her. The priestess did not go far from camp, just enough that she was sure their conversation would not be overheard by prying ears. Stopping, she spun to face him. "Who are you?" she demanded, voice hard.

After a moment of silence, he replied, "Your guardian, Odhrán."

Shiovra crossed her arms. "Do not jest with me," she warned. "The marking on your back is the same as the one for the clan of Dún Fiáin. Who are you?"

Odhrán's face was impassive. "It would seem to me you already know the answer to that."

"I want to hear it from your mouth," she said firmly, her eyes narrowing on him.

Odhrán exhaled irritably. "I am Odhrán, son of Culann, chieftain of Dún Fiáin," he told her. "I did not lie, though, when I said I came to Tara to serve as your guardian."

"However, you did not tell me *who* you were," she countered, her anger mounting. "You allowed me to grow close to you, to struggle against burning feelings I should not have for my guardian, to feel guilty for bringing danger to the alliance each time we coupled." Shiovra took a step toward him, followed by another. "You said you wanted to prove that not all Milidh were deceitful, that some could be trusted, and yet you were never honest with me with who you were."

He moved quickly, grabbing her by the arm and pushing her against a tree. "Aye, I did not tell you who I was," he replied, voice dangerously low as he leaned toward her. "But it does not change the truth that I love you and want you as my wife."

Shiovra flinched when he brought his hand up to touch her cheek, his thumb caressing the skin of her bottom lip.

"Would you have preferred that I had never come to Tara?" Odhrán pressed. "That I had left you to marry me without having ever known the kind of man I am? I kept silent about who I was so that you would be more at ease when the time came for our marriage, so you would not be as apprehensive." He slid his hand into her hair, his thumb continuing its ministrations on the back of her neck.

His closeness, his touch, brought a surge of warmth in Shiovra. She cursed her body thoroughly for reacting. Leaning back against the tree, she watched his face carefully, her breath quickening.

"You said once I bear the mark of a druid and your words were spoken true. I did serve as council to the sons of Míl, but I only did thus for the sake of my village," he continued, "just as you were prepared to wed the enemy for the sake of your people. The sons of Míl seek retribution from the Túath High Chieftains for Ith's death. While I do not condone what was done to Ith, I have no desire for needless bloodshed. I became a druid so that I could keep my people safe, to keep war from my village."

Shiovra closed her eyes as he leaned closer, his hot breath gracing the skin on her neck. She clenched her hands, digging her nails in her palms in an attempt to quell the rising desire within her.

"When my father was approached with a possible union between clans, I did not hesitate to agree," Odhrán breathed in her ear. "And when I learned that not only did Ailill seek your capture, but the sons of Míl as well, I took it upon myself to come and serve as your guardian." He brushed his lips across her neck. "I may not have spoken true of who I was, but my want for an alliance between our people, my desire for you, was no ploy. I know I have wounded your trust in me, and if you want to push me away, I understand completely."

She felt his other hand tilt her chin up before his lips touched her own. Shiovra remained still, unwilling to shove him away, wanting to believe his words were spoken truthfully. Even though she felt betrayed, she still trusted him with her life. She still wanted him at her side. Bringing her hands up slowly, she let them rest against his chest to feel the beat of his heart.

"If the two of you are quite done, it is time to set out."

Odhrán pulled away abruptly at the sound of Ceallach's voice.

Face flushing, Shiovra turned her attention to the Fomorii man as he approached them.

Ceallach's face was as impassive as ever as he looked between them. "The horses have been prepared," he told them. "We are waiting on you. If you are finished *speaking* I would suggest we leave. We have tarried long enough." Turning, he walked back towards their camp.

Shiovra watched as Ceallach disappeared into the trees.

"The choice has always been yours to make," Odhrán said abruptly, his voice still husky from their intimacy. "I will not force you to wed me, though I do hope that we can still achieve an alliance between our villages." He brought his hand up to cup her cheek. "Peace between our people is possible. All you have to do is reach for it." Dropping his hand, he turned and began to walk away. "We should return."

The priestess hesitated. "Odhrán."

He paused without turning to face her.

"A promise was made and I have every intention to keep it," Shiovra said. "Perhaps you are right. Knowing you will be my husband does bring a sense of ease. You have proven yourself to be a fierce warrior and capable leader. And I believe that, together, we can protect our people. Together we can forge a strong and powerful alliance."

Odhrán turned and smiled, holding his hand out to her. "Then let us go, together."

* ~ * ~ * ~ * ~ *

Gráinne's hand lashed out, striking Cúmhéa full and hard across the face. Her long nails raked down across his skin as she pulled her hand away, drawing a trickle of blood. "You have failed!" she hissed at him, striking once more. "Three well trained Fomorii at your disposal and you still managed to fail. Now you dare to come running back to me with your tail between your legs?!" Gráinne crossed her arms and looked at him lividly. "You are no hound of Mide, Cúmhéa. You are nothing but a mere pup!"

"And the priestess would have been mine if Morgan had not interfered!" Cúmhéa growled in return.

Gráinne frowned, unfamiliar with the name. "Morgan? Is he one of the Milidh?"

Cúmhéa shook his head, wiping the blood from his cheek. "No, but he is from across the sea, just as the Milidh did," he replied. "He dared to breach the boundaries of Dún Scáth, proving he was capable of defeating many of Caillte's best warriors not only with bow, but sword and fist. Caillte requested that he join him and serve as his right hand man. Initially Morgan refused Caillte's offer, but he was swayed when Caillte promised to help him find his brother."

She turned away, approaching the fire. Of all her time among Caillte's men, Gráinne had never met a man by the name of Morgan. "And this man, this *Morgan,* managed to best the Hound of Mide?" she laughed.

"He has been taught how to manipulate Fomorii fog," snarled Cúmhéa. "I never saw him coming. He attacked me before I could make the priestess mine. It would seem that Caillte has sent his own guardian to watch over the priestess and keep you from getting your desires."

Gráinne watched the fire dance upon the wood, a cruel smile slowly twisting the corners of her lips. "Men are easily swayed," she purred. "Morgan will be no different." She turned back to Cúmhéa, reaching a hand up to run her fingers down his chest. "With him on our side, the priestess will be all ours…"

* ~ * ~ * ~ * ~ *

The companions only paused a moment as the wheat fields along the outer borders of the village came into sight before continuing along the path. As large as Tara's high fort itself, Dún Fiáin had a strong stone outer wall for defense against attacks. As they neared, a horn sounded on the wind, announcing their arrival.

The village's entrance was well guarded with four warriors armed with spears standing at the gates, while six more stood on platforms above. The warriors stepped aside, allowing passage into the village. Cottages lay clustered closely together while short fences made of woven hazel penned in sheep.

Odhrán took the lead, guiding the priestess and her companions along a well worn path through the village.

All around them villagers stopped in their daily tasks, gathering around to watch as Shiovra and her companions rode through, greeting them warmly. Giggling children pushed past their parents to watch, waving their hands at the priestess with bright smiles on their faces.

The main cottage stood on a small hill, surrounded by a stone wall of its own. Three men waited at the base of the hill and, as the companions neared, approached Odhrán.

Odhrán pulled Shiovra's horse to a halt and helped the priestess dismount before handing the reins to one of the men. Looking her over, he noticed Shiovra studied her clothing with a frown knitting her brow. Though the tunic she wore was clean, her shift beneath was torn and stained from all they had been through. "Our journey here did not go unhindered, they will understand," he told her. Glancing at the companions, he leaned close and asked in a low voice, "Are you prepared?"

Shiovra nodded, replying without any hesitation, "Aye."

"Then it is time," he said, stepping away from the priestess and heading towards the cottage. As he approached the wicker door-lintel, the man standing guard gave him a slight bow before pushing the door open and stepping aside. Nodding to the men, Odhrán gestured for the companions to enter before following himself.

The chieftain of Dún Fiáin sat on a bench by the fire. He was a stout man with dark hair and beard that were streaked with grey. A thick torc circled his neck while a rich forest green tartan woven with bands of blue and gold adorned his left shoulder. To his right sat a slender woman, her long brown hair falling over her shoulder in a simple braid, and to his left a maiden of at most fifteen years of age.

Odhrán followed Shiovra as she walked towards the fire, offering the chieftain a small, respective bow. Her movements were relaxed, much unlike her initial meeting with the chieftain nearly a year prior.

"Merry Meet, Lord Culann, Lady Álainn," Shiovra said kindly, a smile on her lips.

"We welcome you once more to Dún Fiáin, Shiovra Ní Coughlin," said Culann, leaning forward on the bench. "Merry Meet to you as well, Ceallach Neáll of the Fomorii. It has been many years since our last meeting."

The Fomorii man nodded. "Aye, that it has. May I present the Lady Shiovra's companions: Daire, cousin to the priestess," he said, gesturing to each in turn, "Meara of the Neimidh and Eiladyr."

Culann's gaze drifted over the companions before turning his attention to Shiovra and Odhrán, lingering. "It would appear that your journey here did not go without hindrance."

"Aye," replied Shiovra calmly, "however the hunter failed to capture his prey and fled. My injury was only minor. It was your *son* who suffered a greater wound."

The chieftain's brows rose with mild surprise. "Ah—" Culann breathed, leaning back. "So you are aware that my son is actually Odhrán?"

Shiovra met the chieftain's eyes firmly and nodded. "Aye."

"What—?" began Daire, only to be cut off as the priestess held her arm out, silencing him.

"And you are still willing to wed him for the sake of alliance between our villages?" pressed Culann.

"Aye." Her reply was simple.

Odhrán glance at the woman from the corner of his eye. Despite all the strength she presented to the chieftain, he could see weariness in her eyes. "Perhaps we can continue this talk after the priestess has had time to rest."

Culann nodded in agreement. "Of course," he said. "Rest for now and join us in a feast come nightfall to welcome your arrival to our village." He turned to her daughter. "Caoilin, could you please guide the Lady Shiovra to the bathing hut and bring her some fresh clothing?"

The girl rose to her feet and nodded. Offering the priestess a warm smile, she led her from the cottage.

"A cottage has been prepared for your stay," continued Culann as his wife stood. "Álainn will take you there. Your packs should already be waiting inside."

Ceallach gave a short bow. "We thank you for your generosity."

Odhrán tarried, watching as the priestess' companions followed his mother from the cottage before turning back to his father. "The attack was neither from Ailill nor the sons of Míl," he reported, circling the fire, "but from Gráinne. Her ambitions lie with Tara and she will do all within her power to gain control of the village." Odhrán paused beside a table, running his fingers along the edge of a cup. "She sees the High Priestess as a threat that needs dealt with and waited for her to depart from Tara. With the Hound of Mide on her side, she made her attack, separating us using Fomorii tricks while the priestess was hunted."

Culann leaned forward, resting his elbows on his knees. "How many Fomorii?" he asked.

"I found three, one of which gave me this wound," replied Odhrán, gesturing to his side. Pouring water into the cup from a pitcher, he brought it to his lips and took a drink. "When I finally found the priestess, Cúmhéa had already fled. She suffered an injured ankle falling from her horse, but aside from that she was unscathed."

The chieftain rubbed his chin. "Was it the priestess who turned the Hound away?" pressed Culann.

Odhrán shook his head. "She was weaponless and the Fomorii fog interfered too greatly with her power as a priestess," he told him. "It would seem that Ailill has eyes on the priestess, watching and studying her."

"And of Méav?"

"Only silent riddles." Odhrán sat the cup down and returned to the fire. "Unlike Gráinne, Méav is very subtle and will remain quiet until she makes her move. Though she has turned her back on kin and clan, she refuses to allow Milidh to hold sway over Tara. In a sense, we can be reassured that she will not kill the priestess, let alone hand her over to anyone who might."

Culann looked into the fire with a heavy frown, lacing his fingers together tightly. "It would seem we will need to proceed with caution."

* ~ * ~ * ~ * ~ *

Shiovra followed Caoilin through the village to a small hut not too far from the main one. A fire burned brightly in the hearth with water already warming above it. Cloth to wash with and empty basin sat on a small table beside a bench. Several dried herbs hung from the support posts for scenting the water with. The scent of meadowsweet filled the air heavily.

"I shall fetch some clothing for you while you wash," Caoilin told her. "I will not be long."

"My thanks," Shiovra replied kindly. She watched the young Milidh woman leave before walking to the hearth, testing the water with a fingertip. Finding it comfortably warm, she filled the basin and returned to the bench. Removing her shoes, Shiovra cringed at the amount of dirt covering her legs and feet. Setting them aside, she pulled Morgan's tunic off and looked it over then folded it neatly and placing it on the table. Her shift, unfortunately, was ruined beyond repair.

Wetting a cloth, Shiovra cleaned all the dirt and traces of Odhrán's blood from her skin. Emptying the basin, she refilled it and poured it over her hair, repeating the process several times until clean. Drying herself off, she sat on the bench, leaning against a support post as she waited for Caoilin's return. Her thoughts were drawn to Odhrán and the words he had spoken in the woods.

I may not have spoken true of who I was, but my want for an alliance between our people, my desire for you, was no ploy. I know I have wounded your trust in me, and if you want to push me away, I understand completely.

Beltaine was drawing near, only but a few days away. She would become Odhrán's wife and their two clans, once enemies, would become allies. With many eyes set on gaining control of Tara, Shiovra would do whatever was necessary to protect her people. Though she heard great truth to the words Odhrán had spoken in the woods, she could not prove that deceit did not lay hiding beneath.

Peace between our people is possible. All you have to do is reach for it.

Odhrán had asked her once what she would do to defend her village. He told her to be prepared because the actions she took, the battles she fought, would set the fate of Tara and her people. The alliance with his village, the peace they would gain, was one battle she refused to lose. Even if the Túath were to succumb to Milidh rule, she would not allow the peace forged between their villages to crumble.

Shiovra closed her eyes and took a deep breath, slowly releasing it. Letting her body relax in the warmth of the hut, she listened to the snap and pop of the fire. The sound was soothing, lulling her to sleep.

She stood alone in the middle of Tara while the darkness of night stretched across the sky. Looking around she found no hearth fires to ward off the chill of night, no torches to illuminate the way, only the light of the moon. The village was quiet; a heavy, deafening silence with hardly the chirrup of crickets or rustle of wind.

The feeling of loneliness and loss filled her as she walked through the village, each step coming quicker and quicker. Calling out, she received no response. It was as if Tara herself, so full of life, had just simply been abandoned.

As she neared the main gates, she could see the Banqueting House in the distance. At first all she saw was a small flicker of light that quickly grew, consuming the feast hall in flames. She froze at the sight, her heart clenching. It was then that the sound of keening reached her ears, soft at first and growing in intensity, laden with heavy sorrow as the bean sidhe lamented their grief.

The darkness of night swelled around her.

Looking up, she watched as a black shadow grew across the moon, slowly engulfing it. And, just when she feared the moon would be consumed entirely by darkness, light returned, leaving behind a moon the crimson color of blood.

Turning away, she found the luminous, transparent form of a woman with hallow eyes standing before her; one of the bean sidhe.

The woman's hair and garments were long, pale, and her face grief stricken. When she spoke, her voice was distant, "When the moon bleeds, the time of the Túath shall fall into eclipse…"

Shiovra woke with a start, a painful feeling gripping her. Rubbing her face with shaking hands, she strove to calm the beating of her heart. Just as when she had dreamt of Ainmire's death, this dream too held the same intensity. However, unlike the dream with Ainmire, there was no clear enemy.

The door clattered open with Caoilin's return, pulling the priestess from her thoughts.

"This is for you," said the maiden, handing Shiovra a small bundle of clothing. "A gift from myself to welcome you into our clan."

She took them, looking over the garments. "Thank you," she said, quickly dressing into the warm, dry clothing. The shift was a long sleeved line, lightly colored and the dress-tunic a soft wool dyed a deep, rich blue-violet hue. They fit nicely, if not a bit longer than she was accustomed to.

"Please allow me to help with your hair," Caoilin offered as the priestess sat down to put her shoes back on. Stepping up behind Shiovra, she carefully braided her hair then tied it off with a thin leather strip. "The wind is strong today. This will help keep your hair from your eyes."

Shiovra noticed the girl hesitated for a moment.

"Was it frightening?" Caoilin asked abruptly. "When you were attacked?"

"A bit," replied Shiovra honestly. "The Hound of Mide is a very dangerous man. His heart is black, his actions violent and cruel. Though Túath himself, Cúmhéa hates the High Chieftains for occupying themselves with the sons of Míl while turning their backs on kin and village." She offered the girl a tight smile. "Cúmhéa has not been the first to hunt me, to make me his prey, and he will certainly not be the last. I am most fortunate he was unable to succeed in his plans." Shiovra shuddered at the mere memory of the dark lust she had seen burning in his eyes and the feel of his fingers on her skin. When she spoke again, he voice was low and tight, "What he sought to do to me…it was truly horrendous."

A horrified look crossed Caoilin's face. "How did you escape?"

"An enemy of my enemy," replied Shiovra, reaching a hand out to touch the tunic folded neatly on the table. "It was a man by the name of Morgan. Though he claims to have been sent by Ailill to study me, he stopped Cúmhéa's attack and sent the hound fleeing back to Gráinne. Injured as I was, without any means to defend myself, Morgan did not capture me, only left me with a warning. Though I am certain I have not seen the last of either man."

"That must have been truly terrible," said Caoilin. Approaching the door, she opened it and sent a gust of wind into the tiny hut. "I would have been utterly frightened had it been me."

Standing, Shiovra grabbed Morgan's tunic and followed the maiden out the door.

"You will be safe here," Caoilin continued. "Father will keep warriors well posted and you will have my brother at your side to protect you." A sad smile crossed her lips. "I have overheard mother and father discussing possible betrothals for me. They have not decided on whom yet, but they began speaking of it after sending for you." A strained laugh passed the girl's lips. "Is that how it always is, a marriage to forge an alliance?"

"Aye, unfortunately." Shiovra took a deep breath and sighed. "To strengthen the clan and defeat your enemies, marriages of alliance are formed; intricate stratagems to ensure the control and affluence of the clan. My impending marriage with Odhrán is no different."

"Do you… loathe …my brother?" asked the maiden hesitantly, fidgeting with the folds of her skirts.

"Nay," Shiovra said honestly, "although I am very angry with him." She offered the girl a tight smile. "Odhrán and I—we came to trust one another as priestess and guardian. To learn that he kept who he was from me left me feeling betrayed. I am wary to trust his words for fear that perhaps they are not entirely truthful."

Caoilin nodded. "I understand," she replied softly.

Shiovra paused, glancing at the main cottage. "Do not fret," she reassured the girl. "I shall keep my promise to wed Odhrán."

Smiling, Caoilin nodded. "Shall I show you about the village?"

"Perhaps later, if you are still willing," Shiovra told her. "I would like, though, to speak with Lord Culann."

"Aye." Giving a small bow of the head, Caoilin walked away.

The priestess made her way up the path and back to the main cottage. The guard stepped aside, allowing passage. Pushing the door open, she found Culann and Álainn sat alone.

The chieftain looked up as she approached, his gaze questioning.

"Might we speak a moment?" she asked.

Culann nodded.

Shiovra stood before the chieftain and his wife, studying them as equally intense as they did her. "I am certain you can understand my caution," she told them calmly. "I have been hunted and attacked more than once. I have had my own kin turn on me. And now my trust has been wounded by the very man I am to wed. Thus I am a bit wary of what your true intentions with my village and myself may be."

"I will not lie. Since our arrival on Éire, one thing alone has remained on the thoughts of Míl's sons: gathering a strong battle host," replied Culann simply. "And so, for nearly eleven years, they have maintained a strained pretense of peace all the while preparing their battle strategies. Odhrán has been closely watching their movements, preparing means of defense for when the time of war comes. We want, at all costs, to keep the battle from reaching this village."

His words were of no surprise to Shiovra. Through all the pretenses of alliances and treaties, the Milidh clan ever had a dagger waiting for the backs of the Túath clan.

"And my village?" questioned the priestess, her thoughts lingering on the ominous dream.

"More than vengeance for Ith's death, Tara lies at the heart of their plans." Culann rose to his feet and stepped around the priestess, adding wood to the fire. "War will come to Tara, of that you can be certain. We will do what we can to aid in the protection of your village, but we must defend our own as well." He crouched down beside the fire, poking it with a stick. "The warriors we sent are all I can spare without Dún Fiáin's own defenses suffering. I cannot reassure you that Tara will not fall, but I can assure you that my son will do everything within his power to defend it and your people."

~~*~*~*

"You told me once I was possibly a fool for trusting you," began Daire, paying little heed to the increasingly steady rainfall as he leaned against the village wall. "I believe I finally understand the meaning behind your words." His eyes drifted to Odhrán as the Milidh man came to stand beside him in the fading light. Daire exhaled heavily, continuing, "Though I do not believe myself to be a fool."

"Can you be certain of that?" questioned Odhrán.

Without a moment of hesitation, Daire nodded.

The Milidh man chuckled lightly. "No, you are a fool," Odhrán told him, a grin twisting his lips. "A fool in many ways indeed, but not for trusting me." Leaning against the wall, he crossed his arms. "My intentions were never to betray."

Daire nodded.

"For years I have been closely watching the movements of Míl's sons as one of their druids, gathering what information I could and preparing my own means of defense," continued Odhrán. "Thus I have been allied with Ráth Faolchú for many years, and thus I have placed my lot with your mother and father."

"And their terms for alliance with Tara was to wed Shiovra?" asked Daire.

"Perhaps," replied Odhrán, his eyes focused elsewhere. "The sons of Míl are skillful tacticians, more so than you realize. Aye, you know that Ailill has allied himself with the Milidh, but the truth of the matter is that he is manipulated by the sons of Míl. They feed his anger for his brother's death at the hands of the High Chieftains. They nourish his anger at Méav's betrayal.

And, using Ailill as a distraction, the sons of Míl are slowly pulling the Túath clan apart, weakening Tara. Soon this pretense of peace will crumble and bloodshed will fall."

Daire ran his hands through his hair. While clan and kin fought among themselves, the Milidh were gathering strength.

"You understand now, do you not?" came the deep voice of Ceallach.

Daire turned to see his father approach.

"Battles of the past such as Magh Tuireadh will pale in comparison to the one we shall soon face," the Fomorii man continued. "From the moment Ith's blood stained the rich soil of Éire, the storm of battle has been brewing. Réalta and I have done all within our power to strengthen our defenses yet, unless we stand together, we will fall."

Daire remained silent.

"The decision for Shiovra to wed Odhrán was not made lightly," Ceallach told him firmly. "Réalta remained wary, knowing there was great risk in trusting one of the Milidh after already losing so much to them." He turned his cold gaze to Odhrán. "She feared what his intentions with Shiovra and Tara may be. Odhrán may be a dangerous foe, but he is a strong and powerful ally. And so we agreed to the alliance and marriage, for the sake of Tara's people, even should the village fall."

5. BELTAINE RITES

Beltaine had come upon the land of Éire and Dún Fiáin was alive with celebrations that did not dwindle even as night stretched across the sky. They honored the marriage between the Great Mother and Horned Father with the hopes of good harvests to come in warmer days. Great fires were built outside Dún Fiáin's walls while the villagers danced around it to ensure good health, fertility, and abundant crops.

Walking through the moonlit village, Shiovra made her way to the bathing hut where she would purify her body before taking part in the Beltaine rites and wedding Odhrán. Pushing the door open, she found three familiar faces waiting for her and the slight nervousness she felt faded away.

It had been over a year since Shiovra had last seen Réalta's handmaids. During her years of training on the isle of Rúnda, the three women were always at hand to help her prepare for rituals. Seeing them again kindled old memories.

The women bowed low in their greeting.

Shiovra could not help the smile that crossed her lips as she greeted each woman in turn. "Muirean, Niamh, Radha…merry meet."

"Merry meet, Lady Shiovra," said the eldest of the women, Muirean. "Lady Réalta sent us to help you prepare. Come, we allow us purify your body for the rites of marriage."

Nodding, Shiovra followed Muirean to the hearth fire and paused beside a bench where a basin of water rested. Removing her clothing, she handed them to Niamh. Closing her eyes, Shiovra took a deep breath and relaxed her body. She felt the touch of cold water against her skin, but remained still and allowed the women to wash her body with the herb steeped water.

As the women washed her, they began to chant in a singsong manner.

"Blessed be by Dana," came Muirean's voice at Shiovra's left. "Child of hers you shall always be."

"Blessed be by Áine and Óengus mac Óc," Niamh added softly from her right. "May their love fill you."

"Blessed be by Brigid," sang Radha from in front. "May she grace you with healthy children."

"And blessed be by the Dagda," the women spoke in unison. "For we are all his children."

Shiovra opened her eyes, welcoming the warmth of the fire on her cooled skin as the women stepped away to gather her clothing and adornments.

Muirean approached first with a simple white shift that Eithne had made and helped the priestess dress. Niamh took hold of a meadowsweet bundle and lit one end on fire. Quickly blowing it out, she circled Shiovra, wafting the smoke over the priestess. When both women finished, Radha placed the clan tartan over Shiovra's left shoulder before securing it on her right hip with a broach. Stepping back, she adjusted the folds of the cloth till she was satisfied. Niamh returned to Shiovra's side, slipping bracelets onto Shiovra wrists and a torc around her neck.

"One last thing," Radha told the priestess. She placed a crown of white flower blossoms woven together upon Shiovra's head then stepped back and smiled. "You make a lovely bride, Lady Shiovra."

"It is time," said Muirean.

Shiovra nodded silently in return and followed the women through the door. Stepping out into the cool night air, she was greeted by four warriors who stood waiting to guide them.

One of the men stepped forward. "Lady Shiovra."

The priestess returned his greeting with a nod. The time had come.

* ~ * ~ * ~ * ~ *

Caillte stood looking into the hearth fire, his face dark with irritation. Beltaine had come and with it the awaited union between Tara and Dún Fiáin. He did not see the alliance as a threat as many did, however he did find Gráinne's actions a growing vexation. She had made her intentions quite clear when she sent Cúmhéa after the priestess. Had it not been for Morgan's actions, the Hound of Mide just may have succeeded in sinking his teeth into his prey.

"Your orders, Lord Caillte?" questioned Eimh, pulling the Fomorii man from his thoughts.

"Morgan is to maintain his watch over the priestess," replied Caillte, turning to the man. "I do not doubt that Gráinne will continue to lash out, sending hunters after the priestess. And, with Cúmhéa's defeat at Morgan's hand, she will undoubtedly have taken an interest in him. Should Morgan find any of Gráinne's hunters, he is to dispose of them. By siding with Gráinne they have lost their usefulness to us."

Eimh nodded hastily. "Aye, my lord." Bowing, he turned and quickly slipped out the door.

Caillte slowly followed the man, stepping out into the cool night air. His cloak flapped in a sudden gust of wind, moving like great black wings behind him. Looking up at the moon, a smile twisted Caillte's lips. Gráinne was sorely mistaken if she thought he would sit idle while she sent huntsmen after the priestess.

~~*~*~*

Réalta stood on the sandy shore of Rúnda while cold waves lapped wildly around her bare feet. The wind was growing in strength, bringing with it a light fog that obscured her view of Éire. She felt as restless as the sea as it churned and lurched. Beltaine had finally come upon them and with it the union of clans. The peace she had fought to secure was in her grasp and yet she could not shake the consuming feeling that it had all been for naught.

"Réalta?"

She turned to see Gráinne's son, Anlon, approach her with a worried frown marring his brow. He was followed closely by her Neimidh handmaid, Dubheasa.

"It is late. Should you not rest?" asked Anlon.

"I am unable to sleep," she replied, turning back to the fog covered sea. "Beltaine has come."

He looked at her curiously. "Aye, it is Beltaine, but—"

"The Túath clan of Tara and the Milidh clan of Dún Fiáin shall join with the marriage of Shiovra and Odhrán," continued Réalta. "Such a strong alliance should ease my fears...yet they continue to grow."

Anlon remained silent.

Réalta stepped deeper into the water, not heeding Dubheasa's protest. "Everything I have done was to protect this clan, to protect what kin I have remaining to me," she said, her voice tight with sorrow. "The battle I had foreseen long ago, that continues to linger in my dreams, only becomes more and more terrible. Éire will be soaked in the blood of battle. I have strove to prevent such a fate, but at what cost?" She shook her head. "Dubheasa, please have my boat prepared."

"My lady?" questioned Dubheasa, concern in her voice.

Réalta turned to face the Neimidh woman. If a battle was to be fought, she would not face it alone and neither would Shiovra. "I am going to Dún Fiáin," she stated. "There are broken bonds in need of mending."

~~*~*~*

Mahon stood in the moonlight, his eyes narrowed upon the Stone of Destiny. After a moment's hesitation, he reached a hand up and touched the cool stone. The granite standing stone did not react and he had not expected it to; it had already spoken for Odhrán. Still, deep within it, Mahon could feel a light pulse. With each passing day, the pulse grew slowly in intensity. And now, with the Beltaine moon high in the sky, the pulse throbbed wildly beneath his fingertips.

Eithne came to stand beside him, her unbound hair rustling in the breeze. "She will be fine."

Mahon abruptly dropped his hand, turning to the woman. She knew where his thoughts lie all too well.

"I understand that you worry for your sister," continued Eithne. "Especially after learning that Odhrán is the one she is to wed. But Kieran has assured me that Odhrán is a good man and will continue to protect the Lady Shiovra just as he has already done."

He remained silent for a moment. "Can we be so sure?" he questioned.

"Nothing is certain," said the woman, offering him a sad smile. "Nevertheless, we have long trusted Kieran and if he trusts Odhrán, then I believe we can as well."

Mahon exhaled loudly, his eyes turning back to the Stone of Destiny. "Trust…it is a difficult thing," he said in a low voice, reaching a hand out to run his fingers along the rough granite. "More so when a foreboding feeling hangs to heavily in the air."

~~*~*~*

Gráinne stood before the fire, sipping at a cup of mead in her hand. She had given Cúmhéa one simple task. A task he had, most irritably, failed at. The notorious Hound of Mide had been defeated by one man. What more, the Fomorii curs she had sent with him had been slain. Had Caillte not interfered, had he not sent Morgan, she would have the priestess in her grasp, broken.

Face contorting with wild furry, Gráinne screamed her rage and flung the cup into the fire. She was the youngest of the three sisters, the one with the least power as a priestess. For years she had struggled to prove her worth, to show her strength, only to be denied. Her mother treated her as if she were nothing more than a fledgling child. Ailill used her as a pawn before casting her aside.

Time and time again she was denied what she desired. And what she desired most of anything was control of Tara. If she could break the High Priestess, if she could gain control of Tara, then she would be noticed as the powerful woman she was. She would return Tara to her former glory and show all the Milidh that the Túath clan would bend to no one. And with that she would be respected, honored, and *feared*.

A wicked smile twisted her lips. "Deasún! Cúmhéa!" Gráinne shouted.

The door clattered open behind her.

She spun to face them, her skirts swirling with the sudden movement. Stepping up to Cúmhéa, she thrust a finger on his chest. "For your failure, you are to bring Morgan to me," ordered Gráinne coldly. "Prove your worth, *hound*, and bring me the man who managed to best you." Her eyes narrowed as he stood silently before her, his jaw set hard. "You *will* bring him to me," she said, voice low and dangerous. "Is that understood?"

The man's gaze hardened further, yet he nodded.

"Good," purred Gráinne, letting her fingers slip down his chest before turning her attention to Deasún. She walked slowly toward him, a seductive smile playing across her lips. "You have done well for me, Deasún, very well," she told him. Gráinne circled him, her eyes trailing over his body. "And you shall do well for me once more. I have an important task for you."

"And what would that be, Lady Gráinne?"

She paused behind him, brining her mouth to his ear. "Shiovra's death," she whispered seductively. "Just as you took Ainmire's life, you shall take the High Priestess'. I no longer have the desire to play games."

A malicious grin spread wide across the Milidh man's lips. "As you desire," he replied.

Gráinne returned to the fire, smirking. Laughter swelled within her as she watched the flames dance upon the wood. Soon she would have all that she longed for. Soon the High Priestess' life would be forfeit and Tara would be hers.

* ~ * ~ * ~ * ~ *

Shiovra approached a great fire that had been erected outside the village walls. The path she took was flanked with villagers who had gathered to watch the union. The priestess' step fell in rhythm with the steady beat of a bodhrán, a pulse that pounded as loudly as her own heart. All around her she could feel the elements, their power dancing wild and free. Even the very wind seemed to whisper to her, calling, urging.

Shiovra only smiled lightly as she walked past the people of Dún Fiáin. Though she had known Odhrán for a year, though they had grown closer than priestess and guardian should have, she could not help the slight nervousness that filled her. That night they would join together, not only in body, but their clans in alliance. And alliance she would strive to strengthen.

Nearing the fire, she found Ceallach waiting with his hands behind his back. The fire gave the Fomorii man's pale skin and platinum hair an appealing warmer hue. At his side stood Odhrán, garbed in the Dún Fiáin tartan: a deep green cloth woven with bands of vibrant green-blue and yellow.

Pausing before them, she gave a slight bow and brought her gaze up to meet Odhrán's briefly. Following Ceallach's gesture, Shiovra took her place beside her Milidh intended.

Ceallach's ice-blue eyes looked at them each in turn. And, when they nodded in unison, his gaze settled on Shiovra as began the marriage ritual. "Shiovra Ní Coughlin, High Priestess of Tara, do you come willingly into this union?" he questioned.

"Aye," Shiovra replied, a wave of heat rushing through her body.

The Fomorii man turned his attention to Odhrán. "Odhrán, son of Culann and Álainn, do you come willingly into this union?"

"Aye," said Odhrán in a clear, even tone.

Ceallach gazed upon the gathered villagers. "People of Dún Fiáin, bear witness now the bond of marriage sought by both Shiovra and Odhrán," Ceallach stated loudly, gesturing to the priestess and her guardian. "Join hands," he ordered Shiovra and Odhrán.

The beating of the drum increased.

The priestess placed her hands within Odhrán's without hesitation. They were warm and the gentle caress of his thumb across the skin of her fingers made her heartbeat quicken.

Ceallach placed his hands upon theirs. "Mother of all, fair Dana of the Light, Danu of Darkness, whose womb is the earth, who brings happiness and mirth with every loving touch. Please come to us now and join these two in this sacred rite. Give them your love and light!" he called. "Dagda, Father of places wild and free, who brings pleasure, joy, and mirth. Who is the Sun that shines above and warms us with his light and love. Who brings us health, prosperity, and changes all as it should be. Please come to us now and join these two in this sacred rite. Give them your love and light!"

The gentle breeze grew in strength, wrapping around Shiovra and Odhrán. The fire strengthened, reaching for the moon resting high in the velvety folds of the night sky.

Ceallach pulled forth a dagger and pointed it at Odhrán's chest, waiting. "Bear witness now, that which they have to declare!"

"I, Odhrán, do come here of my own free will, to seek partnership of Shiovra," Odhrán stated firmly. "I come with all love, honor, and sincerity, wishing only to become one with her whom I love." His eyes turned to Shiovra, a small grin tugging the corners of his mouth. "Her life I shall defend before my own. May the dagger be plunged into my heart should I not be sincere in all that I declare. And this I swear in the names of Dana and the

Dagda. May they give me strength to keep my vow. So mote it be."

Ceallach turned his dagger towards Shiovra, pointing the tip at the priestess' breast.

Once more the steady pulse played out upon the bodhrán quickened.

"I, Shiovra, do come here of my own free will, to seek partnership of Odhrán," Shiovra declared loudly. "I come with all love, honor, and sincerity, wishing only to become one with he whom I love." She held Odhrán's gaze with a smile of her own. "His life I shall defend before my own. May the dagger be plunged into my heart should I not be sincere in all that I declare. And this I swear in the names of Dana and the Dagda. May they give me strength to keep my vow. So mote it be."

The Fomorii man lowered the dagger.

"As you give love, so you will receive love. As you give strength, so will you receive strength," Ceallach continued. "Together you are one, apart you are nothing. Know that no two people are exactly alike. No more can any two people fit together, perfect in every way. It is no weakness to admit a wrong. More, it is strength and a sign of learning. Ever love, help, and respect each other, and then know truly that you are one in the eyes of Dana and the Dagda." He paused, his voice low and hard when he continued, "As well as all of Éire."

"So mote it be," the three of them said in unison.

Muriean approached, holding two simple bronze bands in the palm of her hand.

Taking them, Ceallach thanks the woman. "A gift from Réalta and myself. One for each, a sign of the strong alliance and union which has been forged between the two of you," he said, handing Shiovra and Odhrán each a ring.

Only after the rings were placed upon their fingers, and a kiss exchanged, did the steady rhythm of drums stop.

* ~ * ~ * ~ * ~ *

The rites of Beltaine stretched late into the night. As the villagers of Dún Fiáin continued their celebrations, Odhrán led Shiovra away and into the village. Two warriors stood guard at the main cottage, stepping aside as they approached. The cottage itself was pleasantly empty and a low fire had been built in the hearth, softly illuminating it with a warm glow.

Shiovra watched as Odhrán added some more wood to the fire before removing his tartan and tunic, setting them aside on a bench. Her eyes drifted over his toned body, lingering on the blue woad marking on his back. Reaching a hand out, she traced the dark blue lines with her fingers. Odhrán remained still beneath her touch and, as she drew her hand away, he turned and caught her wrist.

Odhrán brought her hand to his lips, trailing light kisses across her fingers and onto her palm. "You once feared my touch," he said, continuing his ministrations without looking up. "Loathed me and detested my very presence."

The priestess watched his movements carefully, his lips leaving paths of fire across every inch of skin he touched.

"And now you are wed to me, a man who was once the enemy." Closing the distance between them, Odhrán pulled her into his arms. "Together we are joining two clans, no longer enemies, but allies," he said, mouth close to her ear.

Shiovra felt his fingers brush her neck, pushing aside her hair before bringing his lips to the skin. Closing her eyes, heat rushed through her body, consuming her with want. Heart racing, she pressed her body closer to his.

"My love for you, my *desire* for you, was no lie," continued Odhrán, voice low and husky. He moved a hand to her hip and removed the broach holding her tartan. "You are a woman I want more than anything. A woman who will one day carry my child." Odhrán pulled the tartan from her shoulder and let it fall to the ground.

His mouth was hot against her neck, his breath caressing her ear. Shiovra remained still, relishing every touch, every kiss he bestowed upon her. She felt his hands brush against her breasts as they unlaced the neckline of her shift before pushing the cloth away, letting it fall to pool around her feet. Opening her eyes, Shiovra watched as his gaze drifted across her body, looking over the woad markings trailing down her arm and leg.

"Forever marked," said Odhrán, his eyes not leaving her body. "You have been hunted and attacked...all for being a High Priestess." He ran his fingers along her arm, tracing the twisting pattern as it wove over itself.

The priestess suppressed a shiver, her breath quickening.

Slipping one hand around her waist and digging the other into her hair at the nape of her neck, Odhrán pulled Shiovra hard to his chest once more, bringing his mouth down upon hers. His kiss was hot and hungry, full of desire.

Shiovra felt his hand tighten in her hair while the other wandered across her back, gliding light across her skin.

Breaking the kiss, he lifted her into his arms and carried her to a bed, lying her down upon it. Pulling the curtain closed behind him, Odhrán leaned over her, one knee pressed between her legs. He looked down at her as he played idly with a lock of her hair. Letting the strands slip slowly from his fingers, Odhrán grazed his fingers across her cheek and jaw, gliding slowly down her neck.

A soft moan passed Shiovra's lips when his hand found the tender flesh of her breast, her body arching slightly in response. Even the simplest of touches from him filled her with want.

Keeping a hand on her breast, Odhrán made quick work of his breaches with his other. "Shiovra," he said in a low voice, his breath hot against her ear, "my priestess." Capturing her lips in a fervent kiss, he stifled Shiovra's soft gasp as he pushed into her without warning.

Shiovra wrapped her arms around him and welcomed each demanding thrust with one of her own. She moaned his name softly as his mouth trailed kisses across her jaw and neck, her nails digging into his back. Her breathing was rough, matching the wild pace he set. And, just when she thought the mounting heat would completely consume her, she found her release. Waves of pleasure pulsed through Shiovra's body, leaving her trembling when they subsided.

Odhrán remained joined with her till long after his own release, his hand tight in her hair while the other rested on her hip. "Túath Priestess and Milidh guardian," he whispered in her ear, his voice low and firm. "Together we shall show both the sons of Míl and the High Chieftains just how formidable we can be."

* ~ * ~ * ~ * ~ *

Mahon was not pleased to having been woken early in the morning, especially when the first graying of dawn had only just begun to tinge the sky. Sleepily dressing himself, he prepared to greet whoever had arrived to Tara and in the wee hours of the morning. To his surprise and irritation, Réalta Dubh stepped into the cottage. "Why have you come so early in the morning?" he asked, stifling yet another yawn.

The woman sat down on a low bench beside the table and poured herself a cup of water. "I am only stopping to rest and will not trouble you for long," Réalta replied. "I am on my way to Dún Fiáin."

Mahon crossed his arms, his gaze narrowing on his aunt. "Dún Fiáin?" he pressed coldly with a deep frown. "What are your intentions with my sister? Despite my protest, she still followed through with your wishes and wed that Milidh man, forging the alliance you so greatly desired. I will not allow you to twist her life to your means anymore."

Réalta looked down solemnly into the cup. "I have come to seek forgiveness," she told him.

Her words caught Mahon off guard. Though he heard truth weighing heavily in them, he could not bring himself to believe her completely. "Do you believe Shiovra will forgive you?" he demanded harshly. "You and Ceallach desired to use her as a pawn; however, in the end, she defied you."

"All that I have done was to protect our clan," admitted Réalta. "I had thought that forging an alliance between Tara and Dún Fiáin would ease my fears, yet all it has done was feed them. The battle I foresaw all those years ago, the bloodshed, continues to plague me, growing more and more terrible." Her hands were pale as they gripped the cup tightly. "My desire to protect our clan has only pushed us apart. I have suffered greatly for my actions and have no desire for Shiovra to follow my path. I must mend the bond that I severed and seek forgiveness with Shiovra."

Mahon was silent for a moment, then asked, "How long will you rest here?"

"A few nights, if you will allow," she replied.

Studying her, Mahon took note of the weariness on her face and sighed heavily. "Aye, you may rest as long as you wish," he told her. "Tara is, after all, your home as well."

Réalta met his gaze, a small smile touching her lips. "You have served well as chieftain since Ainmire's death," she said gently.

"I am not the one the Stone of Destiny has spoken for," Mahon stated bluntly.

She nodded. "I am aware." Réalta took a drink of the water. "You have shouldered this burden well, Mahon, and I am sure you shall continue to do so." She paused, turning her attention back to the water. "Have you found yourself a wife yet?"

Mahon sat down across from her. He knew she would ask sooner or later. Even Earnán had been pressuring him to take a wife. "No," he replied, "I have not."

"You should. The blood of our clan grows thin."

He remained quiet.

Réalta met his gaze. "I am not demanding that you take a wife, I only request that you do for the sake of our bloodline."

Mahon looked away. His sister had wed one of the Milidh for the sake of clan and village; the time had come for him to do the same. "Bring me a wife and I will wed her, no matter her clan."

~~*~*~*

Caillte lounged on a fur covered bench beside the fire, cup of mead in hand. Taking a long drink from his cup, his eyes drifted over the buxom woman kneeling before him. The woman, Turiean, did carry a slight allure that piqued his interest. The curve of her hips and delightful swell of her breasts were quite inviting. And, with Gráinne dismissed, he no longer had anyone to fulfill his needs.

Turiean looked up at him with pleading eyes. "My brother Eimh has served you for many years," she began, "is there nothing that I can do for you?"

A smile twisted the corners of Caillte's lips. "Perhaps there is," he said, leaning towards her.

The woman flushed, but did not turn away. "I will do anything you desire of me, Lord Caillte."

The Fomorii man reached out and grabbed her arm, pulling her to her feet as he stood. "I know how you shall serve me best," he said heatedly in her ear as he pulled her roughly to his bed.

Turiean made no protest, though the slight fear that crossed her face did not go unnoticed.

"Ah, you are afraid," he commented with amusement, his hand pausing on the curtain. "Do you fear me? Fear coupling with a man such as myself?"

Hesitating, the woman nodded. "Aye, but if this is how I can best serve you, then I shall bear it," she told him, voice quivering.

Caillte spun the woman about so her back was to him. "Is that so?" he chuckled lightly. Reaching around Turiean, he firmly gripped her breasts as his brought his mouth down on her neck. A surprised gasp passed her lips bringing a smirk to his own. "Aye, you shall serve me well..."

* ~ * ~ * ~ * ~ *

Odhrán woke early in the morning when the sun had only begun to peek over the horizon. Careful not to wake Shiovra, he slipped from the bed and dressed. The hearth fire had long died down, leaving only dimly glowing embers. After a quick glance around the dark cottage, he secured his sword and daggers around his waist before throwing on his cloak and slipping out the cottage door.

None of the warriors posted guard questioned him as he made his way through the sleeping village and out the main gates. Pulling the hood of his cloak up, Odhrán wove his way through the fields and into the woods.

Walking through the trees with light, careful steps, his hand remained on the hilt of his sword. He kept a wary eye and ear out, searching and listening. At first he found nothing that garnered his interest. However, as he reached the eastern edge of the village borders, what he noticed brought a moment of pause to his step.

Crouching down, Odhrán ran his fingertips along the slightly scuffed ground. They were not created by an animal and the village warriors would not deliberately cover their tracks. Glancing up, Odhrán scanned the trees surrounding him, eyes narrowing on a snapped branch. Standing, he looked at it more closely. The break was fresh and, from the bend of the grains, their path was taking them towards the village.

A dark frown crossed his face, his hand tightening on the hilt of his sword. Knowing that Morgan managed to elude the village warriors day after day on their rounds did not sit well with Odhrán. He was not overly fond of Caillte having eyes on his priestess, especially one so skilled at hiding his presence.

Subtle movement caught Odhrán's attention; the muffled snap of a branch followed by the slight rustle of brush. He was not alone in his hunt. Ducking behind a tree, Odhrán drew his sword and listened once more. The movement came from his left. Slipping silently from one tree to the next, he followed the subtle sounds until he came up behind a man who walked slowly with bow and arrow ready in hand

Moving swiftly, Odhrán slipped out from behind a tree and brought his sword up to tap the man on the shoulder with the flat of the blade.

The man stilled suddenly, dropping the bow and arrow before slowly bringing his hands up.

Odhrán shifted his hold on the sword, bringing the blade toward the man's neck. "You are losing your touch, Kieran of the Neimidh," he said, a grin twisting the corners of his lips.

"And you are as dangerous as ever, Odhrán," replied the man with a strained chuckle.

Stepping around the man, Odhrán lowered his sword. "What brings you to Dún Fiáin?" he asked, returning his blade to its sheath before bending and returning Kieran's bow and arrow.

Kieran ran a swarthy hand through his dark brown curls, his face weary. "Not to exchange pleasantries, I am afraid," he replied, looking around. "Might we speak?"

Odhrán shook his head. "Not here," he told the Neimidh man, eyes searching the trees around them. "Much has happened since our departure from Tara. There are hidden eyes in these woods."

Kieran did not question his words, only nodded.

Glancing up into the tree branches high above his head, Odhrán added, "Eyes who have gone too easily unnoticed."

6. SPIDER'S WEB BROKEN

Réalta Dubh stood before the Stone of Destiny, bathed in the early morning sunlight. Reaching up a pale hand, she touched the cool, rough stone. Deep within it she could feel a slight vibration; a lingering pulse that was ever present. Closing her eyes, she took a deep breath and slowly released it. Never before had she felt so at a loss.

Réalta leaned forward, resting her head on the cool stone. She wondered how everything had gone so far awry. All she had suffered, all she had done to protect kin and clan, seemed to have been for naught as the darkness she had foreseen continued to fester and grow. What more, she could feel her power waning.

For many years Réalta had relied on her ability to foresee what was to come. She had prepared all she could to counter the bloodshed and in the end had nearly lost everything.

"It has been many years since Réalta Dubh set foot in Tara."

Réalta opened her eyes and straightened. "Aye, that it has. Far too many years," she murmured, turning to face Earnán. It had been nearly eleven years since she had last see the man, eleven years since she had brought his sister Deirdre to wed Ainmire. "So long that Tara is no longer my home."

"Are you sure about that?" Earnán asked her gently as he came to stand beside her. "Not once have you turned your back on this village. While it stands true that you have lived nearly your entire life away on Rúnda, Tara has remained foremost in your thoughts. Regardless of where you make bed, you shall always be a child of this village."

Réalta sighed and looked up at the bright colors splayed warmly across the sky. "I fear we will not be able to call Tara home for much longer," she told him softly.

Earnán stretched his arms, exhaling. "Perhaps, but until that time comes, I will defend this village with my life," he replied. "Why *have* you returned, Réalta Dubh?"

"To mend a broken bond," she replied simply. "And now, it appears I am to find Mahon a wife."

"I have told him for many years he needed to take a wife." Earnán chuckled lightly and crossed his arms. "He was adamantly against it, but now, with Shiovra willingly entering into a union for the sake of her people, perhaps he has realized that he, too, can do something." He glanced at her. "Do you have someone in mind?"

Réalta nodded, turning to him. "Aye. There is a girl in the village of Traigh Lí who is of age to wed. Though she is Milidh, her village has been on good terms with our clan for many years." She hesitated a moment, then said, "She is younger than Shiovra, but I believe the match would be well made."

"What is her name?" asked Earnán.

"Aislinn."

* ~ * ~ * ~ * ~ *

Upon Odhrán's return to the village, Shiovra hardly had a moment to question Kieran's presence before she was pulled into the main cottage. And, when the Milidh man quickly ordered a guard to fetch her companions and his father, she knew whatever tidings Kieran brought were not good. Sitting down at the table, she watched as Odhrán and Kieran spoke quickly in hushed tones.

Shiovra studied their faces carefully in the firelight. While Odhrán remained calm, Kieran appeared weary and apprehensive, a deep frown marring his brow. His clothing was heavily travel stained and, though within the safety of the village, he stood tensely with a hand resting on the hilt of his sword.

It was not long before they were joined by Culann, who was followed quickly by Daire, Eiladyr, Meara, and Ceallach. The chieftain took a set on the bench by the hearth fire while the companions gathered around their priestess.

Kieran offered Culann a hasty, short bow before straightening. "Please forgive any rudeness at my sudden appearance in your village, Lord Culann," he began, "but it is imperative that we speak."

Culann nodded. "Go on," he commanded.

"In my watch, I have found war hosts heading northward. All Milidh," he continued, pacing beside the hearth fire. "At first, their numbers were small, hardly of any concern, however, in the past few moons, they have drastically grown in number."

Culann leaned back on the bench. "It would seem Míl's sons are moving far sooner than we had anticipated," he murmured, rubbing his chin. "How close have they come within our borders?"

"Fairly close," replied Kieran, "though my concern lies more for Tara."

Shiovra tensed at his words.

"Though Méav turned her back on Tara, she had remained a powerful priestess. And now that Caher Dearg has fallen and the threat of Méav dwindles, Tara has grown weaker. She lacks ample warriors to defend her, leaving her open for attack. Though they still fear the power of Tara's High Priestess," he explained, eyes turning to Shiovra, "their caution continues to fade. There will come the time, very soon, that they will cross Tara's borders without hesitation. When that time comes, war will fully be upon us."

"And we shall be prepared," Odhrán said simply from his place as he leaned against a support post. "This battle cannot be prevented, only delayed. If they seek to play games, then we shall do the same in turn."

"What is it that you propose?" questioned Ceallach coolly.

A smile played across Odhrán's lips. "Break them," he replied. "The sons of Míl rely on their manipulation of Ailill to draw the High Chieftain's attention away from the army they gather. If we remove Ailill, they will be forced to stay their hand a bit longer." Odhrán meet the priestess' gaze and held it. "What more, enemies to the sons of Míl can become our allies with a bit of…persuasion."

"And what will keep them from thrusting a dagger in our backs?" countered Daire.

Shiovra turned to her cousin. "Nothing," she told him firmly, rising to her feet, "in spite of that more than once an enemy has proven to be a valuable ally." She gestured to Ceallach and Odhrán. "Are we to deny how many times they have risked their lives for our clan?" questioned Shiovra, anger rising in her voice. "While I am not claiming all enemies can be trusted, there are a few I believe who can." Her gaze shifted to Eiladyr. "Morgan just may be such an ally."

Daire lurched to his feet, slamming his hands down on the table. "Morgan?!" he shouted. "You would trust a man who was sent by Caillte to watch you and learn our weaknesses? Eiladyr's brother or not, he cannot be trusted!"

"Had it not been for Morgan, Cúmhéa just may have fulfilled his desires," she countered coldly. "I was injured and defenseless. Not only did Morgan stop Cúmhéa, but he even gave me his tunic to cover myself with. Morgan did not threaten me, did not turn his weapon on me, did not even try to *touch* me. He only offered me a warning and left."

"I agree with the priestess," Odhrán said, stepping away from the support post. He pulled a dagger from his belt and crouched down near the table. "Morgan has, quite successfully, managed to linger along the borders of this village." He etched the village into the dirt floor with the dagger's tip. "Since our arrival, I have walked the village borders every morning and found traces of his presence here, here, and here." Odhrán marked the places with crossing lines. "As each day passes, he has moved closer and closer, yet has not once been noticed." He looked up at them. "Morgan would make a highly valuable ally."

Daire sat down roughly. "I do not agree."

"Morgan is the only brother I would trust my life with," Eiladyr said abruptly. "I do not know how he came to be on Éire let alone why he would side with Ailill, but I believe he would join us if given the chance." He paused, rubbing the back of his neck. "I just…need to talk to him…"

A loud, anxious knock on the cottage door interrupted them before it clattered open and one of the village warriors hurried in. He stepped up to the chieftain and bowed low. "Please forgive me," he said, straightening, "but the Hound of Mide has been spotted along the northwestern borders. He is followed by another warrior with lime-washed hair and a small battle host."

Shiovra frowned. One man with lime-washed hair stood out in her mind: a Milidh man with mad eyes who laughed at death. "Deasún…" she breathed.

"How many men?" implored Culann.

"At least fifteen," replied the warrior.

Odhrán straightened. "We shall have to continue this discussion later," he said, returning his dagger to his belt. "It would seem we have some *guests* to welcome." He turned to the warrior. "Prepare the horses and gather a few of the men. We leave immediately."

The man nodded and left quickly.

"We will split into two groups and take them by surprise," continued Odhrán, walking towards the door. "If Gráinne desires to play games, then we shall oblige."

* ~ * ~ * ~ * ~ *

Réalta Dubh secured her packs, double checking that all straps were tight for the journey to Dún Fiáin. She could not help but feel slightly apprehensive about the trip. Though she did not believe Gráinne would be so vindictive as to attack her, it did not mean that there would be no enemies lurking about. Belting a sword about her waist, Réalta accepted the hand offered by one of her guards and mounted her steed.

"Aunt."

Taking hold of the reins, she looked down at Mahon as he approached.

"You would depart without a farewell?" he questioned.

"I did not wish to trouble you during your meal," Réalta told him. "Besides, I believe I have tarried long enough."

"Bidding you farewell could hardly be considered a bother," Mahon said, crossing his arms. "You are kin and a valued priestess to the clan. Sending you off properly is the least I could do."

A smile touched her lips. "You speak like a true chieftain of Tara now. I can see you have grown stronger in the years I have been away," Réalta remarked. "It suits you well."

Mahon remained silent.

"Midday is nearly upon us," she continued. "I must make haste if I desire to reach Dún Fiáin within a week's time."

Mahon nodded. "May your journey go swiftly and unhindered," he told her, reaching a hand up.

Réalta placed her hand in his and gave it a slight squeeze before releasing it. "*Slán.*"

"Farewell," he replied.

Giving her horse a light kick, Réalta continued her journey.

~~*~*~*

The Priestess only paused at the main gates of the village briefly to watch as Odhrán and her warriors rode off before turning away. Walking along well worn paths, Shiovra made her way to the back of the village, away from any eyes and ears that might take notice. Once she believed that she was alone, she called out softly on the wind, "Morrigú."

The wind gathered strength, twisting around her, whispering.

"Morrigú, mistress of battle, please heed my request," breathed Shiovra, turning her face to the sky.

Overhead a crow drifted through the air, cawing as it passed over her.

Shiovra watched it turn and swoop down to circle her.

After one final circle, the crow glided towards the ground, shifting from the body of a bird to that of a woman with pale skin and a cloak of black feathers. Her clothing was dark with the faintest hue of crimson along the bottom hem while thin braids embellished with feathers lay nestled within the thick waves of her long ebony hair.

"Badb of the Morrigú," said the priestess, offering it a small bow.

The woman's dark eyes looked Shiovra over. "Last we met, High Priestess of Tara, you were pursued by a host of Fomorii."

Shiovra nodded. "Aye," she replied. "And once more I call upon you. All is not well, neither with the Milidh nor within our own clan."

Badb frowned. "The meetings with Míl's son Amhergin have gone more smoothly of late," she remarked.

"Pleasant smiles hide hidden daggers," countered the priestess. "Surely you have not been blind to the Milidh war hosts that have been moving northward?" questioned Shiovra, tone hard. "A storm is approaching, and if we do not confront it with every sword we have, we *will* fall." Her eyes narrowed on the woman, waiting.

Badb remained silent for a moment and then asked, "Are you prepared to do all that is needed to defend Tara, High Priestess?"

Shiovra stood firmly. "Aye."

"Then you shall need to seek allies in unlikely foes," stated the woman. "There are two men who would best serve as allies. While you have seen the worth in one, the other is not quite as apparent."

A frown crossed Shiovra's face. "Who?"

Badb shook her head. "I cannot say," she replied. "It is for you to see the value that lies buried within him." Taking a step back, she turned her gaze toward the northwest. "This is where we part, High Priestess. The battle will soon be upon your companions." With a swirl of her feather cloak, the woman's body once more took the shape of a crow. Circling Shiovra, the words she spoke reached the priestess' mind, "This ally will prove his worth with Ailill's death."

* ~ * ~ * ~ * ~ *

As midday approached, the woods grew denser and the village borders were within reach. Odhrán knew his way through the trees well, taking led of half the group while Kieran branched off with the rest to make a wide arc around. Their plan was to take Deasún and Cúmhéa by surprise, flanking them.

Deep within the trees came the shrill caw of a crow, echoing around them. Moments later the crow flew past them, crying out once more before disappearing into the thick leaves overhead. The birds departure was meet with stifling silence.

Odhrán slowed the pace of his steed, his eyes narrowed on the woods surrounding them.

"What was that?" questioned one of the warriors.

"A warning to be heeded," replied Odhrán, tone hard. He had planned to take the enemy by surprise, but it would seem that they had the same strategy in mind. Where the Morrigú flew, death was always close at hand. "Daire, ready your bow," he ordered, pulling his steed to a halt. "We are not alone."

"Aye."

Meara pulled her steed up beside Odhrán as he dismounted. "Let us hope the Morrigú favors us," she murmured.

Odhrán did not respond, only pulled a dagger from his best. His eyes never left the trees as he listened carefully for even the slightest sound in the all too quiet woods. Over the shifting of steeds, he heard it: the slightest rustle of movement. The Milidh man cursed under his breath. They were surrounded.

"Draw you weapons and stand ready," ordered Odhrán. "We will let them come to us."

His command was obeyed without question.

Odhrán took a few steps to the right and glanced back at Daire, who nodded and readied an arrow. Raising his hand, Odhrán continued forward. The sound of a branch breaking underfoot reached his ears, startlingly loud in the quiet woods. And, when the shrill shriek of an arrow pierced the air, Odhrán dropped his arm and Daire let an arrow fly loose.

~~*~*~*

Though some of their warriors had gone to battle, the villagers of Dún Fiáin were calm as they continued their daily tasks. The gates remained wide open, however they were more heavily guarded than the priestess had seen since her arrival. The chieftain himself continuously walked the sturdy stone wall surrounding the village, his hand resting on the hilt of his sword.

Restless, Shiovra walked through the village. As she passed by, the villagers would pause and greet her warmly. Children giggled, offering her small flowers, even tidbits of food, before running off to their mothers. Shiovra accepted each with a grateful smile.

Patting a small boy on the head, Shiovra continued along the path up the hill. She found Caoilin sitting outside the main cottage with her loom leaning against the clay-daub walls. Though the girl appeared to be focused on her task, though from the faltering movements of the shuttle Shiovra could see Caoilin's thoughts lie elsewhere.

Nodding to the men standing guard, she placed a gentle hand on the girl's shoulder and told her, "Do not fret, we are well protected here."

Hand pausing, Caoilin glanced up and met the priestess' gaze. "I have heard may tales about the Hound of Mide," she murmured. "Terrible stories that haunt my dreams. How am I not to worry when he lurks close to my home with warriors at his side?"

"Aye, the threat Cúmhéa brings should not be taken lightly; he *is* a very dangerous man, as is Deasún," said Shiovra firmly. "However so are *my* warriors. Let it be a lesson to not only Gráinne, but all who would seek to destroy the peace we have gained, just how formidable the High Priestess of Tara and her warriors can be."

~~*~*~*

Kieran pulled his steed to an abrupt halt. The woods had suddenly grown quiet; there were no calls from birds, no murmur of the breeze, only silence. All around gathered thick shadows that clung to the trees. The Neimidh man watched the woods around them with wary eyes as he dismounted and drew his sword. Though he could not see them, Kieran knew they were surrounded. "It would seem out own ploy has been used against us," he said, looking back at Ceallach and Eiladyr. "They knew we would come, knew exactly what tactic we would make."

"Should we attack then?" asked Eiladyr as he dismounted.

"No, we will keep moving on foot towards Odhrán," Kieran stated, voice low. He gestured for the warriors to draw their weapons. "Let them think they have the upper hand and before they make their move, we strike first and break them. They will be forced to follow and we will no longer be surrounded."

Continuing through the trees and brush, they kept a steady pace.

Kieran kept his footsteps light, treading softly on the ground as he watched the shadows shifting cunningly around them. The slightest rustle of movement caught his attention. Letting the horse's reins slip from his fingers, he brought his hand up in a subtle gesture. The sound of weapons being drawn reached his ears. "Now!" Crying out, Kieran rushed forward, meeting the blade of a huntsman who stepped out from behind a tree.

Pushing back the man's attack, Kieran brought his foot up and kicked him. As the huntsman staggered back, two more pressed closer: one from the side and the other from behind. Turning swiftly, the Neimidh man blocked the first attack, letting his sword slide across the length of his foe's. Ducking down quickly, he twisted his blade and struck the man in the thigh while also dodging an attack of a spear from the third huntsman.

Tugging his sword free, Kieran kicked his foot out and knocked the huntsman's feet out from beneath him. As the man feel to the ground, he rolled away to avoid another attack from behind. Lurching to his feet, he turned to the huntsman.

The man thrust his spear at Kieran.

Slipping to the side, the Neimidh man brought his sword down on the length of the spear. Though the ash wood did not break, but the blade had left a notable bite in the weapon.

Cursing, the huntsman thrust again.

Kieran did not dodge, only turned his body and allowed the spear to brush past him. As the huntsman stumbled forward, he twisted and thrust his sword through the man. Tugging his blade free, he did not wait for the man to fall before spinning to bock the sword of another foe.

The huntsman's attack was strong, managing to force the Neimidh man back a few steps.

Gritting his teeth, Kieran struggled to knock the man's sword aside.

The huntsman was quick, swinging his sword in once more for the attack.

Kieran blocked once more. From the corner of his eye, he saw the huntsman whom he had wounded in the leg approaching with his sword ready to thrust. He held his attacker's sword at bay and, just as the huntsman moved for the kill, shifted his stance and allowed the men to strike each other.

The previously wounded man slumped lifelessly to the ground.

While the remaining huntsman pulled his sword free, Kieran approached from behind and struck the man violently through the chest before kicking him to the ground and jerking his blade free.

Looking around, the Neimidh man found the rest of the huntsmen had been felled by the others. Exhaling loudly, Kieran swung his sword roughly through the air to rid it of excess blood before wiping it on his cloak and sheathing it. "Are any of the men injured?" he questioned at Ceallach approached.

"Only minor injuries, no deaths," replied the Fomorii man.

Nodding, Kieran walked the area, looking at the fallen huntsmen. A deep frown crossed his face. None of the men were Cúmhéa or Deasún.

The cry of a crow sounded, drawing Kieran's attention. The bird broke through the trees and blocked his path, beating its wings as it turned a piercing black gaze on him. Cawing once more, the crow suddenly shot into the trees to their left.

Kieran's hand tightened on his sword. "The Morrigú…"

* ~ * ~ * ~ * ~ *

The arrow whistled past Odhrán's ear to fly through the trees. He watched as it disappeared into the shadows. At first only silence greeted him, then he heard it; the undeniable thud of something heavy falling to the ground. A smirk crossed Odhrán's lips. They had managed to make the first strike.

Shadows began to shift, moving towards them. One man in particular approached first, naked sword in hand. His lime-washed hair stood stiffly and his green eyes danced with delight. "Ah, what a grand welcome," said Deasún, holding his free hand out. "Look, lads, the chieftain's son has come to greet us personally!"

Laughter came from the huntsmen who began pressing closer in.

Odhrán watched them from the corner of his eye, counting at least six men, though he did not doubt more still hid within the shadows. As he brought his hand slowly to the daggers around his waist, he could hear the tightening of a bow as Daire readied another arrow.

Unrestrained laughter swelled within Deasún. "Are you still sore about Ainmire's death?" he sneered. "That pathetic fool of a man should have never been called chieftain of Tara! Your beloved priestess shall be next!"

Tugging his dagger free, Odhrán swiftly threw it at Deasún.

The man ducked and the dagger landed in the heart of a huntsman behind him. A twisted grin spread wide across his lips as the man fell lifeless to the ground. Raising his hand, Deasún ordered indifferently, "Kill them."

Odhrán paid little mind to the huntsmen rushing in. Instead he focused solely on Deasún. Eyes narrowed on the man, he slowly stalked towards him. Dodging Deasún's attack, Odhrán brought his sword up and cracked the man hard on the jaw with the pommel.

As Deasún staggered back, Odhrán was caught off guard when his tunic was grabbed from behind. Pulling his remaining dagger from his belt, Odhrán twisted and stabbed the man in the shoulder.

Hissing in pain, the huntsman released him.

Without hesitation Odhrán spun on the man and plunged the dagger through his heart. Turning to his next target, the Milidh man brought his sword up to block the attack, all the while thrusting the hand with the dagger up and into the huntsman's gut. When the man slumped forward, Odhrán shoved him away roughly.

Several more men rushed out from behind the trees at Odhrán.

Dropping down to a knee, he set his weapons aside and placed his hands on the ground. The earth beneath him fingers trembled in response and a wave rippled out all around him.

The huntsmen surrounding him stumbled as the ground heaved beneath them and they struggled to maintain their footing.

Odhrán grabbed his weapons and stood, charging one of the men.

The huntsman managed to bring his sword up and block Odhrán's, but failed to notice the dagger before it pierced his side. Ripping his dagger free, he thrust his sword into the man. Odhrán moved from warrior to warrior, blocking attacks and dealing his own. He moved through the battle with ease, taking down huntsmen one by one.

"Odhrán!"

He turned at Daire's voice to find the man in combat with a warrior nearly twice his size. Daire's bow lay discarded at his feet as he struggled to push back the huntsman's sword with his own.

Before Odhrán could act, a spear struck the huntsman through the throat and he fell to the ground.

Following the path of the spear, Odhrán found Kieran and the rest of the village warriors rushing into the fray. Looking over the faces of huntsmen who were now terribly outnumbered, he found Deasún was nowhere to be seen; the coward had managed to slip away. Cursing, Odhrán swung his sword hard, blade meeting the arm of an attacking huntsman. As the man cried out in pain, he struck the finishing blow.

The attack was quickly quelled and, once the last huntsman had fallen, Odhrán retrieved his missing dagger. Looking over his men and companions, he found most wounds superficial. It was Daire who concerned him the most. The priestess' cousin had received a great blow across his chest and the wound bled heavily.

Daire pushed Meara away as she tried to tend to his wound, insisting he was fine.

"That wound begs to differ," countered Odhrán sternly as he approached. "Let the Neimidh woman bind your wound till Shiovra can tend it properly in the village."

Reluctantly, the man nodded.

"Has Deasún fallen?" asked Eiladyr as he sheathed his sword.

Odhrán shook his head. "No, he fled," he replied coldly. "What of the Hound?"

~~*~*~*

Morgan sat in the open field, running a whetstone over his blade as the sun dipped lower in the sky. More than the wind rustled the grass nearby. He knew the Hound of Mide would come for him and, even as Cúmhéa approached, he did not look up. It was not long before the Hound's filthy shoes came into view. Morgan paid Cúmhéa little heed as he continued sharpening his blade.

"I would take your life here if it were not for Lady Gráinne's...*request*," growled the Hound of Mide.

Morgan snorted, raising his sword to inspect the edge. "The desires of your wench mean nothing to me."

Cúmhéa chuckled. "To think the Lady Gráinne would want you at her side," he scoffed, "all because you managed to wound me."

His hand stilled as Cúmhéa's shadow fell over him.

"That was a mistake I shall not allow to happen again," remarked Cúmhéa.

Morgan heard the slow draw of a sword from scabbard.

"If you do not live, then Lady Gráinne will have to see my worth," he continued, "and then the High Priestess of Tara will be mine!"

With the twist of his wrist, Morgan thrust his sword up into the man's abdomen and slowly met the Hound's stunned gaze. "I warned you before," he said coldly, pushing the sword in deeper. "I will not allow you to taint the priestess nor take her life. This ends now!" Violently twisting his sword, he ripped it free.

Cúmhéa stood frozen for a moment, his sword falling to the ground with a heavy thud.

"You never were much of a *Hound*, Cúmhéa," taunted Morgan.

Cúmhéa coughed before slumping to the ground.

Standing, Morgan slipped his whetstone into a pouch at his side and looked down at Cúmhéa. Cleaning his blade off on Cúmhéa's cloak, Morgan inspected it once before sheathing it. Stretching, he gathered his packs and tossed a small, engraved stone on the ground beside Cúmhéa's body. "Soon, brother," he said in a low voice, then turned and made his way back into the light woods nearby.

* ~ * ~ * ~ * ~ *

Shiovra stood on the platform at the village gates while the darkness of night stretched across the sky. Holding her cloak shut to ward off the slight chill carried by the breeze, the priestess ran her fingers lightly along the wooden rail. She stood among the village warriors, looking for any movement in the dark fields surrounding Dún Fiáin.

She did not doubt the abilities of her companions to defend them. Nevertheless when the sun began to set and the waning moon rose high in the sky, an anxious feeling lingered at the back of her thoughts. For a long while she saw nothing, but then she saw it: a small speck of flickering light in the distance.

As one of the warriors sounded a horn loudly, the others prepared bows and spears. Below the platform, the gates were closed securely in preparation for possible attack.

"Perhaps you should return to the main cottage, Lady Shiovra," suggested one of the warriors, a man by the name of Bradan.

Shiovra shook her head. "No," she replied firmly. "I will see their faces first."

Bradan nodded without protest, but did not leave the priestess' side as he stood with his spear in hand.

The light moved closer and closer, while figures gradually took shape in the darkness.

"Stand ready," ordered Bradan.

The sound of bows pulled tight reached Shiovra's ears. Hands tightening on the railing, her eyes narrowed on the approaching figures. In the flickering torchlight, she could make out Odhrán's face and relief washed over her. "Stand down!" she ordered. "They have returned!" Brushing past Bradan, she rushed down the ladder as the gates were opened.

Odhrán lead the group in, holding a torch in one hand and his steed's reins in the other. Daire sat slumped over on the back of the Milidh man's horse, his face pale in the torchlight.

Shiovra paused at the sight of her cousin, eyes falling on the blood stained bandages wrapped around his chest. A frown crossed her brow. "Daire…"

Odhrán pulled his steed to a stop and handed the torch off to an approaching warrior. "We stopped the bleeding, but the wound needs further tending to," the Milidh man told her.

Shiovra nodded. "We should get him to the cottage immediately," she said, gesturing. Though Daire offered her a weak smile as they made their way along the path and up the hill, his bloodstained bandages left her wary. Cresting the hill, she found Culann and Álainn waiting at the cottage door.

Upon seeing Daire, Álainn released a startled gasp.

"What happened?" demanded Culann.

"The enemy anticipated our strategy and employed one of their own," replied Odhrán as he helped Daire down from his steed and into the cottage.

Shiovra gestured for Odhrán to help her cousin sit down on the bench near the hearth while she began digging through her bags. Pulling out a small sealed clay jar and fresh bandages, she moved to sit beside Daire.

"Though we had sought to take them by surprise," continued Odhrán, "we were the ones who were caught off guard. The huntsmen lay dead, but Deasún fled during the fray." Removing his cloak and weapons, he sat them aside on the table and poured water into a small basin, handing it to the priestess.

"What of Cúmhéa?" pressed Culann, sitting down at the table?

Odhrán helped Shiovra remove Daire's bandages and tunic. "Kieran and I searched the woods carefully," he replied, tossing the soiled garments into the fire. "There was no trace of the Hound."

Shiovra glanced at Culann as she wet a cloth in the water.

A deep frown crossed the Milidh chieftain's face. "It would seem, then, that the threat continues to linger." He rubbed his brow wearily and poured himself a cup of mead, glancing at Shiovra. "How do his injuries fair?"

"Daire will need to rest at least a fortnight to be sure his wound heals properly," she told the chieftain as she began cleaning the dried blood from Daire's skin. Rinsing the cloth, Shiovra carefully cleaned the wound and felt her cousin flinch more than once under her touch. Setting the cloth and basin aside, she removed the tie and leather cap from the clay jar and dipped her fingers into the thick salve. Glancing up at Daire, she warned, "This will sting."

Daire nodded in return and turned his face away.

Shiovra brought her fingers to the wound and gently began working in the salve. Once the wound was thoroughly coated, she wrapped the bandages tightly around him and secured the end. Sighing, Shiovra ran her fingers carefully over his skin, checking for any swelling or hot patches. Finding none, she stood and took the basin to the door, dumping it outside before washing her hands.

"It is late. You should rest," ordered Odhrán as he handed her a towel to dry her hands with.

The priestess shook her head. "Not until I have looked over all other injuries," she told him, grabbing her pack and walking for the door.

"Our healers can tend to the wounded," offered Culann.

Shiovra paused in the doorway, glancing back over her shoulder. "Those men were wounded because of me," she told the chieftain. "I will do my part as priestess and tend to their wounds."

* ~ * ~ * ~ * ~ *

Odhrán crouched down beside the lifeless body that once was the Hound of Mide. From what he could see, the man bore one single wound: a single stab cleans through. From the angle of the wound, whoever had taken Cúmhéa's life had been most likely sitting. Straightening, Odhrán searched the area carefully. Eyes narrowing, he bent to pick up a small stone which lay on the trampled grass beside Cúmhéa.

Upon closer scrutiny, he noticed a simple design engraved into the stone. He did not know what the stone meant, but he was pretty sure he knew who it was meant for. Rubbing his thumb over the surface, Odhrán turned to Bradan, who stood close at hand with the horses.

"Did you find something, my lord?" questioned Bradan.

"A message of sorts." Bringing his fingers to his lips, Odhrán whistled; the sound mimicking the call of a bird.

After a brief moment, his call was met with a slightly different, lower reply.

"Return to the village," ordered Odhrán. "Gather some men and come back to burn the body."

Bradan nodded and mounted his steed. Giving the horse a sharp kick, he rode off.

Odhrán looked down at Cúmhéa's body. Though the Hound had not fallen at his own hand, he was pleased to see there was one less threat to be dealt with. Bending, Odhrán picked up Cúmhéa's sword and looked it over. The blade bore several nicks from battle and was pitted quite a bit.

It was not long before the heavy sound of horse hooves galloping caught his attention.

Odhrán did not turn as Eiladyr pulled his steed to a halt beside him and dismounted. "The Hound of Mide will trouble the priestess no longer," he said, tossing Cúmhéa's sword aside. "Your brother would indeed make a valuable ally."

"Are you certain it was him?" asked Eiladyr as he circled around Cúmhéa's body.

"Depends," Odhrán said. "Does this mean anything to you?" He tossed the stone to the man, who caught it with ease, before crouching back down to search Cúmhéa's pouches.

"Aye…" Eiladyr said slowly. "When I was a child, mother gave us amulets to ward off bad dreams. This one was Morgan's." He rounded

Cúmhéa's body once more before crouching down himself.

"And what message is he trying to give?" asked Odhrán, dumping the contents of a small pouch into his hand.

"It is more of a promise," stated Eiladyr. "A promise to ward off those who would threaten our priestess."

* ~ * ~ * ~ * ~ *

Several days had passed since Gráinne's attack was quelled. And, though there were no signs she would retaliate, Odhrán maintained his constant watch of the village borders. Leaving the protection of the village walls, Shiovra walked the fields. Running her palm across the tips of grass, she watched as sheep milled about nearby.

Pausing in the shade of a lone tree, the priestess watched two children as they brandished sticks, fighting in a mock battle while their father tended to the sheep. A smile crossed her lips as the little girl began chasing her elder brother around, the boy's stick broken under her attack.

A soft rustle from behind told the priestess she was no longer alone. From the heavy scent of smoked herbs carried by the wind, she knew who it was. It had been a year since she had left the isle of Rúnda, a year since she had defied the wishes of her mentor.

Shiovra stood in silence for a long while, simply enjoying the gentle breeze and rustle of leaves overhead.

"The darkness I have long foreseen is growing viciously," began Réalta, breaking the silence. "The battle will soon be upon us."

The priestess only spared her a slight glance out of the corner of her eye. Though it had only been a year since she had last heard the woman's voice, it had felt like much longer. "War between the Milidh and Túath is inevitable. There will be no avoiding it."

"I have regretfully come to understand such," Réalta continued with a heavy sigh. "And so I have come to mend a bond which should never have been broken."

Shiovra glanced at the woman as she watched the children who continued to play, taking note in how worn and weary Réalta appeared. In all her years on Rúnda, she had never seen the woman look quite so tired. "Our clan has already grown far too weak with Ainmire's death and Gráinne's betrayal," said the priestess in a firm voice. "If the bond between us is to be mended, I want you to keep one thing in mind. Just as I told Ceallach, I am the High Priestess of Tara and you will follow my word."

Réalta nodded without hesitation. "I understand."

"I have spoken with the Morrigú," stated Shiovra. "There are two enemies who will prove as useful allies, just as Odhrán has. One lingers close by, most likely watching at this moment."

"And the other?" questioned Réalta.

Shiovra shook her head and said, "I am not sure of whom she spoke, but his worth will be proven with Ailill's death."

The breeze picked up, carrying a light earthy scent.

Taking a deep breath, the priestess sighed. "Rain will be upon us soon," she continued. "We should return to the village."

7. CREEPING EVIL

Daire found Shiovra sitting near the main cottage, watching the village women as they carded wool. Slowly, painfully, he sat down beside her and joined her in her watch. His wound had begun to close, but it would leave a terrible scar to remind him of the battle fought. "We should not tarry here much longer," he said after a moment. "Tara needs her priestess."

Shiovra nodded. "We shall return soon enough," she replied simply. "Your wound needs to heal more before making the journey."

He remained silent for a long while, his eyes following the trailing path of blue woad markings on Shiovra's left arm. "Marked for life..." he muttered bitterly.

"Many have said those very words, as if they are some terrible burden to endure, though I do not see them as such," stated the priestess.

Daire looked up to find she continued to watch the village women.

"High Priestess or no, I will do all within my power to protect our village," continued Shiovra, "regardless of what dangers it may bring upon me." She turned to meet his gaze. "We cannot deny the threat the sons of Míl bring upon us. There is a terrible storm brewing and we must face it."

He could not deny the truth behind her words, despite however unpleased with them he was. Daire exhaled and rubbed the back of his neck. "Gráinne will only add to our troubles, in spite of the blow that has recently been dealt," he told her.

"Thus the need for a more cunning strategy on our hand," said Shiovra firmly. "To win this battle, we must be willing to take a few risks."

Exhaling, Daire shifted to lean back on his elbows. "I do not believe welcoming Morgan into our ranks would be worth the risk," he countered. "He may have stopped Cúmhéa, but his warning holds true. He will not hesitate to take you to Caillte."

The priestess rose to her feet and looked down at him with a frown marring her brow. "If Morgan can become an ally, if we can have his sword on our side, then it is a risk *worth* taking!" Shiovra told him harshly. "We cannot afford to be precautious anymore, not when war looms so close. Think of the villagers. Think of Úna and your children."

"Shiovra is right," came Meara's voice as she approached. "We need every sword on our side that we can get. Morgan *could* have turned his weapon against Shiovra, *could* have taken her to Caillte despite whatever orders he was given, but he did not. I agree with Shiovra and Odhrán that he would make a valuable ally."

Daire looked away.

"The Hound of Mide will trouble us no longer and we have Morgan to thank," said Shiovra softly. "I do not wish to think of what Cúmhéa would have done to me had Morgan not stepped in. For my sake, will you please reconsider? As Eiladyr said, given the opportunity, I believe Morgan would join us."

Though he remained wary to trust Morgan's intentions, he conceded defeat and nodded. "I shall trust your decision," Daire told her, standing and dusting off his clothing, "but until he proves himself as Odhrán has, I shall not trust him."

∼∼*∼*∼*

Clouds drifted across the night sky, shifting across the moon as Shiovra walked through the village. She held her cloak tightly shut, warding off the rough, damp wind. A heavy mist rolled across the ground, tinted with the slightest blue hue in the moonlight. The villagers had long turned in for the evening, leaving only the nightly watch by the warriors as her company.

When she reached the village gates, Shiovra gathered her skirts and climbed the ladder. The men posted on the wall did not question her presence, merely nodded a silent greeting as she walked toward Kieran.

The Neimidh man stood with a bow in hand and quiver of arrows on his back. Upon her approach, he turned and offered her a small, respectful bow. "Lady Shiovra," he said softly.

Shiovra moved to stand beside him. At first she said nothing, only watched the man who had once served as her guardian; a man whom she had called companion since her childhood. Though he was no longer her guardian, Shiovra knew he continued to watch over her. Looking out over the dark fields surrounding Dún Fiáin, she said, "I have a request of you, Kieran."

"What is it that you need, my lady?" asked Kieran, offering her his full attention.

Her hand tightened on her cloak. "By sending huntsmen to this village, Gráinne has made her intentions quite clear," she told him. "She has betrayed our clan and attacked her own kin, all to gain hold of Tara." Glancing at the man, she met his gold-brown eyes in the flickering torchlight. "I ask that you travel to Tréigthe. I understand that the journey will take a little over a fortnight, but for our tactics are to hold strong, we need to know how many men Gráinne holds sway over and what other strategies she may hold. Can you do this for me?"

Kieran nodded. "I shall tarry no longer then and prepare to depart immediately," he said. "Is there anything else you desire of me, Lady Shiovra?"

She shook her head. "Nay."

"Then I shall take my leave," he began, moving to step around her.

Shiovra reached her hand out suddenly, touching his arm.

Pausing, Kieran looked at her in question. "My lady?"

Her hand tightened on his sleeve. "Keep a wary eye out, old friend," she told him quietly. "The brewing storm only grows more dangerous."

He nodded. "Aye."

Letting her hand slip from his arm, Shiovra pulled the hood of her cloak up to ward off the rain as it began to lightly fall.

"Gráinne will not submit easily."

Shiovra turned at the sound of Ceallach's deep voice.

The Fomorii man stood to her left, his pale eyes narrowed on the darkness beyond Dún Fiáin's walls.

"I know full well Gráinne's determination," she replied, "as well as her *desperation* to prove herself." Shiovra sighed. "She is the youngest of Méav's daughters and the least skilled as a priestess. In Caher Dearg, Gráinne made it quite clear that she seeks to prove herself and will use whatever means necessary to do so."

Ceallach remained silent for a moment. "What is it that you plan to do?" he questioned.

She closed her eyes and took a deep breath, slowly releasing it. "Protect my village and people." Opening her eyes, she glanced at Ceallach to find the Fomorii man regarding her silently. "Gráinne may be kin, but her betrayal of the clan will not go without retribution."

Ceallach nodded, looking away.

As silence settled over them, Shiovra listened to the soft pattering of rainfall. Glancing at Ceallach, she realized how little she actually knew of the Fomorii man. During her ten years of training, she had come to know his cold, impassive nature well. However, since her departure from Rúnda, she had seen emotions in him that she had never seen before: anger, surprise, and even worry. Looking him over, she noticed that his jaw was tense and he stood stiffly. "You are troubled," she said, abruptly breaking the silence.

"Dún Fiáin is a well defended village with a strong wall," Ceallach told her. "Though you may not wish to sit idle, I believe you should tarry here a bit longer."

Shiovra frowned, eyes narrowing on him as he continued to look out over the dark fields. "I have no desire to leave Tara without her priestess much longer," she told him. "I only lingered this long to ensure that your son's wound heals properly."

Ceallach exhaled and turned to her, placing his hands on her shoulders. "I do not order, but *request* that you tarry a bit longer," he urged in a low voice, leaning towards her. "You are a strong woman and powerful priestess, Shiovra Ní Coughlin, but even you can fall under an enemy blade. As you said, had it not been for Morgan, Cúmhéa would have had his way."

The priestess remained still as Ceallach brought his mouth by her ear.

"Delay your return to Tara and use this time to train. Take your sword in hand and show your *strength*," he whispered before releasing her and walking away.

* ~ * ~ * ~ * ~ *

Gráinne struggled to maintain an air of calm while undeniable furry boiled within her. Nails digging into the bench she sat upon, her narrowed gaze drifted over Deasún as he knelt before her. "You dare to fail me as well?" demanded Gráinne, her voice dangerously composed.

The man did not flinch when he met her eyes. "The priestess' warriors are formidable men," he told her. "If you are dissatisfied, then *you* deal with them yourself."

Lunging forward, she grabbed him roughly by the tunic and brought her face close to his. "I could kill you where you kneel," she hissed.

Deasún smirked. "Ah, but you will not," he said, moving closer as he brushed his lips across hers. "You need me." Bringing his hands up, he pulled hers from his tunic. "You have lost many of your men to the priestess' warriors. You *need* me."

Gráinne stiffened at his words, but her anger quickly subsided as the man pressed his mouth fully against hers. "And why is it that I need you?" she questioned when he trailed his mouth along her neck.

"You need strong warriors at your side," replied Deasún, his hands moving to her hips as he began to gather the length of his skirts. "A man such as me can help bring more huntsmen to your side."

Gráinne shifted closer. "Such as?"

"Aichlinn."

Gráinne frowned and opened her eyes. She knew the name well. Aichlinn was the man who had burned Cúlráid to the ground and fatally wounded Deirdre, wife to the former chieftain of Tara, Ainmire. Nonetheless Gráinne also knew where Aichlinn's loyalties lay. "He is Ailill's man," she said harshly. "If you have forgotten, Ailill cast me aside."

"Perhaps…" murmured Deasún, unlacing his breaches before his hands returned to her hips.

Gráinne gasped as his fingers dug painfully into her skin.

"Aichlinn's loyalties are easily swayed," he told her as he pressed himself between her legs. "He will serve you…for the right price."

* ~ * ~ * ~ * ~ *

Night brought heavy rain and brine off the sea. Caillte walked through Dún Scáth with a cup of mead in hand. Pausing at the edge of the cliff, he looked down as the waves battered mercilessly against the rocks far below. Caillte brought the cup of mead to his lips, taking a long swig as he savored the flavor. Over the din of the waves, he heard the muffled approach of footsteps. Lowering the cup, he asked, "What tidings do you bring, Eimh?"

"Morgan has slain Cúmhéa," the man replied bowing low. "The Hound of Mide shall interfere no longer." Eimh paused, hesitating. "My lord, Ceallach Neáll has been spotted in Dún Fiáin."

Caillte's hand tensed on the cup.

"From Morgan's report, both Ceallach Neáll and the priestess' warriors are aware of his presence, however there has been no move against him. Only increased guard of the borders. Should I have him withdraw from his watch, my lord?"

"No," replied Caillte. "Morgan shall maintain his watch. Should the need arise, he is perfectly capable of defending himself." He paused a moment to take another long drink from his cup. His brother's presence in Dún Fiáin offered a promising opportunity. "As for my brother, I have something in mind for him."

"Aye, my lord."

The Fomorii man stood in silence for a moment and then glanced over his shoulder at Eimh, brow raised. "Was there something else?"

Eimh nodded, then said hesitantly, "My sister, Turiean…does she serve you well?"

"Aye, very much so." Finishing off his mead, he took a deep breath of the brackish breeze and turned to the man. "Tell the men to prepare. We shall soon have a guest."

"My lord?" asked Eimh in confusion.

A smile crossed Caillte's lips. "My brother shall be visiting."

* ~ * ~ * ~ * ~ *

Odhrán made his rounds along the village borders as evening approached. An intense, earthy scent hung in the air, carried by the wind. Rain was moving in quickly. However, something about the heaviness in the air did not sit right with Odhrán. A thick mist had begun to gather, crawling across the ground.

Entering a small patch of trees, Odhrán slowed his pace. In the fading light, he noticed a large gouge in one of them. Pausing, he ran his fingers along the broken bark, checking the depth of the wound. It was fairly fresh, the gash deep. Crouching down, he brushed his fingers lightly across the scuffed turf. Unlike the subtle tracks Morgan had left, these were heavy.

A branch snapped to his left.

Swiftly drawing his blade, Odhrán rose to his feet and looked around. He could see no movement in the growing darkness. Stepping softly, he began to walk slowly in the direction the sound came from. Rounding a hill, he found a cloaked figure walking through the trees with hood drawn.

Ducking behind a tree, Odhrán waited and listened. As the cloaked figure stepped around, he slipped out and approached from behind. Bringing his blade up, he reached around the figure and brought the edge of the sword to the man's neck.

The man stopped and quickly brought his hands up.

"You tread upon the borders of Dún Fiáin, state your purpose here," Odhrán ordered.

"I come by request of Lord Mahon," replied the man, voice steady though his body was tense.

Odhrán's eyes narrowed at the familiarity of the man's voice, though he could not place it. Stepping slowly around him, Odhrán held his sword poised and ready. Only when he turned his gaze upon the man's face did he lower his sword and sheathed it. He nodded to the Neimidh man who was often at Meara's side. "Ainnle."

The man released a heavy breath and dropped his hands, nodding in turn. "Lord Odhrán."

Looking around the man, Odhrán asked, "You come alone?"

Ainnle nodded. "Aye," he said. "The others remained at Tara to maintain the village's protection."

Gesturing for the man to follow, Odhrán retraced his steps back to the small grove. "Why has Mahon sent you?" he questioned, pulling the hood of his cloak up as rain began to fall lightly.

"To bring a message."

Weaving his way through the trees, Odhrán found the one bearing the wound. "Of what sorts?" he asked, crouching down to inspect the tracks more closely before the rain washed them away. When Ainnle hesitated to

84

answer, Odhrán glanced up at him.

The man looked uneasily around the trees surrounding them. "Ailill," Ainnle said in a low voice.

It was a name Odhrán took no pleasure in hearing. Standing, he met Ainnle's gaze firmly and demanded, "Speak."

Ainnle took a step forward, his eyes continuing to search the darkness around them. "Ailill has been seen moving southward," he replied quietly. "Though we do not deem Tara to be in any immediate threat, we do believe he may be heading for Dún Scáth. This village may face the threat of an attack."

"The threat of attack already lurks dangerously near," retorted Odhrán, gesturing to tree. "That wound was born from a Fomorii blade. From the looks of it, fairly recently as well. And those tracks are Fomorii. The village is already threatened."

"What shall we do?" asked Ainnle.

Odhrán's hand moved to rest on the pommel of his sword. "We wait."

～～*～*～*

Shiovra shivered as a chill rushed through her body despite the warmth of the hearth fire. Rubbing her arms, she tried to ward off the shuddering cold seeping into her bones. She could feel it hanging heavily in the air: an ominous, dangerous feeling. Rising slowly to her feet, she looked toward the cottage door as it rattled under the force of the howling wind.

"What is it?" asked Meara, the Neimidh woman standing as well.

Shiovra did not respond, only walked to the door and reached her hand out. A biting spark of energy brought a moment of pause to her actions. Something indeed was terribly amiss. Pulling open the door, Shiovra stepped out into the pouring rain.

A thick, heavy fog filled the village, twisting and swirling in an eerie dance.

Shiovra took a few steps away from the cottage. The fog did not part, only reached for her, small tendrils stretching out to lick coldly at her body. Taking a deep breath, she slowly exhaled, watching her breath disappear on the wind. A stifling weight hung in the air, dampening her powers as a priestess.

"This fog…" breathed Meara as she came to stand beside the priestess.

"Fomorii," replied Shiovra bitterly.

"Are we under attack?" asked Meara in concern.

Shiovra looked down the hill at the village as it lay blanketed in the heavy fog. "Quite possibly, but I cannot be sure," she told the Neimidh woman. Bringing a hand up, she tried to move the fog, to stir it, yet it remained untouched by her actions. A dark frown crossed her face. "Make haste to the main gate. Inform Lord Culann that all men should remain alert. There are misshapen Fomorii about."

Meara nodded. "Aye. What of the men on patrol?"

"I shall go," came Ceallach's voice.

The priestess turned to see the Fomorii man approach, cloak hood drawn.

"Being Fomorii myself, the fog cannot hinder me," he continued. Gesturing a hand out, the fog parted quickly in response. "I will warn the men watching the borders."

* ~ * ~ * ~ * ~ *

Odhrán crouched down, running his fingers lightly over tracks marring the rain laden earth. Despite the heavy downpour of rain, the footprints were undeniably Fomorii. Upon closer inspection, Odhrán took note that they did not head directly for the village, but more as if they circled around it.

Straightening, Odhrán cleaned his fingers off on his cloak as he followed the tracks. It was not long before he found more, many more. Though he could not be certain, Odhrán was quite sure there were at least fifteen misshapen Fomorii lurking about.

Pausing, his eyes turned to the darkness engulfing Dún Fiáin. He could hear nothing over the wind and pounding rain; no clash of weapons, no shouts, nothing.

"My lord?" questioned Bradan's voice.

Bringing his hand to his sword, Odhrán drew the blade slowly. "The village is surrounded."

"Should we return?" asked Bradan.

"Aye," replied Odhrán.

* ~ * ~ * ~ * ~ *

Perched high in a tree and well hidden by thick leaves, Morgan watched as one of the misshapen Fomorii walked beneath him. He pulled the sting of his bow back slowly, aiming the arrow for the creature's head. Exhaling, Morgan began to release the shaft, only the stop as two more Fomorii stepped into view.

Lowering his bow, Morgan frowned as he looked down at the creatures.

In the dim light offered by the cloud obscured moon, the pale flesh of the Fomorii was a sickening shade of green-gray. Scraggly hair covered the head of one, while another only bore on eye. Webbed fingers clutched spears tightly as the creatures spoke in a guttural tone of speech.

Shifting on the tree bough, Morgan leaned down closer to listen. The words spoken were strange to him, incomprehensible. Hand tightening on the bow, Morgan reluctantly withdrew his arrow. To attack would be foolish on his part. Hindered by the darkness of night and rain, Morgan could not be sure how many more of the creatures were nearby.

Returning his arrow to his quiver, Morgan leaned back against the trunk of the tree to wait.

* ~ * ~ * ~ * ~ *

Shiovra woke with a start from a restless sleep filled with terrible, dark dreams. She had not wanted to sleep with Fomorii about, but Álainn had insisted. Gazing up at the dark thatch roof above her, she could hear the din of heavy rainfall. The priestess sat up and crawled to the foot of the bed, pulling aside the curtain.

The hearth fire had dwindled down to meager flames that crawled across the wood. Across the cottage, illuminated softly by the dying fire, Daire leaned against the wall by the door. He sat with a knee drawn up and his sword beside his hand, ready should the need arise.

Slipping from her bed, Shiovra grabbed a blanket from a bench and draped it over Daire. Turning her attention to the hearth fire, she added more wood and stirred up the embers, encouraging the flames to grow.

Behind her, the wicker door lintel rattled in the onslaught of the wind.

The priestess shuddered unconsciously. She could still feel the undeniable chill in the air brought on by the Fomorii. Tossing a cloak over her shoulders, Shiovra approached the door and opened it.

In the darkness of night, she could see the heavy fog creeping and twisting as it heavily blanketed Dún Fiáin.

Shiovra paid little heed to the cold rain carried by gusts of wind, her eyes drifting over the village carefully; searching. When a hand came to rest gently on her shoulder, she only spared Daire a quick glance before resuming her watch.

"Unable to sleep?" he asked.

She nodded silently.

"Come away, your clothing is getting wet," Daire chided, urging her from the storm and to the fire. "You will fall ill if you are not careful."

Exhaling in frustration, Shiovra sat down on a bench. "What do they wait for?" she questioned with a frown.

"The misshapen Fomorii?" asked Daire in turn.

"Aye." The priestess leaned forward, resting her elbows on her knees as she watched the fire. "We are undoubtedly surrounded, susceptible to attack with this fog, and yet—nothing. I do not understand. What are they waiting for?"

"That is just what I want to discover," came Odhrán's voice.

Shiovra looked up to see Odhrán standing in the doorway.

Closing the door behind himself, the Milidh man removed his cloak and wrung it out. "I found tracks all around the village," continued Odhrán. "There are over a dozen Fomorii out there in the darkness, waiting." He moved to stand beside the fire, warming his hands. "Until a move is made, we cannot be sure of what their ploy may be." He turned his attention to Daire. "I want you to join the watch at the main gates. I will remain here with the priestess."

8. SEAL OF THE BROTHERS

She stood alone near the edge of a cliff looking out above a turbulent sea. The brackish breeze licked at her skin while waves crashed viciously below her feet. Taking a cautious step forward, she stared down the sheer face of the cliff. Her breathing was hard and quick, and her legs felt as if she had been running for a long time.

Turning away from the cliff she found a pale figure standing not too far away.

He regarded her silently with pale eyes. The wind tugged wildly at his cloak, fanning it out behind him like great wings.

Calling out Ceallach's name, she began walking toward him.

The long, low note of a battle horn drifted across the wind, bringing pause to her step.

Looking around, she listened as the sound of the horn echoed off crumpled walls. Her heartbeat quickened and she was filled with the sudden urge to flee. Glancing back at Ceallach, she found he had turned away from her. She called out his name, but he did not heed her as he walked away.

It was then that she saw him, a dark cloaked figure who beckoned to Ceallach.

Running towards them, she reached her hand out and desperately called Ceallach's name. He did not stop, did not heed her voice, only continued to walk away as his body was consumed by thickening fog...

Waking with a startled gasp, Shiovra sat up quickly. Her breathing was hard and labored, just as she had felt during the dream, and her legs ached. Hands clenching on the blankets, she strove to calm the wild beating of her heart. Shiovra closed her eyes, focusing on the soft snap and crack of the hearth fire. The sight of Ceallach's retreating back was vivid in her mind. "Ceallach, what have you done—?" he breathed.

Dim light stretched across her bed as the curtain was pulled open and Odhrán looked in. "Shiovra?"

Meeting his gaze, the priestess demanded simply, "Where has Ceallach gone?"

"What do you mean?" he asked.

Shiovra frowned at his words. Shifting to the foot of the bed, she slipped past him and stood, pulling a dress-tunic over her shift. "Ceallach left the village to warn the patrols of Fomorii presence," she told him. "Where did he go after?"

Expression darkening, Odhrán turned away and walked to the cottage door, flinging it open to flood the cottage with bright daylight. "Bradan!"

A shadow stepped into the doorway. "Aye, my lord?"

"Question all the guards," ordered Odhrán. "Anyone who has seen Ceallach or may have seen where he has gone is to report to me *immediately*."

Shiovra reached for her cloak but Odhrán's hand stayed her movements. Meeting his hard gaze, she asked, "You never saw Ceallach, did you?"

The Milidh man's silence was her answer.

"We need to search for him," she stated.

Odhrán's hand tightened on her arm. "No," he said firmly. "We will search for him, you will remain here."

Shiovra frowned and tugged her arm free. "I will *not* sit idle," she told him harshly.

A knock on the door interrupted them and one of the village warriors stepped in, offering Odhrán a quick bow. "My lord, Ceallach Neáll left the village walls late last night and never returned. One of the other men said they had seen him take an eastward path," he reported. "None of the other men report having seen him."

"Dún Scáth," came Réalta's voice.

Shiovra looked up to see Réalta approaching the fire, blanket wrapped around her shoulders.

The woman's face was pale and weary, her normally bright eyes dull from lack of sleep. She circled the fire and came to stand before Odhrán, meeting the man's gaze. "Ceallach has gone to his brother, Caillte."

Meara, who sat at the table, rose to her feet. "Dún Scáth is nearly a three day journey from here on horseback," she said.

"Then we should leave as soon as possible. The less time Ceallach remains in enemy hands the better," Odhrán said. Pulling his dagger from his belt, he crouched down and began to draw lines in the dirt floor. "There is a small breach in the western wall," he said, marking the spot with crossing lines. "It is not very large, not enough to pass through as it stands now, but we can easily remedy that. There is no eastern wall for it borders the sea. The drop is a long and dangerous one that would most likely take your life in the waves and rocks beneath."

Meara looked at him in surprise. "Have you been there?"

"More than once," he replied. "I prefer to keep an eye on anything that might pose a threat to kin and village." Odhrán turned to Shiovra, stepping close to the woman. Leaning down, he brought his mouth near her ear. "Do not leave these walls without proper guard. I will not have Caillte getting his hands on you."

The priestess nodded silently, the heat of his breath sending an unconscious shiver down her spine.

Straightening, Odhrán grabbed his cloak and fastened it around his shoulders. "Gather your weapons and horses," he said. "We leave immediately."

~~*~*~*

Shiovra stood on the platform above the village gates, looking out at the fields surrounding Dún Fiáin. One day had passed since Ceallach's disappearance and the departure of the warriors. She could not begin to understand where his thoughts lie in walking into his brother's grasp; however his departure brought reminder of the Morrigú's words.

It is for you to see the value that lies buried within him…this ally will prove his worth with Ailill's death.

There were not many men who could get close enough to Ailill to bring about his death; not many who held the man's trust. There was only one man she knew of who held both, one man who was dangerous in his own right: Caillte. The Fomorii man was more than capable of taking Ailill's life, but he was not one who would easily be swayed.

Nevertheless, if Caillte was whom the Morrigú spoke of, the blow the Milidh would face would be great. With Ailill's death, the threat of attack on Tara will diminish and the sons of Míl would no longer have a pawn to manipulate in the shadows. They would be forced to find other means of weakening the High Chieftains.

Shiovra knew the risk was great, but if she was to plant the seed of betrayal in his mind, she would need to meet with Caillte and speak with him. Turning away from the fields, she gathered her skirts and climbed down the ladder.

"Shiovra."

Shiovra turned to find Réalta waiting for her, horse reins in one hand and sword in the other. Glancing around the woman, she found the horse had already been prepared with bags. "Are you leaving?" asked Shiovra.

Réalta shook her head. "Nay," she replied. "However, I knew *you* would not sit idle for long." She held out the sword. "Take this. You will not walk onto Fomorii territory without a means to defend yourself."

Nodding, the priestess took the blade and belted it around her waist.

"Ride fast and hard," continued Réalta. "May Dana and the Dagda watch over you."

Grabbing the reigns, Shiovra climbed astride the horse. With one final glance at Réalta, she gave the steed a swift kick and rode swiftly through the gates, past befuddled village warriors who shouted in her wake.

Maintaining a steady gallop, Shiovra urged the horse through the southern fields and into the light woods to the east. She had not been riding long before she noticed movement ahead of her. In the shifting sunlight through the thick blanket of leaves, she saw a shadowed figure standing alone, waiting.

He was exactly where she had expected he would be, lingering along the borders of Dún Fiáin with bow in hand and arrow drawn and ready. If Odhrán desired for her to be properly guarded, then she would be thus, even if it was not who the Milidh man had in mind.

Tugging on the reins, Shiovra pulled her horse to a sudden halt.

Meeting her eyes, Morgan lowered his bow before slowly approaching.

The priestess looked down at him, her horse pawing the soft turf restlessly. "You told me, not too long ago, that should we meet again, you would take me to Caillte," she said firmly.

Morgan nodded, returning his arrow to the quiver. "Aye."

"Prove your words. Take me to Caillte."

The man studied her a moment, then crossed his arms. "Where are your guardians, priestess?"

"I am quite sure you already know the answer to that question," replied Shiovra.

"And why is it you have come to *me,* an enemy?" pressed Morgan, circling her horse.

Shiovra's hands tightened on the reins. "Perhaps foolhardiness? Regardless, I ask that you prove your words and take me to Caillte," she told him firmly.

Morgan remained silent a moment, then turned away from her. "Return to the village," he ordered.

"No."

He paused, back to her. "I have been watching you for a long while now, priestess," Morgan said. "You are a strong woman, but even the likes of Caillte could break your beautiful spirit."

Shiovra urged her steed to follow. "Either you take me to Caillte, or I go to him *alone.*"

Morgan turned back to her, holding his hand up for the horse to smell.

Rubbing the steed's nose, he moved his hand to the mane before grabbing the bridle. "Tell me then, priestess, why you desire to meet with Caillte?" he questioned.

"To deal a blow to the Milidh they never imagined," she replied coldly.

He raised a brow in surprise before a smile crept slowly across his lips. "Then perhaps I shall oblige to your request."

* ~ * ~ * ~ * ~ *

Odhrán pulled his steed to a halt near a small stream and dismounted. It was well past midday and they had ridden far, but the horses needed to rest as did they. "We will pause here for a bit," he said, meeting Daire's questioning gaze firmly, "unless you would prefer to continue to Dún Scáth on foot."

After a quick glance around to see who was tending to the horses, Odhrán began gathering water skins before crouching down beside the stream to fill them. They still had much ground to cover and would not rest for long. There would be time for a meal later when they stopped for the night.

Eiladyr dropped down to a knee beside him. "If we keep moving at this rate, we will reach Dún Scáth just before nightfall on the morrow," he said in a low voice, casting a quick peek back over his shoulder. "You are planning on attacking under the cover of night, am I right?"

Odhrán nodded, sealing the water skin before dipping another into the water. "Aye," he replied. "Ceallach was taken under the cover of night, why not use that very same tactic to our advantage? There are too few of us to risk a frontal attack in the middle of the day. Discretion is our best option."

* ~ * ~ * ~ * ~ *

She could feel his eyes on her as she sat watching the low fire he had built to ward off the slight chill in the air and cook the hare he had found for their meal. Morgan had not bothered to tie her up nor secure his weapons from her reach; instead he sat with his bow, quiver, and sword resting on the ground carelessly between them while he prodded the fire with a stick. Embers drifted up from his actions, drifting along with the breeze for a short moment before dying out.

Shiovra glanced at Morgan, meeting his gaze.

"You seem to be quite at ease in the presence of an enemy," he mused.

"That is because you are...different," she replied, looking at the fire. "I have learned that not all *enemies* are quite what they appear to be. At times, even the most hated enemy can surprise you with kindness, though that is not true for all." Shiovra paused, pulling her knees to her chest and wrapping her arms around them. "You did not need to save me from Cúmhéa, did not have to let me go, yet you did. You even gave me your tunic to cover my torn shift. You are *different*."

Morgan was silent a moment, then asked with a note of amusement, "You trust me?"

She rested her head on her knees. "I trust you will keep to your word and not harm me." Shiovra thought a moment. "You have not only been watching me, but your brother as well."

Silence greeted her and for a moment she thought he was not going to speak.

"Aye. What of it?"

A smile crossed her lips. "Eiladyr does not speak fondly of his life before coming to Éire, and even less of his own kin," she told him. "The only kind words I have heard him speak are of his mother and for one lone brother." Shiovra turned her head to look at Morgan. "You."

A short laugh passed his lips as he grinned. "Is that so?" Morgan turned his attention back to the fire, prodding at the fire covered wood. "It has been three years since Eiladyr and I have spoken. He may not see me quite the same as he once had."

Shiovra watched him in silence for a moment, then asked, "Why is it, if I may ask, that you chose to side with Caillte?"

Morgan leaned forward on his knees, his auburn hair bright in the light of the fire. "He made me a promise," replied the man. "Eiladyr does not know this, but I followed him onto that ship the night he left home, wanting to be free as well, but then the storm hit." Morgan's jaw tensed, his hands clasped tightly. "I fell into the sea and when I came to, I could not see my brother anywhere. Eventually I learned to speak Éire's language and found myself treading upon the borders of Dún Scáth."

The priestess watched as the man rose to his feet and stretched.

"I have never had need of Caillte's offers and still find no use for them," continued Morgan, "but he did promise to help me find my brother and, in a way, he has." Bending, he added some wood to the fire.

Stifling a yawn, Shiovra lay down on her cloak and looked up at the star filled sky. She could hear Morgan shift beside her. Though she did not fear him, she was quite aware of even his most subtle movement. A gentle hum reached her ears, one that held a note of familiarity. Shiovra listened to the slightly melancholy melody before she realized where she had heard it before; it was the song Eiladyr sung on their way to Dún Fiáin.

The humming stopped and Morgan began to sing in a smooth, low tenor voice:

Child of fire, you lie so fair
My hopes you hold in your tiny hands
Born in strife and captured there,

As if the whole of all the land
In your sleepy gaze were braced,
Keep us me in your infant dreams,
Of crowns and chieftains and other things
And glory given more to fate unseen,
But in your mind's eye in your infant dreams.

When his song ended, Shiovra glanced at him only to find he was already watching her. When she met his warn brown eyes, an embarrassed heat rushed to her cheeks and she looked away quickly.

Morgan chuckled lightly. "It is late," he said. "You should rest for the night. I will wake you come morning."

~~*~*~*

Daire watched the fire with a narrowed gaze. They had ridden hard since early morning and now that they rested for the night, his body was greatly protesting even the smallest of movements. He greatly welcomed what little sleep he would get. Daire was pulled from his thoughts as Odhrán sat down across from him.

"We should formulate a plan of attack now. We can alter it if need be later," he said, gesturing for Eiladyr, Meara, and Ainnle to join him. Smoothing a patch of dirt, he pulled his dagger from his belt. "Now, as I said before, Dún Scáth is built along the edge of a cliff," Odhrán continued, scratching a line in the dirt with a semi-circle coming off it. "The cliff is sheer with a few narrow, weak ledges, thus why the need for using the breach in the wall."

Daire frowned as he looked over the drawing. He could see nothing promising for what they needed to do.

"The main gates face the southwest and are heavily guarded. The outer walls are stone," Odhrán explained. "As I said, the breach is not large enough to pass through. We will need to make it larger, and with haste. Use whatever you can on the loose stones: sword, spear, anything. Speed and silence will need to be our priority." He scratched cross markings near the entrance as well as two more near each of those. "These are wooden watch towers, built up so that they may fire arrows over the walls. It is essential that the men posted there do not see us. Perhaps, if it comes down to it, we can set them aflame as a distraction."

Daire swore under his breath and rubbed his neck.

"We will need to move fast once we are inside," the Milidh man continued. "Locating Ceallach should be easy. He will most likely be held within the main cottage and heavily guarded. We must deal with the guards as quietly as possible. Do not attack unless you have been seen, otherwise you *will* draw attention to us."

Meara leaned forward, her eyes intent on the etched map. "This will be quite the challenge…" she said with a frown.

"And certainly not the last," muttered Daire.

* ~ * ~ * ~ * ~ *

Ceallach woke on fur pelts in a dimly lit cottage, his head throbbing. Groaning, he sat up, his entire body protesting the movement. The cottage he had been placed in was small and bare with naught but a meager fire burning in the hearth. Over the crack and snap of the fire he could hear the muffled crash of waves nearby. His mind felt as clouded as fog itself.

Light flooded the cottage, bright and painful.

Shielding his eyes, Ceallach lurched to his feet. The sudden movement sent his head spinning and he was forced to lean against the wall lest he fall. He could not control the trembling of his body as weakness flooded him. Running a shaky hand over his face and into his hair, his pale eyes coldly met that of his elder brother's. "What have you done to me?" he demanded, voice tight and harsh.

"Such cold words, brother," replied Caillte, crossing his arms. "Is that all you have to say to me after eleven years?"

Ceallach did not respond, his eyes narrowing on his brother as he struggled to regain his strength. He would not allow Caillte to bait him.

Approaching the fire, Caillte stared down into the flames. "Do not worry, it will wear off in due time," he told him.

Hand clenching against the wall, Ceallach took a slow step toward the man. "What are you planning, Caillte?" he pressed calmly, his eyes not leaving his brother for a moment. "What do you seek to gain by sending Morgan to watch Shiovra?"

"Does it truly matter? He has nothing to do with you, only the priestess," replied Caillte, glancing up to meet Ceallach's gaze as he slowly circled the hearth. "We are Fomorii and as such we bear no allegiance to the Túatha Dé Danann. It is only you who remains among them—all because of that woman, Réalta Dubh." He paused, offering him a small grin. "You have already lost too many years at her side. Your duty as her guardian has long ended. There is no need to remain beside her, no to protect that High Priestess. Join me here, brother."

Jaw tensing, Ceallach allowed bitterness to encroach upon his voice when he replied. "Because of you, our sister Saibh is dead. You believe that you can so easily bring me to your side?"

Caillte shook his head. "There was nothing I could do for her," he replied. "I nearly lost my life that day as well. Does that hold no meaning for you?"

Gaze darkening, he took another step forward. "It lost meaning when you allied yourself with Ailill," Ceallach said callously.

"It was Túath blood that took Saibh's life!" barked Caillte. "Had it not been for Ailill, I would have died that day as well, but he tended to my wounds. He gave me the opportunity to grow in strength and seek my revenge."

A frown crossed Ceallach's face. "You allied yourself with Ailill for retribution?"

"Aye." A grin spread wide across Caillte's lips. "For hundreds of years we Fomorii have suffered at the hands of unwanted guests. The Parthalon, the Neimidh, the Fir Bolg, the Túatha Dé Danann and now the Milidh. Éire is rightfully *ours*. For the sake of our people, I will play this game of war. And, when the battle comes, I will sit back and watch as the Túath and Milidh clans kill each other."

"Tell me then: what part does Shiovra truly play in this?" Ceallach questioned in an even tone. "To what purpose do you truly intend to use her?"

"The High Priestess is crucial to everything," he replied. "She is sought by Ailill for her power. She is a threat to the Milidh. She is valued by the Túath chieftains. Though Gráinne may want her dead, I find that her life is highly valuable to my plans."

Hands clenched tightly, Ceallach watched his brother with a narrowed gaze. "I will not let you use Shiovra as your pawn," he said.

Caillte chuckled heartily. "How is what I plan for the priestess any different than what you and Réalta Dubh have done?"

Anger rising, Ceallach swung his fist at his brother.

Caillte was faster, grabbing Ceallach's wrist and pulling the man into his arms. "Forgive me, brother, for not being able to keep Saibh safe," he said in Ceallach's ear. "But her death opened my eyes. If you will not join me, then you must not interfere."

Ceallach felt a prick on the side of his neck and, as numbness began to fill his body; his brother's words reached his ears just before darkness consumed him.

"Sleep for now, my brother."

* ~ * ~ * ~ * ~ *

Odhrán crouched amongst the trees and brush, eyes scanning over Dún Scáth as he carefully scrutinized the sentry towers rising high above the stone walls, illuminated by torchlight. He drew back a bit when the gates opened, allowing passage for six huntsmen before closing once more. The night was quiet, save for the sound of waves crashing upon the rocks below the cliff from a restless sea, and the wind carried the heavy scent of salt and rain.

Slipping away and returning to the others, Odhrán ordered, "Tether the steeds."

Daire nodded and quickly took to the task himself.

"This will not be a simple task," continued Odhrán, his eyes drifting back to the village. "The ditch surrounding the wall is steep and it will be difficult to keep our footing." He watched as the huntsmen move away then gestured. "Move quickly and keep to the shadows."

Leaving the safety of the trees, Odhrán crept his way toward Dún Scáth. He only paused a moment to glance at the guards before sliding down the ditch to land in a small puddle of water at the bottom. A muffled cry reached his ears and he turned just as Eiladyr lost his balance to land face first in the mud.

Odhrán offered the man a hand up then turned to the breach in the wall. Running his fingers along the stones, he searched for loose ones. They would have to move quickly and quietly. Their closeness to the wall kept them well out of sight of the watchtowers, but it was the men who had left the village that concerned him the most.

Pulling a stone free, he set it aside before turning to another. Eiladyr and Ainnle worked alongside him while Meara kept watch. Within a short amount of time they had widened the breach enough for them to slip though with a bit of effort.

Odhrán slipped through the breech first, pausing to look for huntsmen before signaling for the others to follow. Standing aside, his hand remained on the hilt of his sword as he watched a warrior sleeping against a cottage, snoring loudly. Turning his attention back to his companions, he noticed Ainnle lingered outside the wall.

Meara gestured for the man to follow but he merely shook his head.

I cannot fit, he admitted in a series of hand gestures.

Odhrán stepped forward. *Keep a careful eye out that you are not seen,* he signed back to the man.

Ainnle nodded.

Turning, Odhrán focused his attention on the cottages around them. One in particular, close to the cliffs edge, caught his attention. Two men stood guard outside the feeble wicker-work door. And while he had assumed that Caillte would have kept his brother in the main cottage, he could not help the feeling that the Fomorii man was in there. Tapping Meara and Daire on the shoulders, he gestured to the small cottage. *There,* he signed.

They followed his line of sight and nodded.

Several sleeping and drunken huntsmen lay between them and their target.

Do not get too close to the sentry towers, Odhrán gestured. *If they spot us, the whole place will be woken up and make it very difficult to reach Ceallach.*

Perhaps it would be better to take out some of these guys who have been drinking, signed Daire. *Make it look like they drank too much mead. The other guards won't even think anything of it if we do it right.* He glanced at Eiladyr, a mischievous light flashing in his eyes. *Help me get those two.* Daire gestured to some men sitting near a cottage to their right.

Eiladyr grinned broadly and his gold-brown eyes burned with all the mirth of a hunting wolf as he nodded. *This is going to be entertaining.*

Do not do anything too foolish, signed Meara.

* ~ * ~ * ~ * ~ *

Daire stalked toward the cottage with Eiladyr following. He paused, gesturing Eiladyr to circle around the opposite side of the cottage and when the man nodded in agreement, he pressed his back against the cottage wall and waited a moment before slowly creping his way toward one of the men. Reaching a hand out, Daire tapped the huntsman on the shoulder. As the man turned in response, he brought his fist flew up and struck the huntsman in the face between the eyes.

The man teetered a moment in drunken haze, then slumped unconscious to the ground.

Daire looked up just as the other warrior fell under a blow from Eiladyr's sword pommel. Grinning, he made his way further to the right, moving towards another cottage.

The men there were sound asleep, several empty mead cups surrounding them.

Daire started as he was suddenly seized by the arm and roughly pulled into the shadows. Glancing at Eiladyr, whose grip on his arm had not lessoned, he signed, *What?*

Eiladyr gestured with his head.

Following the man's gaze, Daire noticed two quite sober huntsmen step around a cottage and head toward them.

Daire cursed under his breath, pressing further into the shadows. His eyes scanned the area frantically, searching for any sign of the rest of his companions only to find they were too far to be of any help. "Damn."

Beside him, Eiladyr's hand tightened on his sword.

Shaking his head, Daire moved slowly around the back of the small cottage. Unfortunately, his retreat was quickly brought to a halt as he realized just how closely they had come to the watch towers. That realization was followed by a string of low curses.

Eiladyr tapped him on the shoulder, grinning. Reaching up to the thatch roof, the man grabbed a clump loose and pulled a leather tie from inside his tunic to wrap around the bundle.

Daire frowned. He had a terrible inkling on what the man was planning and it would go completely against Odhrán's plans of *quiet*.

Eiladyr's eyes narrowed on the small bundle. Wisps of smoke began to rise from the bunch, quickly followed by small flickers of flame that rapidly grew as they began to consume the thatch. With a triumphant grin, Eiladyr hurled it onto the watchtower.

* ~ * ~ * ~ * ~ *

Ainnle walked to the edge of the cliff, hoping to find some means in which he could get into Dún Scáth. The crumbling sheer face and waves crashing into sharp rocks below proved that the cliff was indeed a nonviable course of entrance. Muttering to himself, Ainnle relented to sit down upon a large stone and keep his lonely watch on the breech.

He nearly fell from his perch, though, when fire suddenly erupted on the thatch roof of a watchtower. Despite the dampness carried by the air from the sea and incoming storm, it burned brightly. A wild charge of energy danged in the air along with the flames, fueling them.

Stumbling to his feet, Ainnle heard a battle horn sounded warning on the wind. His eyes snapped to the main entrance.

The doors had been flung wide open and the huntsmen who had been keeping guard were nowhere in sight.

Ainnle cared not why they were open, only that his opportunity to join in stood waiting.

Drawing his blade, he slowly made his way toward the gates. The din of battle was quick to reach his ears. Pressing close to the wall, Ainnle peered inside Dún Scáth.

Utter chaos filled the village.

A grin crossed his lips. He cared not how everything had fallen out of place, only that his chance to take part in the ensuing battle was upon him. Laughing heartily to himself at his good fortune, Ainnle drew his blade and rushed into the fray.

* ~ * ~ * ~ * ~ *

Ceallach moaned as he opened his eyes, head throbbing horribly. Sitting up, he rubbed his face wearily and looked around the cottage to discover he was alone once again. A frown crossed his face as he could hear the muffled din of battle. Clambering to his feet, Ceallach made his way to the door while grabbing on to the wall for support. Whatever his brother had done to him continued to affect his body, leaving him feeling a lingering weakness he was unable to shake.

Through the door he could hear shouts and the clash of swords. Pulling on the door, he found it would not move. Ceallach tried to use the weight of his body against the door, but in his weakened state his efforts were useless.

He was, in a sense, perfectly trapped. Worn, he leaned against the door and rubbed his temples.

"Ceallach."

Ceallach's anger mounted at the sound of the priestess' voice. Gaze snapping up, his attention fell upon the fiery form of a woman standing in the hearth. His eyes narrowed. Though it was only an ethereal form of the priestess being channeled through the flames, he could *feel* her presence close by. "Do not be foolish," he muttered, his voice close to pleading.

"You were the one who walked willingly Caillte's grasp, Ceallach Neáll," replied Shiovra in a voice that echoed in the small cottage.

Ceallach's hands clenched. "You should have remained in Dún Fiáin," he countered angrily. "Instead you linger far too closely to this place."

The priestess gave a small nod. "It is of necessity."

He could not be sure of the meaning behind Shiovra's words, but the sheer simplicity of them did not please him in the least. "Why have you come?" he demanded. "Did I not warn you that even you can fall under an enemy's blade?"

Shiovra offered him a tight smile. "Sometimes risks must be taken. Surely you understand this, Ceallach Neáll."

Ceallach rubbed his face. He knew there were always risks to be taken, but some were better left untouched.

"Please trust me," whispered the woman as the flames dwindled down, leaving him with naught but a mere hearth fire.

"Move aside!"

A frown crossed his face. The voice had come from outside the cottage and sounded very familiar. Heeding the warning, Ceallach stepped away from the door.

There was a sudden loud crack as something slammed into the door, sending it to the ground under the sheer impact. Odhrán stumbled in after the door, torch in hand. The Milidh man's eyes narrowed on Ceallach. "We are leaving. Now," he ordered.

Ceallach raised a brow at the man, but stepped from the cottage nonetheless. Whatever his brother had done to him left him too weak to argue.

Odhrán followed him from the cottage and paused to toss the torch onto the thatch roof, setting it ablaze.

All about them chaos filled the village.

Ceallach watched as several huntsmen rushed passed, hardly sparing him a glace. His eyes carefully scanned the village, searching. "You keep going," he said. "I have something to do."

The Milidh man frowned and asked, "What were you planning, Ceallach Neáll?"

A conceited grin crossed his lips. "That," Ceallach told him, "would be a better question for the Lady Shiovra."

∼∼*∼*∼*

Rain had begun to fall softly as Morgan covered the remaining fire embers with dirt. The horses had long been tethered a safe distance away and Dún Scáth lay within their sights, the watch towers ablaze. Even from the distance in which they stood, the clamor of battle could be heard clearly.

Shiovra glanced at Morgan to find that the man watching her.

"May I touch you?"

She could not deny that his question had caught her off guard. Unsure of the meaning behind his words, Shiovra nodded hesitantly. "Aye."

Morgan reached out, pausing when she tensed. "I will not harm you," he told her. Stepping closer, he took hold of her wrist gently and lifted her arm. Running his finger tips along the pattern, a frown crossed his face. "They are as beautiful as you, priestess."

"Shiovra," she told him.

His gaze met hers curiously.

"My name is Shiovra Ní Coughlin."

Morgan nodded. "Shiovra, then," he said, bringing his other hand up to trace the spiral curling by her right eye. "You said I am *different*. You are as well." He brushed a lock of hair behind her ear.

Shiovra remained still, her eyes not leaving his face. Her heart quickened slightly at his touch, afraid yet curious.

Exhaling, Morgan's hand dropped from her face, joining the one holding her arm. "We best hide these lest they draw unwanted attention," he told her. Digging through a pouch on his belt, he pulled out a long strip of cloth. Morgan wrapped the bandage over her arm, covering her markings, and secured the end. Meeting her gaze once more, he asked, "Are you ready?"

The priestess nodded.

He hesitated a moment before letting her arm slip from his grasp. Stringing his bow and grabbing an arrow from his quiver, Morgan began walking toward the village.

Shiovra took notice that the man no longer bothered trying to hide their presence and headed directly for the main gates.

Flames consumed nearly all the buildings, brightly illuminating the disarray that was Dún Scáth. Several huntsmen lay dead on the ground while a few tried in vain to quench the flames.

"Keep close," warned Morgan.

Shiovra nodded.

As they made their way quickly through the village, Shiovra searched over all faces till she found Daire and Eiladyr. Although in the middle of battle, the men argued with one another over something about the fire and, for a brief moment, Shiovra's eyes met with Daire's before she turned away to follow Morgan.

"Morgan!" came a shout over the commotion. "Why are you here?"

Shiovra turned at the voice, her gaze narrowing. She recognized the Milidh man too well for her liking. Though she had only encountered him once while leaving Rúnda, Árdal was a demented man she had hoped never to lay eyes on again.

"Ah," A malicious smile tugged at Árdal's lips. "You have brought a pretty little wench. Pity we will not be able to enjoy her till these curs are dealt with." He took a step toward them. "She has a familiar look about her—"

Morgan loosed his arrow, striking the ground at the man's feet in warning, and hastily readied another.

The man took a step back, meeting Morgan's cold gaze with outrage. "What is the meaning of this, Morgan?" Árdal demanded.

Shiovra glanced at Morgan from the corner of her eye to find the man's attention completely focused upon Árdal.

"You will not lay one filthy finger on her," said Morgan in a harsh tone as he pulled the string back, arrow aimed for the Milidh man's heart. "I made a promise to someone that I would protect this woman, especially from the likes of you."

A grin twisted Árdal's lips maliciously. "Have it your way then," he replied. With a shout of rage, Árdal made to charge at the man.

Morgan shifted his hold on the bow and let the arrow fly. It struck the ground hard, a mere hairs width away from Árdal's foot. As quickly as he had released the arrow he had another drawn and ready. "I will not hesitate to kill you," he warned coldly.

Árdal hesitated only a moment, then took a step forward.

Shiovra watched as the arrow glanced across Árdal's cheek, leaving a deep gash.

The man stopped and brought his hand up to the wound. Dragging his fingers down, he smeared the blood across his face as his eyes snapped up to meet Morgan's. "Stop toying with me!" snarled Árdal. "If you want to fight, then fight me!"

Morgan scoffed as he handed his bow and quiver to Shiovra, drawing his blade. "Pardon me," he said, "but I must deal with this man."

Árdal's laughter filled the air, low and mad.

Cold rain began falling from the blackened sky.

With the threat of the bow gone and Morgan's sword ready, Árdal charged toward them.

Shiovra took a quick step back.

The clang of blades rang sharply through the air as Morgan's sword met Árdal's full on, leaving it signing from the attack.

Morgan forced Árdal's sword back with his own, kicking his foot out and hooking it behind the man's to sending him crashing hard to the ground. His attack was quickly followed by his foot to Árdal's chest, forcing him onto his back.

The huntsman cursed and his hand twitched on his own weapon.

Anticipating the possible attack, Morgan thrust the tip of his sword into the man's wrist. "You should have heeded my warning," he remarked simply. Ignoring Árdal's pained cry, he wrenched his sword free and turned it to the huntsman's heart. "This ends here." Without a moment's pause, Morgan raised his sword slightly before plunging it down. Pulling the blade free, he cleaned it on his cloak before sheathing it.

"That was quite the display."

Shiovra turned at the deep, oddly familiar, voice. Had it not been for the length of the Fomorii man's silvery-white hair, she would have easily mistaken him for his brother. "Caillte…" she breathed, her voice trailing off.

The man turned his icy gaze to meet her own, a curious expression crossing his face. "And you would be?"

"Shiovra Ní Coughlin, High Priestess of Tara," she replied firmly.

Caillte's eyes shifted to Morgan. "Did I not instruct you to merely watch her?" he demanded. "Why is she here?"

Morgan flashed the man a playful grin. "She was persistent."

Frowning, Caillte turned his attention back to the priestess. "What is it that you seek by coming here, Túath priestess?" he asked. "Do you wish to barter with me?"

Shiovra studied the man's face for a moment. She knew she needed to chose her words carefully; that she needed to plant the seed which would lead to his betrayal. "There is a battle to be fought, Caillte of the Fomorii," she told him. "Where shall your place be? Will you maintain your current purpose? Will you continue to seek using me for your own gain against the Milidh and Túath alike?" When the man's eyes widened slightly, a smile touched her lips. "Aye…I know that which you seek to gain. You wear your intentions far too clearly on your face."

Caillte's face hardened, his eyes narrowing on her. "And what do you propose?" he questioned. "Do you want me to just sit aside and allow my sister's death to hold no meaning?"

Shaking her head, Shiovra replied, "Nay. By all means play this game of war. But first, think of what holds more importance to you: this little diversion of bloodshed or the lost sister you so dear. Will you remain a pawn and stain this beautiful land crimson, or will you protect *her* memory. Would Saibh approve of what you are doing?"

Morgan stepped between Shiovra and Caillte. "I will be returning Shiovra to her guardians now," he told her.

"Do you side with the priestess now?" asked the Fomorii man smoothly.

"Perhaps." Turning, Morgan began to walk away.

With one quick glance at Caillte, Shiovra followed Morgan through what remained of the village.

The fires had been quenched in the rain, leaving the Dún Scáth dark and shattered. Bodies of huntsmen littered the ground, staining the stone and dirt with blood.

Morgan stopped at the gates, turning to her. "This is where we part for now, Shiovra," he stated. "I will keep my watch over you at a distance. We will meet again when the time is right."

Shiovra hesitated a moment, glancing at him. "It was Eiladyr you spoke of when you told Árdal you had made a promise to protect me."

He looked away, but the answer was written clearly across the man's face. "Your guardians wait. Go."

Nodding, Shiovra stepped through the remains of the gates and toward a small flickering light struggling to survive in the rain. As she neared, the faces of her companions greeted her.

Daire greeted her lividly. "What were you thinking coming here with *Morgan* nonetheless?!" he snapped.

"Now is not the time for this," interrupted Odhrán in a cold tome. "Dún Scáth may have fallen but the threat still looms. A safe distance must be made between us and the village before the priestess' actions are discussed."

$* \sim * \sim * \sim * \sim *$

The trees offered little shelter from the downpour of rain. Morning was drawing near, however Odhrán advised that they rest longer before continuing on their journey and no protest was made to counter his orders. Shiovra sat quietly on a fallen tree, running her fingers along the cloth that wrapped her arm and hid her markings. Morgan proved his worth as an ally, although he had not quite joined their side. All that remained was to wait and see what choice Caillte made.

Daire sat down beside her, clasping his hands together tightly. "Why did you come?" he asked in an eerily calm tone.

Shiovra's hand fell to her lap. "To plant the seed of betrayal," she replied. From the corner of her eye, she saw Daire's hands tense and there was no doubt in her mind the anger he held at bay. "The Morrigú spoke of an enemy who would prove his worth with Ailill's death. I can see no other capable of such than Caillte."

He remained quiet for a long while, his eyes focused ahead of them. "And if in the end he betrays us as well?"

"Then we deal with it when the time comes." Shiovra glanced at Odhrán. The Milidh man leaned against a tree, watching her. "Till then, let us deal with current threats." Standing, she touched Daire's shoulder gently before approaching Odhrán.

Gesturing for her to follow, Odhrán turned and walked deeper into the trees. Only when the distance between them and their companions was great enough where they could not be overheard, did her stop and turn to her. Reaching a hand out, Odhrán ran his fingers lightly down her cheek, across her shoulder, and to her wrapped arm. "Setting foot in Dún Scáth was a dangerous choice," he told her in a low voice.

Shiovra held his gaze and told him firmly, "I was not without proper guard. Morgan proved that he is completely capable of protecting me."

Odhrán closed the distance between them, pinning her against a tree with his body. "That does not excuse the seriousness of the situation," he rebuffed. "I stated quite clearly that I did not want Caillte to get his hands on you, and still you walked right to him."

"Such a risk was necessary," she said, trying to ignore the heat of his body seeping through her cold, wet clothing. "To get Caillte on our side would be a great advantage. Not only is he capable of bringing about Ailill's downfall, but to have him on our side would deal a great blow to the sons of Míl."

He brought one hand to her hip while the other took hold of her chin. "Keep in mind that not all risks are worth taking. Some just may cost you your life," warned Odhrán sternly. "You are no help to the people of Tara if you are *dead*." His hand slipped from her chin and brushed a lock of her hair over her shoulder.

Despite the harshness of his tone, Shiovra could always feel gentleness in his touch. When he pressed his body harder against hers, she could feel his arousal, sparking her own.

Odhrán leaned closer, brushing his lips across her neck and nipping it lightly. "Remember your rede," he added. "As ye harm none, do as thou will. Do nothing that would harm another, *nor thyself*, lest it come back to you threefold or cost you your own life. Such is the way of the priestess. By risking too much, you break your own vows to the great Túath Mother and Father." Odhrán slowly gathered the length of her skirts, pushing them up to her waist.

Shiovra shivered as a gust of wind brought cold rain onto her exposed skin. His words were spoken true. If the risk would certainly cost her life, then it was not a risk to be taken. "You know the vows of a Túath priestess well," she said.

"Such is the duty of a Milidh druid: to know thy enemy," he replied, one hand leaving her hip to unlace the ties of his breeches.

"We are enemies no longer," countered Shiovra, her anticipation rising.

"Aye—we are much more." Odhrán's hands returned to her hips, lifting her up slightly. Bringing his mouth to hers, he stifled her gasp as he pushed into her, firm and quick.

Closing her eyes, she wrapped her arms around his neck and clenched the length of his hair. Desire quickly built within her from each hard, demanding thrust. Breaking the kiss, Shiovra tilted her head back.

Odhrán's hands gripped her hips painfully as he guided her movements in rhythm with his own. "One day soon you shall carry my child within you," he breathed heatedly against her ear. "A child of Milidh and Túath blood. *Our* child."

9. KISSED BY THE SHADOW OF DESPAIR

The fall of Dún Scáth was celebrated with a grand feast. However, despite the merriment of celebration, Shiovra felt restless. Ceallach's words continued to play through her mind: *You are a strong woman and powerful priestess, Shiovra Ní Coughlin, but even you can fall under an enemy blade.* Although she maintained her practices as a priestess, calling upon the elements and deities to watch over and protect her people, she had severely neglected her training with blade and bow. Slipping away from the festivities with sword in hand, she made her way into a nearby field.

Pausing, Shiovra held the sword at her side and closed her eyes. She took a deep breath and slowly released it, listening to the gentle whisper of wind through the meadow. Reaching her free hand out, she took a few steps forward and ran her palm along the tips of the tall grass, feeling their caress on her hand. Shiovra titled her head back slightly and relished in the warmth of the sun.

All about her she could feel the elements; the earth beneath her feet, the rustle of the wind, the lingering scent of rainfall, and the fiery heat of the sun. This was the power of the priestess: the power to feel the elements and draw upon them. She was a Túath priestess; a holder of what the Milidh had come to call divine power.

Opening her eyes, she slowly raised the sword. "I am one with the elements," Shiovra breathed. "Nothing yet everything. I am the giving earth and the sturdy rocks, the calm seas and the turbulent storms, the whispering winds and the shrieking gales, the flickering flames and the wild blaze!" Shifting, she brought the blade up into a defensive position and held it a moment before spinning and swinging the blade in an attacking motion, shifting her feet.

Opening her eye, she lowered her blade and paused briefly. Taking another deep breath, she released it slowly before smoothly repeating the movements several times, shifting from one to the next with increasing speed. It was a simple ritual to help her focus upon the weapon in her hands and to call upon her strengths.

The grass rustled behind her, the sound of an approach.

Shiovra paused, altering her hold upon the sword. She waited and listened before spinning and hurling the blade in a swift movement.

The tip of the sword landed in the ground with a firm thud at Ceallach's feet, garnering a quirked brow from the Fomorii man in response.

"I see you have decided to heed my words," stated Ceallach as he tugged the sword free. He looked over the blade before handing it back to the priestess. "Always maintain a proper defense, even within what one would consider the safety of a village," he said.

Shiovra met his gaze firmly, his slit pupils following her every move. "I am quite aware of thus, Ceallach Neáll, though a sword alone will not be adequate enough." She returned the blade to its sheath. "I will hone my skills with spear, bow, and fist. Whatever the circumstances, it is essential that I be prepared. No more shall I allow the Fomorii to make me to feel useless."

"You will tarry in Dún Fiáin then?" questioned Ceallach.

"Aye, for a short while," Shiovra said. "I will not leave Tara without her High Priestess for too long."

The Fomorii man nodded, looking away. "Come dawn, Réalta and I shall depart for Tara and welcome Mahon's bride."

Shiovra could not deny she was not surprised. Her brother had been steadfast for years that he had no intentions of taking a wife. "Mahon's *bride*?" she asked. She stared at the man in disbelief, wondering if she had perhaps misheard him.

"Mahon had agreed to follow your footsteps and, for the sake of clan and village, has agreed to take a bride," Ceallach told her. "A girl from the Milidh village of Traigh Lí was chosen. You have played your part; it is time for him to play his."

The priestess fell quiet for a moment, glancing away. His words left her with an ominous feeling. Though Shiovra wanted to press the man further on Mahon's impending marriage, another question also weighed heavily on her thoughts. "Why did you go to Caillte?"

Silence greeted her at first, and then Ceallach's deep voice reached her ears, "He is still my brother and I wanted to know the reasoning behind his actions. Everything tied to Saibh's death as well as his hatred for the Milidh and Túath clans."

Shiovra studied the Fomorii man for a moment. He stood look "And you, Ceallach Neáll?" she questioned. "How do you feel about the Milidh and Túath clans? About Saibh's death?"

Ceallach met her gaze, holding it firmly. "I grieved the loss of my sister and hated my brother for his failure and betrayal," replied the man in a hard tone. "I hold no animosity for the Milidh or Túath, only indifference. There will always be exceptions to both, though."

She stepped closer to Ceallach and reached her hand out, resting it on his chest. His heartbeat was steady beneath her hand. "You are not the man I once thought you were," Shiovra said, eyes drifting to her hand. "Since my departure from Rúnda I have seen you tense and worried. I have seen anger. I have seen kindness. On Rúnda I only saw the cold, guarded lover of Réalta." Looking up, she met his gaze once more. "I have come to understand you, if even only a little."

The Fomorii man offered a tight smile. "And I you."

* ~ * ~ * ~ * ~ *

Noon had come upon Tara when Aislinn of Traigh Lí arrived. To arrive quickly, they had traveled long and hard during the day, making camp late into the night and leaving at the first graying of dawn. During her journey, she had come to know her guide, Naal, quite well and found him an agreeable, if not somewhat unusual man. Of whom she was to wed, she was told very little, a matter which had come to worry her greatly. She had been told by her mother to produce a child quickly or her husband may chose to find himself another bride and she would be sent home. Her clan desperately needed the alliance, but she could not push aside the apprehension she felt towards the Túath clan. They possessed divine power and great knowledge she could never fully understand, though she was aware how the sons of Míl feared them. Now, after over a fortnight of travel, the Túath village of Tara lay before them in all her glory.

They had dismounted their steeds, allowing them a moments rest leaving Aislinn to stand gazing towards the High Fort in wonder. She brushed her long braid over her shoulder with a fair skinned hand that was in startling contrast to the ebony locks. Her bright brown eyes took in the village carefully. Tara was indeed intimidating. Far larger than the village she hailed from, Tara carried the very air of strength and regality. Aislinn had never felt so much like a lost child than she did at that very moment.

Glancing at the man named Naal, she took notice of the warm, delighted smile that crossed his lips at having returned home.

The sound of horse approaching caught the young woman's attention.

Turning, Aislinn's eyes widened at the sight of a glorious woman with lavender dyed garments and flowing mahogany hair followed by a stoic looking man with pale eyes and long white hair.

When the riders came to a stop before Aislinn and Naal, the man quickly dismounted, moving to the woman's side to help her down.

Aislinn studied the man and stiffened in realization. Although she was not overly familiar with them, she knew the man was one of the Fomorii, an often misshapen and very cruel race. Hesitant to break her watch of the Fomorii man, she looked at the woman. A pair of the most unusual eyes returned her watch: the right eye was blue while the left was green. Aislinn had never seen such eyes before.

The woman turned her attention to Naal. "Ah, Naal, I see we have returned just in time," she said with a smile.

"We have just arrived ourselves, Lady Réalta," replied the man.

"Welcome, Aislinn of Traigh Lí, to Tara," Réalta stated, gesturing to the village. "I am Réalta Dubh, aunt to your intended, and this is Ceallach Neáll." She handed Ceallach her horse's reins. "Naal, go ahead to the main cottage and announce Aislinn's arrival."

Naal nodded. "Aye." Offering Aislinn a comforting grin, he walked quickly through the village gates and disappeared from sight.

Réalta turned back to Aislinn. "I trust your journey here went unhindered?" she asked.

"Aye," replied Aislinn, her hands fretfully clutching the fold of her skirts. "Although I am a bit weary."

"Such is understandable." Réalta took a deep breath and sighed, smiling gently. "This is your home now. There is no need to be wary."

Despite the kindly spoken words, Aislinn could not help but feel apprehensive. She had left her home, journeyed far, and now stood within what had been enemy territory. She felt alone and vulnerable. Biting her lip, Aislinn asked, "I have heard of Lord Ainmire's death. Who is chieftain here?"

"Did Naal not tell you? Mahon is serving as acting chieftain until the one whom the Stone of Destiny spoke of steps forward," Réalta answered. "Your role as Mahon's wife is an important one. The burden of being chieftain is a heavy one for Mahon to bear. You will need to lend him your own strength."

Aislinn nodded. Although she found the village intimidating, knowing that would be the wife of the acting chieftain, commanding respect and authority, lessened the fears in which she felt.

"Come, let us continue toward the main cottage," Réalta said, interrupting Aislinn's thoughts. "The time has come for you to meet Mahon."

Nodding, she followed Réalta and Ceallach along a well worn path. She could feel the eyes of the villagers upon her; hear their whispers as they passed. Aislinn spared them small glances, noting the curious looks on their faces. As the path took them up a hill where a large cottage stood, she noticed a woman and man waiting for them.

Aislinn studied them both. The woman appeared to be Neimidh with her lightly tanned skin and dark brown hair. The man, on the other hand, had light brown hair that reached past his shoulders and a blue woad spiral curled beside his right eye, marking him as one of the Túath.

Aislinn found the man's blue eyes watching her as carefully as she watched him. He was older than her by what she could guess around eight or ten years, and weariness was written clearly across his face. She could see kindness in his eyes as he studied her.

Réalta turned slightly, gesturing to Aislinn with a bright smile crossing her lips. "Mahon, this is Aislinn of Traigh Lí, your wife."

* ~ * ~ * ~ * ~ *

Clouds thickened over Tara with the approaching storm, and the wind gathered in strength. Nearly the entire village gathered at the main cottage, awaiting the marriage between Mahon and Aislinn. Naal stood beside his father, Earnán, at the cottage door. His gaze drifted to where Aislinn stood flanked by Réalta and Úna.

The young woman stood nervously with her eyes downcast as she fiddled with the hem of her tartan. Aislinn was a startlingly beautiful woman, even while anxiously biting her lip. The bright crimson shifts she had been dressed in did naught but enhance her magnificence.

Naal worried though. Upon his initial meeting of Aislinn at Traigh Lí, the woman hardly spoke a word, keeping her eyes turned away. As they took to their journey, he noticed that something wore heavily on the woman's thoughts, troubling her deeply. She spoke nothing of her feelings or worries, only asked small, trivial questions about Tara and her people. Naal would have thought the woman would be a bit more curious about the man she was to wed.

He was concerned most for Mahon, whose role as chieftain of Tara was burdensome enough. Although Réalta relished in the alliance that would be forged with Aislinn's union to Mahon, Naal wondered just what the cost may be for such a treaty. Shiovra's union with the Milidh man Odhrán had been a good one; the man had a tactical mind and was more than capable of defending the village. Aislinn did not exhibit the same strength that Tara needed.

Keeping his voice low, Naal leaned toward his father and spoke his concerns, "This does not sit well with me."

Earnán nodded without turning. "I agree," he replied, tone hushed, "yet all there is for us is to wait and see how this union plays out."

The cottage door opened and Ceallach stepped out, followed by Mahon.

A steady beat of the bodhrán was set forth, muffled by the growing intensity of the wind.

Naal tensed.

Garbed in the clan tartan with a torc about his neck, Mahon offered his hand to Aislinn.

Aislinn slowly brought her gaze up to meet Mahon's and, as she placed her hand in his, clouds blotted out the sun.

* ~ * ~ * ~ * ~ *

Kieran waited in the shadows, bow in hand and arrow ready. His eyes narrowed on the man with lime-washed hair as he waited patiently. The man, known as Deasún, spoke with what Kieran could only assume to be a messenger. From what he could hear, Gráinne was expecting the arrival of Aichlinn at any moment. Kieran knew the name well. A little over a year ago Aichlinn had burned Cúlráid to the ground in a vicious attack that had ultimately cost Deirdre, wife of Tara's late chieftain, and her son their lives.

Kieran's grip tightened on the bow. Once he dealt with Deasún, he would make Aichlinn his next target. Although Shiovra had asked that he gather information pertaining to Gráinne's plans, he could not let the opportunity slide to weaken her. When the messenger left, Kieran found his opportunity to strike. Knocking his arrow lose, he let it fly at Deasún.

The arrow struck the Milidh man in the shoulder just above a vital spot. Hissing in anger, Deasún staggered back a few steps before his eyes shot in Kieran's direction.

Moving swiftly, Kieran knocked a second arrow loose and struck Deasún firmly in the leg. Quickly tossing the bow aside, he drew his sword and made his way toward the Milidh man.

Deasún's eyes blazed with unbridled fury as he gripped his wounded shoulder. "Who are you," he growled in demand, grimacing as he tried in futile to wrench the arrow free.

"I bring greetings from the High Priestess of Tara," replied Kieran with a cruel, slightly amused, twist to his lips.

Frown deepening, he drew his sword with a bloodied hand. "Perhaps I shall return the greeting, Neimidh scum," countered Deasún.

Kieran studied the man. Though he pointed the blade towards the ground, Deasún's stance proved he quite ready to attack. "It is most unfortunate that my lady priestess will never be burdened by your *greetings* ever again."

Deasún laughed maliciously in response. "Is that so?"

Hand tightening on his sword, Kieran stepped closer to Deasún. "Why does Aichlinn come?" he asked, bringing the blade up to point the tip at Deasún's throat, though he maintained a safe distance. "Does he not serve Ailill, the man who pitilessly cast her aside?"

"Does it matter?" Deasún took a few steps forward, letting the blade press into his skin slightly, enough to draw a small trickle of blood. Madness danced wildly in his eyes. "Perhaps she would like a new companion for her bed?"

"Gráinne seeks to sway Aichlinn's loyalties to her."

"Aye," replied Deasún. "You are aware of what Aichlinn is capable of, are you not?" A mad grin spread wide across his lips. "With Aichlinn at her side, there is nothing Gráinne cannot do. If you want to keep your precious priestess alive, then you better kill Aichlinn."

Kieran smirked. "Easily done, but you...you will die *first*."

The Milidh man laughed. "I have been awaiting death a long time, but it has never been granted to me." Deasún slowly stepped to the side, allowing the tip of Kieran's sword the drag across the skin of his neck before slipping away from it. His shifted back into a ready stance, bringing his sword up. "What makes you believe you will succeed where so many have failed?!" he shouted, lunging at Kieran.

Having anticipated the attack, the Neimidh man countered easily and blocked with little effort. Holding back Deasún's blade with his own, Kieran stepped closer and kicked him hard on the leg which he had previously injured with an arrow.

Grunting, Deasún managed to keep his balance, but failed in his attempts to break Kieran's counter. Stepping back in defense, his face contorted with pain.

Thunder clapped in the distance.

Kieran grinned as he readied his own defense. Roughly pushing Deasún back, he began to circle to the left as his eyes did not once leave the man's face.

Deasún growled and dipped as if to go low.

Catching onto the ruse immediately, Kieran shifted. When Deasún thrust his blade up, he pushed it aside and only caught a light wound to his left arm. Swiftly moving from his defense, Kieran knocked Deasún's sword from his hand. Stepping in, he brought the sword back and, in one blinding movement, sent the man's head rolling.

Lightning flashed as Deasún's headless body crumpled to the ground.

Kieran stood looking down at his bloodied sword as rain began to fall, softly at first then quickly growing heavier. "I succeeded because there is a strong difference between us," he muttered, watching as the rain washed his blade clean. "You fight for the desire of battle. I fight for the desire to protect those I care about. That is why you never succeeded."

* ~ * ~ * ~ * ~ *

A midsummer storm raged over Tréigthe, tearing through the village. The wicker-work door lintel rattled under the violent gusts of wind. Gráinne knelt before the hearth fire, watching the flames dancing wildly upon the wood as her fingers clawed into the earthen floor.

Deasún's headless body had been found along the village borders, leaving her vivid with anger. Of who had taken the man's life, there was no trace. Gráinne knew she could not afford to lose anymore of her men, especially one as valuable as Deasún. Without men such as Deasún, men who did not fear death, she would never be able to claim Tara and return her to her former glory. Her sister, Réalta, was a fool to allow alliances with the Milidh, the very clan who brutally took their sister, Tríonna's, life. The High Priestess of Tara only enabled such foolishness with her marriage to one of them and welcoming their warriors into the village, tainting it with the Milidh presence.

Laughter swelled within Gráinne. "Soon…" she muttered, rising to her feet and casting a handful of dirt into the fire. "Soon the High Priestess of Tara will fall. Soon I will prove mother wrong and take my place as Lady of Tara. No more shall I be cast aside like a fledgling child." A smile played across her lips. "Once Tara lies within my grasp, I will drive those Milidh hounds from this land and reclaim it for pure Túath blood!"

~~*~*~*

Shiovra woke to the sound of wind slamming violently into the cottage. Rolling onto her back, she stared up at the dark thatch roof looming above her as rain pounded against it. The bed beside her, where Odhrán normally lay, was cold and empty. Shivering, she sat up and crawled to the foot of the bed, pulling the curtain aside.

Even though the fire had dwindled down to little above embers, it was bright on her sleep-ridden eyes. Swinging her feet to the floor, Shiovra stood and wrapped a blanket around her shoulders before grabbing some wood, adding it to the dying fire. With a sigh, she sat down on a bench beside the hearth.

"You should be resting," said Odhrán's low voice.

Glancing toward his voice, she found the Milidh man sitting near the cottage door, running his thumb along the edge of a dagger as he inspected the blade. "I could say the same for you," Shiovra replied in a hushed tone so not to wake the others.

Odhrán did not look up. "I have night watch," he replied, setting the dagger aside and picking up another.

Turning back to the fire, she prodded it with a stick and watched as the embers flared in response. Shiovra remained quiet for a little while, listening to the storm.

The wind continued its onslaught upon the cottage, making the door rattle loudly with each howling gust.

"The wind woke me."

"Is that all?" he pressed.

She exhaled. "Another union has been forged for alliance between Túath and Milidh with Mahon's marriage to Aislinn." Shiovra rubbed her face wearily. "I know nothing of the Milidh clan of Traigh Lí. Can they be trusted? Are they a threat to Tara?" Silence greeted her at first, then arms wrapped around her shoulders and the warmth of Odhrán's body pressed against her back.

"Traigh Lí lies to the west just beyond the borders of Cúlráid," he replied, the heat of his breath caressing her ear. Resting his chin on her shoulder, he tightened his arms around her. "The village is small but well defended. The sudden alliance with Tara does bring their intentions under question." Odhrán paused, brushing his lips against her neck. "I have already decided that eyes shall be placed within the village to determine whether or not they will become a threat to Tara, regardless of what Réalta and Ceallach may have decided." Dropping his arms, Odhrán released her from his embrace and stretched. "There is a long night ahead of us. Go back to bed."

* ~ * ~ * ~ * ~ *

Aislinn lingered in bed well after sunrise, unwilling to move. Midsummer had come to pass and Lughnasadh was but days away. She had been wed to Mahon for a little over two fortnights and her courses had come upon her, early nonetheless. She bore him no child. Before her departure from Traigh Lí, her mother had expressed the utter importance of bearing the Túath man a child. The alliance of her village to Tara relied heavily on conceiving a child, and if she failed, he could send her home and find himself a new wife, one who would help him carry on his bloodline.

Upon her arrival to Tara, she was given the Neimidh woman Úna as a handmaid. At first she enjoyed the woman's welcoming smile and kind nature, finding it comforting. Confiding in the woman, Aislinn had expressed her need to conceive for the alliance yet Úna, the mother of twins, told her in turn to take time and learn more about her husband before rushing to come with child.

Aislinn's thoughts were interrupted as her bed curtain was pulled aside and sunlight flooded the tiny little nook. Groaning, she propped herself up and met Úna's quirked brow.

"My lady, are you *still* in bed?" scolded Úna gently as she leaned in to tug on the blankets. "Come now, Lord Mahon will worry if you lie the day away in bed."

Aislinn reluctantly sat up and crawled to the foot of the bed, standing. "Aye, he will worry that I will become too weak to bear him a son," she said coldly.

"Forgive me, my lady, but you worry needlessly about carrying Lord Mahon's child," Úna told her firmly. "Forget whatever your clan has told you about the necessity of conceiving. Instead, you should speak with Lord Mahon so that you can come to understand the man he is, not whom you expect him to be."

Aislinn's hand lashed out, striking the Neimidh woman hard on the cheek in her anger. "How dare you lecture me, you who are nothing but a servant?" She gestured to the door. "You may leave."

"As you wish, Lady Aislinn." With a small bow, Úna turned and left.

Aislinn spun away from the door, her gaze falling on the bed. She could not stand the sight of it.

"Do not be so harsh on Úna."

She turned to see the woman called Eithne step into the cottage.

"Úna has been nothing but kind to you, even while you childishly pout over being unable to conceive in such a short amount of time," stated Eithne harshly. "You would do best to heed her words."

Aislinn looked away.

"Úna has suffered much and continues to do so. She fell in love with a man, succumbed to his desires, and nearly lost her life bearing his children," explained Eithne. "Her body has never fully recovered, leaving her weak and her heart torn as she fears Daire feels nothing for her. Though you may be Mahon's wife, please consider how your words and actions affect others." Grabbing some clothing from a bench, she handed them to Aislinn. "Now, if you will pardon me, I have duties to attend to."

After the woman left, Aislinn looked down at the clothing. The colors were light and gentle, contrasting the rich ones she had worn upon her arrival to Tara. Aislinn remembered having mentioned to Úna that she quite enjoyed the muted colors the village women wore and wondered if she could perhaps wear some as well. She had never imagined the Neimidh woman would have heeded such a wanton desire. Hands tightening on the soft cloth, she buried her tearful face in it as she sagged to her knees.

* ~ * ~ * ~ * ~ *

Shiovra held the dagger in her hand, testing the weight and balance before gaze shifted to the tree before her. The difference between throwing a sword compared to a dagger differed greatly, but still held some of the same principles. Understanding the blades balance and weight were crucial in striking the target properly. Bringing her hand up, she judged her aim and let the dagger fly. It spun through the air and the pommel hit the tree with a thud before falling to the ground.

"Hmm, not too bad. You have good strength and aim behind the attack," Odhrán said from beside her, handing her another dagger. "Try again."

She tested the balance once more before chucking it at the tree. The blade found its mark this time, only to fall out shortly after.

The Milidh man grinned broadly. "Better. Now, try to release it quicker and build more momentum as it goes." Odhrán offered another dagger.

Shiovra took a deep breath, focusing, before letting it fly swiftly from her fingers. The dagger landed deeply embedded in the tree and a smile crept across her lips.

Odhrán approached the tree and checked the depth of the wound. With a grunt, he tugged the dagger free and ran his fingers along the bark. "Very well done," he told her, tossing the dagger up and catching the hilt deftly in his hand. "Study the weight and balance of this dagger more." He handed her a dagger then slipped the other two into his belt. "Learn how it moves when thrown and after more practice, you will hit every target with confidence."

Nodding, she looked down at the dagger.

"Ah, here comes Daire."

Glancing up, Shiovra followed Odhrán's gaze.

Her cousin ran along the path toward them, looking greatly winded. As he neared, he slowed his pace. "I have been all over the village looking for you," Daire said breathlessly as he sat down roughly in the tall grass beside Shiovra. "Odhrán, Bradan is looking for you. He wants to know if you are still doing the midday rounds along the southern borders."

"I will return for the evening meal," Odhrán told Shiovra. Leaning down, he gave her a quick kiss before turning and making his way back to the village.

Feeling a slight tugging on her skirts, Shiovra glanced down at Daire.

"Sit with me for a moment," he muttered, exhaustion written clearly across his face.

Sitting down, she sat the dagger aside and fell back into the grass.

Daire followed suit with a heavy exhale.

For a while neither of them spoke, simply watched the clouds drifting aimlessly across the sky while the gentle breeze whispered through the grass.

After a long silence, Daire asked suddenly, "Do you think she is well?"

Shiovra glanced at him from the corner of her eye. Though she knew of whom he spoke, she inquired anyway, "Úna?"

Daire nodded. Sitting up, he ran his hands through his hair. "Although she told me to accompany you, I could see something lingering in her eyes and it has continued to plague me since," he admitted. Crumpling forward, he buried his face in his hands. "She was so *weak*, nonetheless she smiled at me and told me to go."

"Do you regret what you have done?" questioned Shiovra. She knew several meanings lay behind her words and when Daire spoke again, she knew his answer was to all of them.

"Every day."

* ~ * ~ * ~ * ~ *

Lughnasadh had come and gone when Kieran finally arrived upon Tréigthe after hard pressed travel. He spent the following day avoiding scouts while taking careful note of the village's strengths and weaknesses. He knew it would be difficult to slip in. Tréigthe was better guarded than Dún Scáth, but Gráinne did not quite instill the fear the Fomorii man had and, for that, her defense was lax at times. Kieran finally found his opportunity quickly. When the guards changed duties, the main gate stood briefly defenseless and that was when he would slip in.

Kieran's hand moved to his sword, his fingers tightening on the hilt as his blood pulsed in anticipation. His eyes narrowed as the time to act drew near. Straightening, he slipped out of the brush and made his way up the sloping hill toward the wall surrounding the village. Kieran pressed against the side and waited patiently.

As the low note of a battle horn sounded, the main gates opened and the guards who had been standing guard entered the village.

Moving slowly, Kieran made his way to the gates and peered in.

The guards stood off to the side near a cottage, leaving a clear path into the village.

A grin twisted the corners of his mouth. Kieran pulled the hood of his cloak up and slipped in, ducking behind a cottage. Keeping to the shadows, he made his way swiftly to the largest cottage.

Two men with spears guarded the door.

Crouching behind a woven hazel fence, Kieran paused.

Once again the battle horn sounded, repeating a pattern of one long note, two short, followed by another long and two short.

The cottage door opened and Gráinne stepped out, her red curls falling unbound over her shoulders. Gesturing for the spearmen to follow, the woman began making her way to the main gates.

Kieran waited for them to pass before casting a quick glance around to see if any eyes were turned his way. Standing, he hastened into the cottage, making sure the door closed behind him. A fire burned brightly in the hearth, creating plenty of shadows from the long curtains which hung from the roof supports. With Gráinne's enjoyment of taking men to her bed, Kieran knew the best way to get to Aichlinn would be to wait in the woman's cottage.

Lifting a curtain aside, Kieran found a small alcove that would suit well as a hiding place. Crouching down inside, he kept his hand firmly on his sword and began his wait.

When the sound of voices reached his ears, Kieran pulled the curtain aside, careful to keep in the shadows.

Gráinne stepped into the cottage first, followed by a man with a naked sword hanging at his side, the blade battered and scared from countless battles.

"You desire for me to destroy the priestess and her guardians?" the man inquired as he slowly walked past the table, fingers trailing across the rough surface.

"No, the priestess' death will be by my hand and my hand only," Gráinne told him sternly. "I need to you remove the threat her guardians bring. I trust you are capable of such, Aichlinn, being how well you handled Cúlráid."

The man nodded. "And what shall you offer me to do such?"

"Cattle, land, riches…" Gráinne's voice trailed off as she turned to him.

"I have no need for such," Aichlinn replied, turning to her. "What more do you have to offer me?"

A smile played across her lips as she brought a hand up slowly to rest on her left shoulder. "Myself." Gráinne pushed the neckline of her shift, letting it slip down to the ground.

The man looked her over, his eyes lingering on the woman's breasts. "That, my lady, is an offer I gladly accept." Slipping an arm around Gráinne's waist, but pulled her close and brought his mouth roughly down upon hers. Aichlinn's tone was low and dangerous when he spoke again, "You are mine now." Leading her to the bed, he shoved her violently onto it.

From the shadows, Kieran was sure he saw fear briefly flicker across the woman's face. He watched as Aichlinn cruelly claimed the woman as his own. The sheer brutality of how the man coupled with Gráinne filled Kieran with disgust and anger. Hand tightening on his sword, he forced himself to remain still.

Once Aichlinn was satisfied, he collapsed on the bed without a second glance to the woman.

Glancing at him warily, Gráinne stood and dressed. "I shall have some food prepared for you," she told the man.

Aichlinn did not reply as he dozed lightly in the bed with one hand behind his head.

Huffing, the woman left the cottage.

Kieran waited a bit before drawing his blade and quietly slipping out from behind the curtain. His movements were slow and careful as he made his way towards the bed. Taking a deep breath, Kieran brought his sword up, exhaling as he plunged it down.

His sword rang loudly off the blade of a dagger.

Kieran's eyes snapped to Aichlinn.

The man watched him with a cold stare. "Did Gráinne send you or did the priestess of Tara?"

Kieran's face hardened as he pressing down against the dagger with his sword. "If you must know, I do indeed serve the High Priestess of Tara," he replied, "although your death was not by her order, but my own desire."

"You believe you can best me?" sneered Aichlinn.

"Deasún perished by my hand. Why would you be any different?" Grinning, Kieran swiftly knocked the dagger aside and it landed upon the earthen floor with a thud.

"I must admit there is strength behind your movements," Aichlinn murmured. "Will you grant me a weapon so that we may fight fairly, man to man?"

Kieran's smiled faded as he leaned over the man. "You lost that chance when you gave Deirdre her death wound and took her child from her," he growled. "No man, however cruel, should *ever* take the life of a woman and child!"

Genuine fear flitted cross the Aichlinn's face and he slowly shifted away, pressing back toward the wall. He was an easy target, weaponless and alone.

"There is only one man who could best me and I would never raise my blade against him." Kieran thrust his sword down without hesitation, piercing the man's heart. He gave it a quick twist before pulling his blade free, wiping away the blood with a blanket, then sheathing it.

Urgency to leave rushed through his body and he searched for one of the small side doors of the cottage. Finding one, Kieran pushed it open and looked out.

Gráinne was heading back toward the cottage, followed by a rather disgruntled looking warrior bearing a large bowl of fruit.

Swearing under his breath, Kieran searched for a means of distraction. Grabbing hold of an earthen pot, he tossed it out the door towards one of the cottages. When Gráinne and the man turned to the sound, Kieran slipped from the cottage and hurriedly ducked behind another. Pausing for a moment, he continued to move from cottage to cottage, making his way to the back of the village. Soon the stone wall was within sight.

The uneven rocks would make it possible to climb, however leave him completely vulnerable to attack.

As Gráinne's scream pierced the air, Kieran knew it was time to leave. Without a concern to what guards may see, he launched himself at the wall, gripping stones with his bare hands. Dampness and moss made it difficult and the Neimidh man struggled to find proper hand and foot holds while keeping himself from falling. As he reached the top, he could hear shouting over the pounding of his heart. Gritting his teeth, Kieran dropped down the other side as an arrow came whistling past his head.

* ~ * ~ * ~ * ~ *

Eithne walked with Naal, trying to ease his concerns as they made their way up the hill to the main cottage. She had gathered a basket full of apples with the hope they would help ease the tension Mahon's wife felt. Her brother, Naal, had found her climbing the trees of the orchard and decided to help, expressing his worries over Aislinn and what she may do to the clan. She could never have foreseen what they would stumble upon once they entered the cottage.

The basket of apples fell from Eithne's grasp and tumbled to the ground, forgotten, as she hastened to Úna's side as she lay in a crumpled heap on the floor. Leaning over the Neimidh woman, she brought her ear to Úna's chest. The woman's heartbeat was slow and strenuous. Sitting up, Eithne brought a hand quickly to Úna's forehead, nearly reeling back at the intensity of her fever. "Naal," she said, glancing at her brother. "Grab some cool water and rags! Úna has a fever and she is hardly breathing."

He nodded and ran out the door.

Eithne pulled the woman toward the bed, struggling to get her into it and covering her with a blanket. She frowned at Úna's pale face and her shallow, labored breathing. As promised, she had maintained a careful watch over the Neimidh woman since Shiovra's departure. Each day Úna appeared to be gathering strength and recovering, yet there she lay thin, weak, and pale.

Her thoughts drifted to Úna's children. Rushing to them, Eithne found the infant children sleeping soundly, the fever absent from their bodies. After reassuring herself that they were indeed well, she returned to Úna's side.

The cottage door clattered open loudly and she turned to see Mahon rush in.

"Naal told me that—" he began, stopping abruptly as his eyes fell on Úna's body. Mahon approached the bed and sat down roughly on a nearby bench. "How long has she been like this?"

"I am afraid I cannot say," replied Eithne. "By all appearances, Úna had been recovering. She was eating well, had no complaints of pain, and had even resumed her duties without pause." She glanced over at the woman. "First she was forced to deal with a difficult childbirth followed by Daire's departure, the lashing out of your wife, and now this…" She shook his head. "May Brigid and Dian Cécht watch over you and heal you."

* ~ * ~ * ~ * ~ *

Shiovra landed roughly on the ground, all breath knocked from her. Groaning, she let herself fall back into the grass and looked up at the sky, her arms and legs protesting the intensive training. A shadow moved to loom above her and she tilted her head back to gaze up at Eiladyr.

He leaned over her with his arms crossed and a frown marring her brow. "You are still too slow," Eiladyr told her. "Again."

Sitting up, Shiovra let him pull her to her feet.

"Now, I want you to do the same as last time. Block my hits and then throw your own." He shifted, placing his feet apart and bringing his fists up, ready to attack.

When Eiladyr thrust at her, Shiovra raised an arm and blocked, quickly bringing the other up to block his next attack before throwing her own.

As before, Eiladyr caught her wrist with great ease but, instead of knocking her to the ground, he spun her around and tugged her toward him. Swiftly spinning her around, he trapped Shiovra's wrist behind her while he wrapped his free arm around her waist and pulled her to his chest. "Still too slow," chided Eiladyr.

Shiovra took his hold on her into consideration. Though his grip on her wrist was tight, her other arm had a bit more freedom of movement. Jabbing her elbow into Eiladyr's ribs, she twisted her writ free from his grip and escaped his hold.

Eiladyr staggered back a few paces, hand rubbing where she had struck him as a smirk crossed his lips. "Better."

"Unconventional but effective," said Daire from where he leaned against a near Odhrán.

Crossing his arms, Eiladyr stated bluntly, "She needs to move faster."

"But she has improved," remarked Odhrán.

Eiladyr scoffed.

Shiovra sighed and rubbed her wrist. "I am aware that I still have much to learn—" Her voice trailed off as she was overcome with a sudden wave of weakness. Reaching her hand out, she grabbed Eiladyr's arm in an attempt to steady herself before sinking to her knees as great pain and unbridled fear coursed through Shiovra's body.

Eiladyr quickly crouched down beside her. "Shiovra?" he asked in concern.

Trembling, Shiovra's hands reached up to clutch his tunic tightly as she rested her head against his chest. The sensations rushing through her body were not her own, however she could feel each labored breath taken that was taken and the burning fever that raged wildly as if they were. As quickly as they had come upon her they were gone.

Odhrán dropped to a knee beside her, touching her shoulder.

Priestess.

The voice was familiar as it whispered in her mind. Eyes snapping to her left, she found a crow perched upon the thatch roof of a nearby cottage, watching her with its head cocked to the side.

The Neimidh woman fades fast. She will not survive much longer.

With a sudden caw, the crow lifted into the air and flew away.

Shiovra turned to her cousin, meeting his gaze. Her throat felt tight when she told him, "Daire, Úna is dying."

Daire's face paled, his hands tightening at his sides. "I—" He stopped and looked away. "Forgive me, cousin, but I must return to Tara."

Shiovra nodded, understanding. "Make haste," she told him. "We will follow after."

Without another word, Daire turned and ran up the path to the main cottage.

"Can you stand?" asked Odhrán from her right, offering her a hand.

"Aye." Releasing Eiladyr's tunic, she accepted his offered hand and rose with him to her feet.

Odhrán turned to Eiladyr. "Find Meara," he ordered, slipping an arm around Shiovra's waist. "We depart immediately."

~~*~*~*

Eithne sat beside Úna, pressing a cool damp rag to her brow as the woman slumbered in a fevered sleep. A week's time had passed and her condition had only worsened. The woman feared Úna would not survive the night. Eithne had watched over the Neimidh woman carefully after her difficult birth. There had been no hints of any illness. Hand tightening on the cloth, she refreshed it in the water and returned it to Úna's brow.

The cottage door opened and Mahon stepped in. "Has there been any improvement?" he asked.

Eithne shook her head. "She will not survive long."

He nodded solemnly, moving to sit beside her. "The children?"

"They are very healthy, but cry greatly for their mother." Eithne hesitated, glancing briefly at Mahon. "Has word been sent to Úna's clan? To Daire?"

"Aye, though I fear it will reach them far too late." Mahon rubbed his face wearily. "Is there nothing that can be done?"

"I am afraid not," replied Eithne, bowing her head. "If only Lady Réalta had not departed, perhaps she could help. Úna loses strength every day and refuses to eat—" She stopped abruptly as Úna stirred restlessly of the bed. Leaning over the woman, she asked, "Úna?"

"Lady Eithne…Lord Mahon…" Úna began slowly, her voice quiet and raspy.

"Do not speak," urged Eithne. "Save your strength."

Úna shook her head, opening dull eyes that were once vibrant and full of life. "Please…watch over my children…and tell my lord husband…to forgive me. Tell Lady Shiovra…to watch over him…in my stead." Several spasms of coughing tore through Úna's body, shaking her weak frame. She clenched her eyes shut, calming the fit. "It has been an honor…to serve the clan…of Tara…"

"Shhh," chided Eithne gently, patting the woman's cheek with the damp cloth. "Do not fret."

"My time has come..." continued Úna between coughs. "I only hope that my children...do not have to suffer such a fate as this..." A small smile graced her lips as her eyes drifted shut. "My spirit shall make its way...to the Cave of Cruachan and we shall meet again in Tir na n'Og..." Her breathing began to slow until the rise and fall of her chest was no more.

"Úna? Úna?" Eithne called out, desperation in her voice. Reaching a trembling hand out, she checked for a pulse and found none. "Úna!" Tears stung her eyes as she turned into Mahon's embrace and wept in his shoulder.

Úna of the Neimidh clan had died.

$$* \sim * \sim * \sim * \sim *$$

Upon his arrival, Daire found a funeral pyre being constructed and his heart dropped. The grief-stricken faces of the villagers as he rode through the gates confirmed his worst fear: he was too late. Cresting the hill, he found Mahon waiting for him at the main cottage with a solemn face. Pulling his steed to a stop, Daire dismounted.

Mahon did not say a word, only pulled Daire into a quick embrace before releasing him and guiding him into the cottage.

Eithne, who stood beside Úna's pale body, turned as they entered.

"How?" was the simple question that came from Daire's mouth.

"Naal and I found her collapsed upon the floor," Eithne replied gently. "Since your departure, I have watched her very carefully. I found nothing that brought my cause of concern. Whatever befell Úna...she hid it very well." Biting her lip, Eithne turned away, busying herself with gathering a pile of clothing. "The fever was too great for her to bear. I am sorry. I did all that I could for her."

Daire nodded, regarding her in silence for a moment. "And my children?"

"They are healthy." She replied as she put the clothing into a basket. "Would you like a moment with her?"

"Aye."

Eithne nodded. Taking the basket in her hands, she turned to Mahon. "Grab that one and follow me," she ordered. "They will need to be burned lest any illness linger behind." Pausing beside Daire, she touched his shoulder gently before leaving, Mahon following behind.

Daire remained unmoving for a long while, simply stared at Úna's lifeless body in disbelief. Knowing the pain she suffered from giving birth to his children, knowing that it had nearly cost the Neimidh woman her life, Daire had been conflicted about accompanying Shiovra to Dún Fiáin. The following morning Úna had offered him a reassuring smile and insisted that he go. Despite his own better judgment, he followed her words.

Looking down at Úna, his hands clenched tightly. He had been the cause of her pain. The cause of the sadness he saw lingering behind each warm smile she gave him. In Daire's eyes, he was the reason Úna had died. Falling roughly to his knees, his body shook violently as tears fell from his eyes.

A pair of warm arms wrapped around him.

"Daire."

Raising his head slowly, he found it was Eithne who held him.

"It is time."

10. RED DESTINY LOST

The sky above the ruins of Dún Scáth was as gray and dreary as the village itself. Caillte stood among what remained of the scorched and crumbling cottages, looking down at the sea as it crashed violently into the cliff side. His thoughts drifted to the High Priestess of Tara, a woman who had defiantly stepped into the very place she should fear and challenged him.

There is a battle to be fought, Caillte of the Fomorii. Where shall your place be?

Her eyes haunted him as sure as her words. The priestess' gaze had not wavered, holding his strong and true. Each night since their meeting, Caillte could feel the woman's presence within his dreams, her fiercely defiant stare watching him. He had seen eyes such as hers before within his own sister, Saibh.

By all means play this game of war. But first, think of what holds more importance to you: this little diversion of bloodshed or the lost sister you hold so dear. Will you remain a pawn and stain this beautiful land crimson, or will you protect her *memory.*

Everything he had done, the blood staining his hands, had all been for Saibh. Caillte wanted the Túath to pay for her death, and the priestess of Tara was vital to his plans. With her, he would have a sword against not only the Túath, but the Milidh as well. He wanted nothing more than to deliver his retribution and watch as the Túath and Milidh clans crumbled around him. Only then did her believe his anger would subside.

Nevertheless the priestess' words, spoken so bluntly, had brought him to question his desires. Each time the priestess' eyes met his in sleep, it was if

Saibh herself watched him in disappointment.

There is a battle to be fought, Caillte of the Fomorii. Where shall your place be?

Running his hands through his hair, Caillte growled in frustration. No matter how hard he tried to block them, the priestess' words continued to invade his thoughts. Turning his gaze once more to the restless sea, his eyes narrowed on the waves slamming against the rocks below, fervently seeking to claim the land above.

Will you remain a pawn and stain this beautiful land crimson, or will you protect her *memory.*

Was he indeed a pawn himself? Would his need for vengeance over Saibh's death truly protect her memory? Dropping to his knees, he shouted into the wind, "I am no one's pawn!"

* ~ * ~ * ~ * ~ *

"I will *not* stand for anymore incompetence!" Gráinne hissed at her huntsmen, gesturing with the hand which held her cup; the mead within spilling over the brim from the sudden movement. "For one man to have managed to breech the walls, let alone reach *my* cottage, is unacceptable!" She threw the cup at one of the men, who in turn ducked and let it shatter on the ground behind him. "Tell me, how was he able to do so?"

"We are unsure, my lady," answered one of the men. "He must have slipped in during the change of guards—"

"You are *unsure*?" Gráinne questioned harshly, pulling a dagger from her belt. Circling the man, she pointed the tip at his throat. "Tell me, what is your duty here at Tréigthe?"

The man swallowed hand, but held his head high. "To guard it and protect it from those who would destroy it."

"And...what have you done?"

"Failed to secure it which in turn allowed an enemy to enter unnoticed."

"Exactly." Gráinne paused beside him, trailing the dagger's tip down his cheek and drawing blood. "That man has long served the High Priestess of Tara. For him to have so simply walked in here and leave a bleeding corpse in my bed is unacceptable. I am sure that it was by his hand as well that Deasún lost his head." She dragged the blade down the man's jaw and throat. "This will *not* happen again." Dropping her hand, Gráinne turned away and moved to stand before the huntsmen once more.

"Lughnasadh has come and gone," she continued. "Soon the days will begin to grow colder. Let us bide our time gathering every willing sword, bow, and spear to our side. If the priestess seeks a war, then she shall have one."

* ~ * ~ * ~ * ~ *

Once again Caillte found that he stood along the cliff's edge. His eyes fell upon a sword he held within his hands. The metal was far from flawless; the blade pitted and heavily battle-scarred. The tip and edge were horribly dull and practically useless. However, he continued to hold onto it for it had been given to him by his father many, many years ago.

There is a battle to be fought, Caillte of the Fomorii. Where shall your place be?

A frown crossed his brow as he was once more plagued by the priestess' words. Caillte could not shake the woman from his thoughts. Was the blood staining his hands any different than that of Saibh's upon the Túath's? Many a life he had taken in her memory, just as the Milidh had done in memory of their fallen kinsman, Ith.

He remembered the day Saibh died vividly. She had been smiling at him just before the Túath warrior's sword pierced her heart. Caillte had been quick to retaliate, but he was no match for the men who surrounded him. He would have died had Ailill not come to his aid and tended his wounds. Ailill had lost his own brother at Túath hands and offered Caillte a chance for revenge. As Ailill's war lord, he had gained the strength and power he needed for just that. It was not long before Ailill had become his pawn in his own strategy of retribution.

Will you remain a pawn and stain this beautiful land crimson, or will you protect her *memory.*

His grip tightened on the sword, a deep frown crossing his brow. Ailill had found him quickly that day, fending off his Túath attackers with ease and sending them fleeing. Caillte had never questioned Ailill's presence that day, never questioned how he had managed to deflect the warriors attacks alone. However the priestess' words had brought it into question. Scoffing, Caillte muttered, "I have been the pawn all along?"

"It does not have to remain as such, Caillte of the Fomorii."

Stiffening at the voice, he turned.

A woman stood before him, her auburn hair falling unbound over her shoulders. She watched him with blue-green eyes that matched the very seas which surrounded Éire.

Only once before had he set his eyes upon the mother of the Túatha Dé Danann, yet he remembered her very well. "Dana," he said bluntly.

The woman nodded.

"Have you come to mock me?" he demanded.

Dana shook her head. "Nay," she replied. "I would not mock a man who has only lost his way."

Caillte snorted in disbelief. "Then why have you come to me, an enemy to the Túath?" he pressed.

"Just as with your brother Ceallach Neáll, you are different." Dana moved to stand beside him and look out over the crashing waves. "Men will always go to war and shed blood, each for their own reasons: greed, power, lust…and vengeance. Unfortunately, there are very few who go to war over the loss of innocent life."

"You speak with a tainted man," he argued coldly, turning away from the woman. Caillte brought a pale hand up and stared at his. "Túath and Milidh blood alike stain these hands, their lives taken in violent rage. I am no different than those who conspire for battle over wanton desires, no different than my misshapen kin."

"Many a man would not hesitate to kill their own kin, yet you have," Dana said in turn. "You may be tainted, but there is still light hidden deep in your heart."

Caillte scoffed at her words.

Dana sighed softly. "It was not the Túath who took Saibh's life, but Ailill himself," she told him suddenly.

His jaw tensed and the hand on the sword clenched tighter.

"It was his sword which pierced her heart," continued Dana. "The attack was a ploy created by Ailill to bring you under his command. All the while, you have been his pawn, fueled by Saibh's death."

"What is it that you want from me, Dana?" asked Caillte bitterly.

"My inquiry is the same as the High Priestess of Tara: where shall your place be in the upcoming battle?" Dana turned away from the cliff, circling around behind the man. "The choice is yours, Caillte of the Fomorii. Either remain a pawn and continue being manipulated by Ailill, or—" she lightly touched his hand holding the sword "—fight for *Saibh*."

Before Dana pulled her hand away, Caillte felt a surge of power and warmth flow from the woman's hand. Bringing his arm up, he looked down at the blade. Still pitted and heavily battle-scarred, the blade now gleamed with renewed life. A frown crossed his face and he turned to face the woman, only to find he was alone once more.

"*I offer you a life, Caillte of the Fomorii,*" whispered Dana's fading voice on the wind. "Your *life*."

* ~ * ~ * ~ * ~ *

Midday was drawing near when she heard their muffled approach. Taking cover in heavy brush, she sat in wait. It was not long before the softly spoken voices drew closer. Peering out through the leaves, her cold blue eyes fell upon a small group of travelers passing by. She would not have spared them a second glance had it not been for one face in particular that caught her attention: a woman with red-blonde hair and twisting blue woad markings along her left arm. It was the High Priestess of Tara.

A smile crossed her thin lips at the promising opportunity that had been presented to her. Shifting quietly, her gaze drifted more carefully over those accompanying the priestess, narrowing on the man who walked closely beside her. It was the priestess' Milidh guardian who would pose the greatest threat. Precautions would need to be made before she could have the priestess once more within her grasp.

* ~ * ~ * ~ * ~ *

Night brought heavy clouds over the ruins of Dún Scáth, blotting out the moon and stars while the wind carried the warning of rain. A heavy, chilling fog filled the defeated village, giving it an air of eeriness as Caillte stood in the middle of it all with a dark cloak draped over his shoulders and naked sword in hand. The fog swirled around him, reaching and bending to his will.

With a subtle flick of his wrist, fog began to part and allowed passage to a lone man, quickly reforming behind him. Caillte remained unmoving, watching as the man approached. He knew several of Ailill's warriors lie in wait beyond his Fomorii fog, too fearful to brave the mists; a wise choice on their part.

Looking around at the destruction, Ailill demanded, "What has happened here? How has Dún Scáth fallen?"

Caillte made no reply, only watched the man with eyes as cold as the thick mist surrounding them.

"I will have answers, Caillte!"

Will you remain a pawn and stain this beautiful land crimson, or will you protect her memory.

"The High Priestess of Tara and her Milidh guardian are more formidable than we could have ever imagined," replied Caillte. "It was by their hands that Dún Scáth met its downfall."

"Your failure is not acceptable," Ailill said callously.

Beneath the folds of his cloak, Caillte's hand tightened on his sword. If Dana's words had been spoken true, standing before him, berating him for the village's destruction, was the man who had forced his hand into bloodshed; the man who had turned him against his own brother; the man who had taken the life of his beloved sister.

As Ailill continued his tirade, Caillte's thoughts turned elsewhere. Had Saibh not perished that fateful day would he have sided with the priestess and the Túatha Dé Danann as his brother had? Would he have risked his life fighting the Milidh for the Túath? If he was to approach the priestess and offer his sword, would she accept him? Would his brother?

Deep in his own thoughts, the man before him continued his enraged rant, face contorted with his wrath. However, Caillte could care less. He was overcome with the need to destroy all that reminded him of Ailill and his bloodstained hands.

The corners of Caillte's mouth twitched in the faintest of grins. Ailill did not seem to grasp with whom he dealt; Caillte was of Fomorii blood, he commanded power over the sea he was born within. He would destroy what remained of Dún Scáth, even if it meant taking him down with it.

The ground beneath the ruined village began to tremble and a low rumble came from deep within the earth, slowly growing in intensity; rising and growling. Whispered protests rose from crumbling stone outer wall as it began to lurch violently. The wind howled as the sea crashed into the cliff in sheer vengeance.

He was of the blood of Balor, leader of all the Fomorii clan. He had command where others did not and to Caillte, the sea itself was a servant to his every whim.

Ailill's lecture fell short as indisputable panic crossed his face. "Do not forget that I saved your life!" he shouted in desperation. "If you turn against me, it shall be your life upon my blade!"

"You shall pierce my heart as sure as you did my sister's?" questioned Caillte, voice dangerously low.

Ailill took a step back, the truth written clearly across his face. "I did not—"

Before the man could finish, Caillte flung his cloak open and thrust his sword through Ailill's heart. "This is for Saibh," he hissed through gritted teeth, pushing the sword deeper and twisting it before wrenching it free. Watching as Ailill's body crumpled lifeless to the ground, he cleaned his blade off on his cloak. "No more shall I serve as your pawn."

Sheathing his sword, Caillte walked toward the remains of the village gates, the earth shuddering beneath his feet in his wake. The outer walls lurched and trembled as large cracks began to form, spider-webbing across the ground. Not once did Caillte look back, even when the remains of Dún Scáth began to break apart from the land, crumbling into the sea.

* ~ * ~ * ~ * ~ *

It was late in the night when Shiovra woke to the gentle fall of rain on her face. Reluctantly rolling onto her back, a frown crossed her brow. Something did not feel right. There was the heaviness of power hanging in the air all around her. Sitting up quickly, she threw her blankets aside and lurched to her feet. Eyes drifting over the faces of her companions, she found them all in a deep sleep. Even their steeds slumbered as they stood tethered to the trees.

The woods surrounding her were completely silent. There was no rustling of leaves, no sweet call of birds, no chirping of crickets; only silence.

Keeping her eyes on the dark trees surrounding her, Shiovra bent slowly and took her sword in hand. Walking over to Eiladyr, she pushed him roughly with her foot and called out his name urgently. When he did not move, she shoved him again. "Eiladyr!"

Still the man did not stir from his slumber.

Shiovra moved to Odhrán, Meara, and finally Ainnle; none would wake.

The silence was broken with the soft singing of a woman's voice. The ghostly melody wove its way through her body, entwining with the very air around her as the pitch rose and fell fluidly with a tone that threatened to lure her away.

Shiovra's hand tightened on the sword. Gráinne by no means held the extent of power she felt within the air, and the Fomorii would only dampen her own abilities as a priestess. Only one other came to mind. "Méav."

The melody suddenly stopped and a cloaked figure strode out from behind a tree. Reaching pale hands up, the woman lowered her hood, her yellow-blond hair falling unbound over her shoulders. Although her beauty had begun to fade, her blue eyes remained as hard as gems. Gone where her noble adornments and rich fabrics. The Méav who stood before her now looked worn and weary.

"Merry meet, Shiovra Ní Coughlin, High Priestess of Tara," replied Méav, slowly approaching the priestess. "Last we met, you scorned what I had to offer." She glanced at Odhrán's sleeping form. "The Milidh guardian…he has become your husband, has he not?"

Shiovra did not reply, only watched Méav carefully as the woman walked leisurely through the camp.

"The Milidh took your mother—my *daughter*—from us," continued Méav, "and now they plot behind false peace agreements with the intentions of war and bloodshed. How many more lives will be lost before they are satisfied?" She stepped around Eiladyr and paused before Shiovra. "Their druids are wise and powerful and we…we priestess' are becoming too few. I do not come this night offering promises. I ask that you join me." Méav lifted her arm, holding her hand out. "Together we have the power to stop them."

Watching the woman, Shiovra thought a moment. Méav was once the High Priestess of Tara before she turned her back on kin and clan; however what had been the reasoning behind her actions? Why would she cast aside duty and clan to lure Ailill with promises of power? What had been Méav's true intention for seizing control of his Huntsmen and Caher Dearg? There were many questions Shiovra wanted answered.

Taking a step forward, the priestess nodded. "I will join you."

~~*~*~*

Odhrán crouched down, running his fingers lightly across the wet ground. His eyes narrowed on the light tracks which were quickly disappearing in the heavy rainfall. From what he could discern, there were no traces of a scuffle having taken place. It was as if the priestess had simply walked away from their camp; a matter which reassured and displeased him all the same.

"Will you be able to track her?" asked Eiladyr, coming to stand beside him.

Odhrán shook his head. "The rain is too heavy," he replied, straightening and cleaning his fingers off on his cloak. "Her tracks are already being washed away." His eyes skimmed over their camp before turning to his left, narrowing on the dark trees. "She has gone to Caher Dearg."

"It lies in ruin," countered Eiladyr.

"Whether Caher Dearg lies in ruins or not does not matter when Méav herself has not fallen," Odhrán told the man as he secured his sword on his belt and tucked his daggers in his belt. "Pack up. We ride for Caher Dearg." Reaching for the reins of his steed, Odhrán paused. It was quiet, nearly missed over the din of the rain, but he heard it nonetheless: the sound of movement drawing near. Letting the reins slip from his fingers, Odhrán drew his sword and took a few steps forward.

"What—"

Odhrán cut Eiladyr off with a quick gesture that commanded silence. Stepping forward once more, he brought his blade up. The rain and darkness of night made it difficult to discern any definite enemy movement among the trees, leaving them at a disadvantage.

Eiladyr and Meara moved in to flank him; Eiladyr drawing his sword while Meara stood in a defensive position with her spear, Ainnle at her side.

He heard it then, the muffled snap of a branch. "Hold until I say," ordered Odhrán in a low voice.

The air around them grew suddenly cold and a light mist rose up from the ground, mingling with the rain.

Odhrán's hand tightened on the hilt. "Show yourself, *Fomorii*," he demanded.

A branch snapped loudly, followed by a deep, familiar voice, "Perhaps if they were not weapons at ready I would be more inclined to step forward."

He knew the voice well. Lowering his sword, Odhrán glanced at Eiladyr and Meara in turn. "Do as he says," he commanded, sheathing his blade.

Though they hesitated, they followed his order.

From the darkness of the trees, a pale figure approached them followed by another much larger one. As they neared, the face of Ceallach Neáll greeted them. Brining his steed to a halt his pale eyes studied each of them in turn before settling on Odhrán. "Where is the priestess?"

~~*~*~*

Standing pitifully among the crumpled and charred ruins of Caher Dearg, one lone cottage remained standing. The thatch roof was mostly unharmed with only a small bit missing near the door which allowed some sunlight to drift in. It was there that Méav had taken her one day prior, a mere cottage in the defeated village she once held sway over. Shiovra counted thirteen men who remained under Méav's command, two of which constantly stood guard at the cottage.

Shiovra knew she would not have much time to gather the answers she sought before her warriors came for her. Pacing the cottage she had been restricted to, the priestess mulled over her options. Méav had not bothered to take her sword from her, leaving her perfectly capable of defending herself should she chose to turn on the huntsmen *watching* her. However, if Shiovra wanted answers, she had a part to play.

Her thoughts were interrupted as the cottage door opened and Méav stepped in. The woman only spared her a small glance before circling the fire and setting a bowl of fruit down on the small table.

Shiovra studied Méav for a moment and then asked, "What shall be done when my guardians come looking for me? Undoubtedly they will track me here. What then?"

Sitting down upon a low bench, Méav ate a piece of fruit. "They shall be dealt with when the time comes," she replied simply.

Adding wood to the fire, Shiovra asked causally, "How are we to stand against the war host of Míl's sons?"

Méav was silent for a moment, eyes narrowed on the bowl of fruit. "I had begun preparing for this day many, many years ago when my warnings went unheeded," she said. "If the High Chieftains would not listen my forewarning, if my husband ignored my counsel, then all that was left to me was to take matters in my own hands."

The priestess turned back to Méav. "You foresaw the coming of the Milidh."

Nodding, Méav met her gaze and rose slowly to her feet. "I had foreseen the coming of Ith to Éire," she replied in a hard, cold tone as she walked slowly around the hearth. "I knew his death would enrage his kinsman, Míl. Furthermore, I knew that Míl would send his sons for revenge. All the blood, all the *death* I have seen." She laughed bitterly. "Nonetheless, the High Chieftains and my own husband believed my warning to be naught but foolish fears. Now they find *they* are the fools."

Shiovra watched the woman carefully.

"If they would dismiss me so easily, then I would have to do the same and take matters into my own hands," continued Méav. "I left kin and clan. Seizing Caher Dearg for my own, I gathered strength and fear. If they would do nothing to prepare for the battle with the Milidh, then I would. When the time of battle came, *I* would be the one to rise victorious. Unfortunately," her eyes flickered to Shiovra, "new tactics will have to be taken. Caher Dearg clearly lies in ruin and my war host has greatly dwindled down. Your actions little over a year ago have greatly hindered my strategy."

Stirring up the embers, Shiovra remained silent.

"You have shown me that my strength alone will not be enough to stand against the Milidh forces," stated Méav. "We must stand together if we are to survive."

A sharp knocking upon the door greeted them.

Exhaling with irritation, Méav ordered, "Enter."

Sunlight flooded the cottage briefly as the door opened and one of Méav's huntsmen stepped in. "My lady, we found a man lingering in the edge of the woods," he said, gesturing toward the door.

Another shadow filled the doorway as a man was shoved roughly into the cottage, his hands bound behind his back.

Shiovra straightened, recognizing him. "Morgan?"

Meeting her gaze, he offered her a mischievous grin. "Shiovra."

Méav approached Morgan, looking him over. "I have seen the priestess' guardians, you are not one of them," she said. "You are not of the Túath clan, Milidh, nor Neimidh and obviously not Fomorii."

He shook his head. "No, I am not," replied Morgan. "However, I have taken quite a liking to remaining close to the priestess' side."

"A lover?" pressed Méav, circling him.

Morgan's gaze flickered briefly to Shiovra, grin broadening, before returning to Méav. "Perhaps."

"Where do you stand in the encroaching battle with the Milidh?" asked Méav, her eyes drifting over his sword and bow.

"My place is at the Shiovra's side," he told her simply.

Méav turned to Shiovra. "Does this man speak true?"

Without any hesitation, Shiovra nodded. "Aye," she answered. "His skill with sword and bow make him a highly valuable ally to which I will not be without." She stepped closer, reaching a hand up to touch his arm as her eyes turned slowly to Méav. "If you desire me to remain with you, then Morgan must be at my side."

After a moment of thought, Méav nodded. "I shall permit his presence for the time being, as long as he heeds my commands," she said, returning to the table. "Untie him."

～～*～*～*

The midday sun hung brightly in the sky when they reached the ruins of the once proud Caher Dearg. After tethering the horses a safe distance away, Odhrán began to study what remained of the village. Méav had kept quiet for good reason. After the fall of Caher Dearg, she was left with a paltry of men under her command, most of which who had not fallen under their attack having joined Gráinne.

"There has been no sign of Méav for a year," muttered Eiladyr as he came to stand beside him, hand twitching on the pommel of his sword. "Why now?"

"I believe the priestess will have the answer," replied Odhrán, tone hard. "She went with Méav for a reason and until she is at our side once more, the reasoning shall not be known." Turning away from Caher Dearg, he walked back to where Meara, Ainnle, and Ceallach waited. "We must move quickly, but with great caution. Only one thing is certain, Méav will not release the priestess without a fight."

"Wisely spoken words."

Odhrán turned at the dark voice, taking note of the slight chill which had suddenly crept into the air around them. His hand moved to the hilt of his sword, ready to draw.

A man stepped around a tree and into the sifting sunlight. His garments were travel stained and worse for the wear. Pale blue eyes with slit pupils drifted over the companions before settling on Ceallach. "Merry meet, brother,"

The Fomorii man stepped forward angrily, his usual calm vanishing. "Merry meet?" he growled venomously. "Have you so easily forgotten our last meeting?" Ceallach's hand flew to his sword, ripping it free from its scabbard with ease. "You will receive no warm greeting from me, Caillte."

"I wish to speak with you, not do battle," replied the elder of the brother's evenly.

Ceallach laughed openly, stepping forward to press the tip of his blade to Caillte's throat. "Surely you jest."

The man stood calmly, his eyes not wavering from Ceallach's. "This is no jest," stated Caillte. "Drop your sword, brother, doing battle here will solve nothing."

Ceallach remained still, his hand tight on the sword.

Odhrán stepped forward, looking Caillte over before turning his attention to Ceallach. "Save your quarrel for later," he said harshly. "Recovering the priestess is of more importance."

"The Milidh guardian speaks true," stated Caillte. "If you wish to punish me for Saibh's death, then strike me down where I stand and be done with it. However, bear in mind, that by taking my life you will become no better than I have."

Ceallach did not move, his hand continuing to hold the sword steady at his brother's throat.

"As I said, I have come to you with the intention of speaking, not shedding blood," continued Caillte, slowly reaching a hand up to push Ceallach's sword aside. "It was the words of your priestess who opened my eyes, and now she lies within Méav's grasp. Will you allow her to remain so?"

"Keep a wary eye on him if you must, but now is not the time to be settling differences," stated Odhrán. "The priestess awaits us." Turning his attention to the village gate, he took note that the two huntsmen had become distracted with conversation, their backs to them. Drawing his own blade, Odhrán gave his undisputed order, "We move now."

~~*~*~*

"I have seen how you move in battle, how well you can hide your presence when watching your prey. You *allowed* Méav's men to capture you," Shiovra remarked when she had finally been left alone with Morgan.

The man grinned at her from across the table as he took a drink from his cup. "Of course," replied Morgan. "Only your Milidh husband is truly capable of such a feat, let alone being able to track me."

"Why allow yourself to be captured?" she asked.

"I could ask the same of you," he countered with a playful note.

Shiovra looked down and ran a fingertip along the lip of her cup. "Méav came to me alone and I took the opportunity to find the answers in which I sought," she told him. "I was a small child when she turned her back on kin and clan, on her own daughters. Her reasoning behind such actions remained unknown. Though Gráinne has openly proven she is a threat to Tara, Méav has not. Since abandoning us, she has made no move against the village or clan. In truth, it was quite by accident that I came within her grasp, and even then, she only made an idle threat. To see if she will become a danger to Tara, I followed her here."

Morgan shifted, leaning forward. "Is she a threat?"

The priestess did not look up, her body tensing as her hand stilled. "I am afraid so," she replied. "Méav has become so focused on gathering strength through fear and warriors that she has failed to see her approach is quickly becoming no better than the Milidh's. Her desire to protect Éire and her people is warranted, but her approach is inexcusable."

"What do you plan to do?" he questioned, taking another drink.

Shiovra hesitated a moment, thinking. "I have destroyed Caher Dearg and drastically reduced her war host to only a handful of men," she told him, meeting his eyes. "However, Méav remains a very powerful High Priestess. If we are to truly impede upon her strategy, then her power will need to be bound."

Morgan remained silent for a moment before asking, "Are you able to bind Méav's power as a priestess?"

Reluctantly, she nodded. "It will be dangerous, but it is possible." Shiovra took a long drink of her water before meeting his gaze once more. "Tell me, Morgan, why did you follow me here?"

A broad grin crossed his lips. "Curiosity?" he replied with amusement. Morgan's eyes drifted to her sword, which lay across the table within arm's reach. "There is strength in you that most women do not have, both in mind and heart. I want to watch that strength and protect it." He rose to his feet and walked around the table, moving to stand behind her. "I did not lie when I told Méav that my place is at your side."

Shiovra felt his hands touch her shoulders gently before the warmth of his breath caressed her cheek.

"And protect it I will, even should it mean following you here," he told her, lips brushing against her ear.

His simple touch brought a slight blush to her cheeks. She couldn't shake the feeling that in some way he was teasing her. Turning her head slightly to glance at the man, the long note of a battle horn caught Shiovra's attention.

Morgan's grin turned mischievous. "It would seem your guardians have arrived."

* ~ * ~ * ~ * ~ *

A horn sounded on the wind to bring warning of attack; however it came too late. They had breached the ruined village wall and gained the element of surprise, felling two men swiftly before turning upon a third. Odhrán approached the huntsman from behind, seizing him by the tunic and thrusting his sword through the man's back.

Wrenching his blade free, Odhrán turned to assist Meara with a huntsman who had managed to gain the upper hand. Swinging wide, he struck the distracted man across the arm, severely wounding him.

"Behind you!" shouted Meara, thrusting her spear at the huntsman as his sword clattered to the ground.

Odhrán spun and brought his sword up just in time to meet that of his attacker. With a grunt, he pushed the man back roughly. As the huntsman stumbled back, Odhrán pulled a dagger from his belt and brought his sword up. Taking a deep breath, he straightened. All around him time seemed to slow. Three men had moved to flank with the huntsman, taking Odhrán's attention away from his companions. Exhaling, his hands tightened on his weapons as he shifted his stance.

His gaze shifted over the four men approaching him before his eyes narrowed on the one to his right. Odhrán lunged at the man, knocking the huntsman's sword down and rolling his shoulder into him. As the warrior fell roughly to the ground, Odhrán turned his attention to his initial opponent. Catching the huntsman's sword on the guard of his own, he thrust his dagger up and twisted it.

Wrenching the dagger free, Odhrán turned without pause to block an attack with his sword. He met the strike with great force, shoving his foe back with ease. Dropping down, he narrowly avoided a sword to his left, the blade grazing across his tunic and tearing it. Straightening, he shoved his sword through the chest of the man he faced while bringing his dagger up to the throat of another.

"Enough!"

Twisting his sword, Odhrán tugged the blade free and let the man fall to the ground. Keeping his dagger poised at the huntsman's throat, he slowly brought his gaze to Méav.

The woman approached them with spear in hand, stopping a safe distance away, her eyes drifting over each of them in turn.

Eiladyr stepped around Odhrán, sword raised and knuckles white with his anger. "Release Shiovra!" he demanded.

Odhrán brought his blade up and pushed Eiladyr's down. "Hold," he commanded sternly.

"Release her?" scoffed Méav, an amused smile crossing her pale lips. "One cannot release something that has not been *captured*."

"What do you mean?" asked Eiladyr.

"Your priestess willingly came here," replied the woman, her gaze turning to Odhrán. "Yon Milidh guardian knows I speak the truth."

Odhrán paid little heed to the stunned look Eiladyr gave him, instead his gaze remained fixed on Méav as he pressed the tip of his dagger harder against his foe's throat. From the corner of his eye, he saw Shiovra step from the lone cottage, sword in hand at her side, followed by a man armed with bow and sword. From the look of him, Odhrán knew he was not one of Méav's huntsmen and his thoughts were confirmed was the name passed Eiladyr's lips.

"Morgan—"

"Cease this bloodshed now and lower your weapons," Méav commanded. "The priestess is no prisoner of mine."

Odhrán shifted his gaze to Shiovra as she stood slightly behind Méav. She met his eyes and nodded. Although he could not be certain what Shiovra's plan was, he lowered his dagger and tucked it back into his belt.

Eiladyr turned to him. "How can you heed her words so easily?" he questioned angrily.

"Do it," Odhrán commanded sternly.

Reluctantly, Eiladyr sheathed his sword; however his hand did not leave the hilt.

"You show great wisdom, Milidh guardian," Méav said softly, her eyes drifting over the companions. "What an odd assortment of companions you have gathered, Shiovra: Milidh, Neimidh, and Fomorii all standing in the service of a Túath priestess." Sighing, she stepped around Odhrán looking him up and down before coming to a stop in front of him. "Tell me, Milidh guardian, why do you protect one of the Túath clan? The treaty of alliance you forged just may be naught but a ruse to gain Tara."

From the corner of his eye, Odhrán took notice that Shiovra and Morgan had begun making a wide arch around Méav toward the rest of the companions. Holding Méav's attention, he replied simply, "True, the alliance I have forged may indeed be an elaborate strategy to claim Tara for the Milidh—however, it could also be the only way your kin and clan will *survive* the oncoming storm." Hand tightening on his sword, he studied the woman carefully as she stood defiantly before him. "What of you? What are your intentions with *my* priestess?"

"To end the bloodshed upon this land," Méav told him.

"By spill more in the process?" countered Odhrán, taking a step toward the woman.

Méav stiffened in response, her eyes flickering briefly to his sword before returning to hold his gaze.

A grin tugged at the corners of Odhrán's lips. "Have you forgotten the rede of a priestess? Harm none."

Frowning deeply, Méav replied bitterly, "A priestess' duty is to protect her people. If I do not take action, who shall? The High Chieftains who did not heed my warning all those years ago? My late husband who laughed and brushed my counsel aside?" Laughing cynically, she walked away from him and spun, her skirts swirling in response. "Look around you, Milidh guardian, at the blood you and your *companions* have shed more than once!" ordered Méav, gesturing with her spear. "What makes you any better than the rest of the Milidh?"

"We are not seeking to start a war, only protect those close to us!" shouted Eiladyr as he took a step forward.

Méav pointed the spear at the man. "You are a stranger to these lands and as thus need not meddle in our affairs." Her attention returned to Odhrán. Gesturing her hand, the remaining huntsmen pressed around him.

Odhrán raised his hand, commanding his companions to remain still. He knew they would move to his defense; however, he did not need them. "You would journey a path laden with blood and death to protect your people?" he questioned coldly. "It is *you* who is no better than the Milidh."

An ugly, livid scowl crossed Méav's face, distorting it with her fury. "I will *not* sit idle and watch Éire be torn apart by war brought on from the ignorance of the High Chieftains and sons of Míl! I will defend her with my own hands, shedding blood if I must," she hissed, knuckles turning white as her hand clenched tighter on the spear, "starting with you!"

Weapons drawn, the huntsmen moved to attack, but Odhrán was quicker. Taking his sword by both hands, he turned the blade down and dropped suddenly to his knee, driving the metal into the ground. The earth beneath him trembled and suddenly heaved like a massive wave, rippling out and knocking his attackers off their feet. As soon as they fell, the companions were upon them.

Straightening, Odhrán began to approach the woman. "This ends now, Méav."

The woman calmed suddenly, her face becoming stoic. "Aye, it does," she told him. Swinging her spear up suddenly, she hurled it toward Odhrán, aiming for his heart.

Odhrán had expected such an attack. What he had not expected, however, was for Shiovra to step in its path.

11. INTIMIDATION TACTICS

Heavy gray clouds moved in swiftly over Tara, blanketing it in shadows while a murmuring, moaning wind circled the village, carrying dampness to it. Birds took off in sudden flight as if fleeing some unseen foe. Restless horses reared and whinnied as they circled in their pens and pulled at their ties. The people of Tara paused in their duties, exchanging fearful looks at the ominous feel they felt weighing heavily in the air.

Within the main cottage, Réalta Dubh came to a sudden pause as a chill crept through her body. Flinging the door open, she ran outside and looked down the hill at the village. She could feel it quite clearly and it terrified her.

Daire came to stand beside her and she only spared him a slight glance. From the look on her son's face, she knew he felt it as well.

"What is it?" he asked.

"It has begun," Réalta told him as she sank weakly to her knees, "the fall of the Túath clan."

Daire stiffened. "How?"

Réalta shook her head, feeling ill. "I…" Her voice trailed off as she brought her hands up to look at them. Though she could still feel the power of a priestess coursing through her veins, could still feel the energy of the world around her, it felt *weakened*. Something had happened that she had not foreseen.

Her son shifted in front of her, crouching down suddenly and grabbing her by the shoulders. "Shiovra!" he said anxiously. "What of Shiovra?"

~~*~*~*

Kieran drew his hood up against the roughness of the cold wind as he stopped to take shelter from the rain beneath a tree. Leaning against the tree, he watched the blades of grass bend beneath the unrelenting gusts of wind. Rainstorms were by no means uncommon in Éire; however this one held an unsettling feeling to it. The palm of Kieran's hand itched as it rested upon the pommel of his sword.

Eras have come and gone many times from Éire and so time shifts once more.

The words his mother had spoken over a year prior echoed in his mind. Kieran frowned, the apprehensive feeling increasing tenfold. He needed to return to Tara and with great haste. The rain and wind were forgotten as he stepped out from the shelter of the tree and broke into a run.

~~*~*~*

Gráinne was not one known for great patience, nevertheless, for the sake of her plans, she would bide her time and use the coming winter months to increase the number of her warriors. Standing beside the hearth fire, she swirled her mead around in its cup as she mused over her strategy. Tara had become tainted with the presence of Milidh and the High Priestess herself had allowed it. Gráinne had no qualms about using Milidh warriors; they were excellent fodder for battle. Yet, to simply *welcome* them into Tara was unforgiveable. Tara belonged to those of Túath blood and Túath blood alone.

Behind her the wicker door rattled under a rough gust of wind.

Frowning, Gráinne walked to the door and paused only a moment before opening it.

Without the door to obstruct its rampage, the gale freely slammed into the cottage and circled the woman, tugging at her hair and clothing.

Gráinne stepped from the cottage and looked up at the gathering of dark clouds. Although she failed in many ways as a priestess, she could still feel it: a shift in power. Tilting her head back, she closed her eyes and raised her arms as a cruel smile crossed her lips.

~~*~*~*

Shiovra took a long, deep breath, closing her eyes. She could hear her name being shouted, but the voices felt distant as she drew upon all the power within her grasp, pulling from every rock, tree, and gust of wind. Even the rain which had begun to fall slowed and paused in its descent from the sky.

Slowly releasing her breath, she opened her eyes.

The spear Méav had thrown hung before her, suspended in midair naught but a few paces from Shiovra's breast. Flicking her wrist, the length of the spear began to tremble and twist. Another flick and it snapped, cracks forming all along the wood before falling uselessly to the ground in pieces.

Shiovra's eyes snapped to Méav. "An attack against my guardians is an attack upon me," she said, taking a step forward.

Méav retreated a step in response, eerie calm written across her face. "What now, High Priestess?" asked the woman. "Will it be my life?"

Eyes narrowing on Méav, Shiovra stated, "A priestess' duty is to protect lives, not take them. Even though you did not thrust the blade yourself, your hands remained stained with blood." She took another step forward and gestured at what remained of Caher Dearg. "This is your punishment, Méav. Your war host has fallen and your defenses in ruin. Admit your defeat."

Méav stiffened, hands clenching tightly at her sides. "And you have sealed our fate!" she shouted spitefully. "How many more lives will fall under sword and spear when the chieftains go to war? I could have *protected* our people! I could have—"

"Enough!" commanded Shiovra, continuing to draw upon the power of the world surrounding her. "The rede of the priestess was simple: as it harm none, do as thou will. Such simple, important words you seem to have forgotten." Her breathing had become labored with the effort, but she pushed it aside, instead focusing on weaving the energy around Méav. "You have harmed many people, Méav, and it ends now. You shall be given fair punishment and have your power bound."

Shiovra closed her eyes, focusing on the power within Méav. Though she could not take that power away, she could bind it and prevent the woman from using it for harm. "Your darkness has ended, you control is done," she breathed, weaving the words around Méav as if they were an impenetrable barrier. "Welcome the light, my battle is won." With those words, Shiovra opened her eyes and released all the power she had gathered before meeting Méav's gaze.

At first the woman did nothing, simply stood in silence and watched Shiovra with a shocked expression. Only a reminiscence of Méav's former beauty remained. Her hair, once a glistening yellow-blonde, had dulled and become threaded with silver strands. With her power bound, Méav appeared as the woman she truly was. Sagging to her hands and knees, she sobbed.

"A priestess' power is not to be used for war and death, but for life," chided Shiovra. "Your power as a former High Priestess remains to you, Méav, I cannot take it away, only bind it so you can no longer do harm."

Without looking up, Méav asked, "What shall be done with me now?"

"As you harm none, do as you will," replied the priestess simply.

"No life remains to me but that of an outcast," cried Méav, turning away from the companions. "Leave me to myself."

Ceallach stepped toward the woman. "You have cause much harm and destruction, not only to the Túath clan, but to your own kin." His deep voice rang harshly in the quiet ruins. "Come with us to Tara and seek the forgiveness of your own blood."

Méav rose slowly to her feet and brought her gaze to his. Gone was her haughtiness, leaving only the appearance of a shattered woman. "You think my daughter will forgive me, Ceallach Neáll of the Fomorii?" she asked bitterly. "Do you think any of them will?" She gestured to Shiovra and her warriors. "No. I think not. Leave me to myself. Banishment is punishment enough."

Shiovra stepped forward. "You cast aside kin and clan," she said, voice firm, "you took lives and shed blood, you broke your vows as a priestess and yet…you did so with the intentions of *protecting*. Your methods were wrong, but your heart was right." She offered the woman a weak smile. "You are not banished and forgiveness can be given, but you must be willing to seek it. Till then, do as you will."

Turning away from Méav, Shiovra was overwhelmed by a wave of tremendous weakness. All the power she had gathered to bind Méav's power had left her with little energy of her own. Her eyes met Odhrán's briefly before she was completely consumed by the darkness of unconsciousness.

* ~ * ~ * ~ * ~ *

Nightfall quickly approached as Kieran reached the village of Tara. Last the Neimidh man had set foot in Tara was well over a year ago, just before Shiovra's departure from Rúnda. Despite the length of time since his last visit, he noticed quickly the somber mood which filled the Túath village. Not far in, Kieran learned quickly of Úna's passing. Quickening his pace, he made his way towards the main cottage.

Cresting the hill, he was surprised to find Daire leaning against the cottage wall, face distant. The last he had seen the man was shortly after Gráinne's attempted attack upon Dún Fiáin. Slowing, he paused to look down at the man. At first Kieran said nothing, simply sat down beside the man and let silence settle comfortably over them.

After a long while, Daire finally spoke, his voice rough, "Do we fight a losing battle?"

Kieran glanced at him. "Perhaps, however it is one that I am willing to fight, no matter the outcome."

A short laugh passed Daire's lips. "These alliances Shiovra forges without hesitation, they worry me," he admitted. "I fear they are only prolonging the calm before the storm."

"Aye, battle with the Milidh may be inevitable, yet what Shiovra does is for the sake of protecting lives. Even if Tara becomes lost, the people of this village will survive through her efforts. You may question some of Lady Shiovra's decisions, but I do not," Kieran told the man firmly. "She is my priestess and I her loyal sword. What more, she is my *companion* and I will do all within my power to help her." He looked up at the sky with a narrowed gaze. Thick gray clouds lingered over the village, blotting out the colors of the setting sun. "Shortly before my arrival, I felt a shift in power. The air was ripe with an ominous feeling."

Daire nodded and rubbed the back of his neck. "I have likewise had such a feeling," he said. "Never before have I seen mother quite as fearful as I did at that moment. She spoke of the beginning of the end to the Túath clan."

Kieran studied the man a moment, noting that Daire's hand trembled slightly as it continued to rub his neck. He knew instantly where the man's thoughts lie. "Lady Shiovra is not here, is she?"

"No," replied Daire, shaking his head. "After she told me of Úna's illness, I left immediately. Shiovra said she would follow after—"

Pulling a knee up, Kieran leaned an elbow on it. "You fear the shift in power has something to do with her."

"Aye."

He could not say he did not understand the man's thoughts, having felt such a moment of fear himself. "Lady Shiovra has always stood defiantly against those who seek to bring harm to Tara and her people, even if it means setting the wheel in motion that will ultimately bring about the Túath's downfall," replied Kieran. "Nevertheless, I will continue to stand beside her and help protect these people." He fell silent a while, watching as the last glimmer of sunlight sank beneath the horizon. When he did speak, his voice was kind, "I am sorry for your loss."

Daire did not respond and Kieran said no more.

"Lord Daire?"

Kieran looked up at the voice, finding a young woman of astounding beauty standing in the cottage doorway, looking at them. Her pale skin and raven hair where bathed with the warm glow of the cottage's heart fire. The woman's eyes met his briefly, widening with a flicker of surprise before she turned her attention back to Daire.

"Eithne said the children are awake," the woman continued.

Daire nodded, standing. "Thank you, Aislinn," he said, glancing down at Kieran. "If you will excuse me."

"Of course." Rising to his feet, Kieran watched as Daire slipped past the woman and retreated within the cottage. When he found the woman watching him he said, "Forgive me, my lady. I am Kieran, an old companion of Lord Daire and the clan of Tara."

She watched him for a moment then gave a flustered, "Ah!"

Courteously offering a small bow, her face flushed. "I am Aislinn, wife of Mahon," she returned. "Please forgive me, but you look so much like my late brother I had thought you were him for a moment and thus have failed to properly greet a companion to my lord husband."

Smiling gently, Kieran said, "No harm done, Lady Aislinn. I am sorry to have intruded so late in the evening, but I must speak with Lord Mahon."

* ~ * ~ * ~ * ~ *

The darkness of night stretched wide across Caher Dearg as Odhrán sat in the lone standing cottage keeping watch over Shiovra as she slept soundly in the bed. Prodding the hearth fire with a stick, he watched with a hard gaze as the embers flared in response. The priestess had taken a great risk to bind Méav's power; one that could have easily taken her life. Roughly tossing a piece of wood into the fire, he ran a hand through his hair and cursed.

He had never felt such unease before, such *fear*. To bind Méav, the priestess had wielded a tremendous power which nearly broke her. Odhrán was left feeling both anxious and irritated over her actions. It was not the first time the priestess had willingly stepped into danger, and although he was quite sure it would not be the last, he was far from being pleased about it.

His thoughts were interrupted as the wicker-work door creaked open. Glancing up, he watched as Morgan and Eiladyr slipped into the cottage, a cold night breeze following in their wake. The brothers appeared as worn and weary as he himself felt.

Morgan's eyes drifted to where Shiovra slept, lingering before turning to meet Odhrán's gaze. "She continues to sleep?" he asked, sitting down across from the fire.

Odhrán nodded and poked at the fire once more, staring at the flames dancing across the wood. "What the priestess did brought risk to her own life," he said in a hard tone. "The question remains is for what reason did she go with Méav." Odhrán's gaze slid up to meet Morgan's, holding it firmly. "I am quite sure you know the reasoning behind her actions."

Exhaling loudly, Morgan leaned forward on his elbows. "While Gráinne has openly proven herself a threat, Méav has not. Shiovra sought to determine if Méav would pose a danger to Tara as well as to learn the reasoning behind her abandonment of kin and clan, and so when Méav approached her, she willingly followed," he told Odhrán. "Shiovra feared that Méav's plans were leading her to be little better than the Milidh and thus deemed that binding her power as a priestess was the only way the remove the threat."

Leaning back on the bench, Odhrán studied the man carefully. From the occasional glance toward the slumbering priestess, Odhrán could easily see where the man's intentions lie. "You have been watching the priestess for some time now," he stated bluntly.

"Aye," replied Morgan.

"Not only that, but you have even raised your weapon more than once against those who would bring her harm," continued Odhrán. "What now, Morgan? Shall you join us as one of her guardian warriors?"

Morgan flashed him a wry smile and stood. "For the time being, I shall maintain my distance unless needed," he said, making his way toward the door. Pausing in the doorway, he glanced over his shoulder and grinned at his brother. "Worry not, brother, I will always be close by, watching and protecting. Tell Shiovra that we shall meet again soon." The door clattered shut behind Morgan.

Rising to his feet, Odhrán stretched. "The night is late and we have a long way ahead of us," he remarked. "Get some rest."

* ~ * ~ * ~ * ~ *

Shiovra woke to early morning sunlight stretching from the hole in the roof and onto her face. Rolling onto her back, her entire body protested the movement. For a moment, she simply lay in the bed, looking up at the thatch roof looming above her. Her thoughts lingered over what had happened. She remembered binding Méav's power; however, after that, everything had gone black. With a grunt, Shiovra sat up and pushed the blankets aside.

Glancing around the cottage, she found that she was alone. Climbing from the bed, she approached the table to find her sword and cloak lying beside a small wooden bowl of fruit and cup of water. As she reached for the fruit, a low, dangerous voice from outside the door drew her attention.

"You are not welcome here, Caillte."

Shiovra recognized the voice as Ceallach's. Walking to the door, she opened it and stepped outside.

Ceallach stood with his back to her, hand resting on the hilt of his sword, while Caillte stood across from him, hands open and weaponless. To her left she found Odhrán watching them with his arms crossed. He only spared Shiovra a small glance before returning to his watch of the brothers. Meara, Ainnle, and Eiladyr were nowhere in sight.

"Do you wish to punish me for Saibh's death?" demanded Caillte. "Her last smile torments me every night! I was a fool to believe I could manipulate Ailill when I was his pawn from the beginning. It was by his sword that Saibh lost her life, and by mine in which he lost his. Your priestess questioned me as to where my place would be in the upcoming battle; if I was to remain a pawn of protect Saibh's memory. I chose *her*."

This ally will prove his worth with Ailill's death.

Badb's words rang clearly in Shiovra's mind. Glancing at Ceallach, she noticed his jaw had tensed, yet he said nothing in return.

Glancing over his brother's shoulder, Caillte met Shiovra's gaze briefly. "I came to offer my sword, not do battle with you, brother. If I am to leave, it shall be by the priestess' order."

"Your hands are stained crimson with Túath blood and yet you wish to stand beside the priestess?" countered Ceallach.

"Ceallach, peace," interrupted Shiovra, placing a restraining hand on his arm as she stepped around him. Ignoring the hard glare he gave her, she turned her attention to Caillte. "Speak, Caillte of the Fomorii."

The man offered her a small bow. "Lady Shiovra," he said, his deep voice smoothly speaking her name. "Your words have plagued me since our meeting. I have decided my place and offer my sword, although it would seem that my brother's disapproval is unyielding."

Shiovra considered his words for a moment. "You have taken Ailill's life?" she asked.

Caillte nodded. "Aye."

"And now, you wish to turn you back on everything to serve me?"

He nodded once more.

"He cannot be trusted," protested Ceallach.

"That is not for you to decide," Odhrán warned sternly, as he approached. "Caillte has chosen to serve Shiovra, not you. If he is to leave, it will be her word alone."

Ceallach met Shiovra's eyes, his displeasure written clearly across his face. "Bear in mind that by welcoming him, you just may be welcoming your own death."

"I am perfectly capable of defending myself, you are well aware of that, Ceallach Neáll," Shiovra told him. "War is drawing near. I am not telling you to welcome his with open arms or to even trust him. I am asking you to accept him as another sword in our defense, just as I have accepted you and Odhrán. As Ailill's warlord, he holds knowledge of not only Milidh movements, but Fomorii as well. His can be of use to us."

Caillte took a step forward and held his hands out wide. "Will you have my sword, brother?"

Exhaling, Ceallach turned away from his Caillte. "Aye, but I will be watching you."

* ~ * ~ * ~ * ~ *

Kieran could only grin as Mahon brought his blade up to block the fierce attack. Although he knew the man was hardly a match for him, he enjoyed Mahon's fighting spirit. Kieran took a step back, chuckling, as Mahon swung at him. It had been many years since they last spared and he was quite enjoying himself. It took his mind off other matters which troubled him.

Grinning, Kieran parried Mahon's next attack with ease and spun, slapping Mahon on the back with the flat of his sword. He was not weary in the least, enjoying their little game of mock battle; however Mahon appeared a bit worse for the wear, sweat rolling down his face and dampening his tunic. A mischievous grin tugged the corners of Kieran's lips as Mahon shifted stances. He knew Mahon well enough to know was thinking and, as the man leapt for him, Kieran casually stepped to the side.

Knocked off balance from the failed attack, Mahon recovered his footing. Twisting quickly, he made to attack from the side.

Blocking, Kieran pushed his blade back and forced his wrists to turn, knocking Mahon's sword from his hands. His victory over Tara's acting chieftain garnered applause from the villagers who had gathered to watch.

Breathing heavily, Mahon wiped the sweat from his brow and gave Kieran a solid clap on the back. "Good fight," he said, sheathing his blade. "But you went far too easy on me, my friend."

Kieran grinned. "Should I have done otherwise?" he asked in a tone of mild innocence. "I believe your lady wife would have been greatly distressed had I gone harder on you."

Mahon chuckled, shaking his head. "Who better to best me than my own trusted companion? It is unfortunate that my wife had to witness my defeat. I am too old for this."

"You are only four years older than me, Mahon," reminded Kieran.

He merely grinned and looked to where Aislinn stood amongst the gathered villagers.

She stepped forward and offered the men a gentle smile. "It is good to know that such a man stands at my lord husband's side," Aislinn said. "To have one who is so skilled is a good thing."

A grin crossed Mahon's face. "Ah, Kieran is the most capable warrior I know; however it is not I whom he serves, but Tara's High Priestess."

Kieran shook his head and chided, "Do not speak such falsehoods, Lord Mahon. You know very well that I can easily be bested by Lord Odhrán."

"You are second only to him. Besides, he is in Dún Fiáin with my sister," replied Mahon. "Your skill if far greater than the warriors who remain here in Tara, do not deny that."

"Kieran is a modest man," said Earnán's voice as he approached. "He has no desire to admit his prowess in battle." He grinned at the Neimidh man. "Perhaps a friendly competition is in order. It has been quite a few years since one was held."

"Aye, I agree with you," Mahon agreed, nodding. "What say you, Kieran? Would you be willing to participate in a competition of skill?"

Kieran shook his head. "No, I afraid I shall have to pass." He nearly regretted the disappointment that crossed his companion's face.

"Is there no swaying you?" pressed Mahon.

"I am afraid not," replied Kieran, stretching his arms. "I must prepare for the priestess' return to Tara. I have yet to speak with her about what I have previously informed you."

"My lord Kieran, would you perhaps not reconsider?" asked Aislinn softly. "From just this little sparing match, it is clear to see that the people of Tara would be greatly entertained by a competition. Would you not like to further hone your skills in battle by testing those of others?"

"Lady Aislinn has a point," added Earnán. "I will even have Naal participate since he has neglected taking up his sword of late." A broad grin crossed his lips. "These days of peace may not last much longer. We should brighten the hearts of Tara's people before darker times fall upon us."

Kieran could not deny the truth to Earnán's word and exhaled in defeat. "Fine, fine," he said. "I shall take part, for the sake of the villagers. However, I follow the priestess' wishes first and foremost. I serve her."

"Daire will surely want a hand in this," remarked Mahon. "He could use a diversion from the ill events that have befallen him recently."

Rubbing the back of his neck, Kieran turned to leave. He could only hope that all was well with the priestess and she would return soon.

"Lord Kieran?"

He turned at the woman's voice to find Aislinn following him down the path. "Do you have need of me, my lady?" Kieran asked, curious as to why the woman had followed him.

"Please forgive me, but I worry that I have troubled you by requesting your participation in the contest. I do not wish for you to feel as if you are forced to take part," she told him. "Mahon has told me you serve the High Priestess of this village. Perhaps if you are concerned about her—"

"My lady priestess is a strong and stubborn woman," Kieran reassured Aislinn. "While it is true that I may worry about her, she is not only perfectly capable of protecting herself, but also protected by her guardian warriors."

"Are you a guardian of the priestess as well?" inquired Aislinn.

Kieran nodded. "Aye," he continued as he walked down the path, hands behind his back. "I served as her guardian from the day she arrived on Rúnda for her training till the day she left and I continue to serve her in any way possible." Studying the woman from the corner of his eye, he asked, "You are Milidh, Lady Aislinn?"

She nodded. "Aye."

"How are you finding life here in Tara?"

Aislinn paused, remaining quiet for a moment before replying, "It is…different from what I am accustomed to as well as what I had come to expect."

Kieran understood the hidden meaning to her words and offered her a reassuring smile. "You have a good husband in Mahon," he told her. "Do not hesitate to express any concerns or fears you may have to him. He will listen. Fret not over whatever your kin or clan may have told you. It matters not here."

The woman nodded, keeping her gaze lowered as she fidgeted with the lengths of her skirts. "It is difficult, though." Aislinn bit her lower lip, looking away. "My lord husband remains a man I know very little of."

"Perhaps then, my lady, you should speak with him," suggested Kieran. "You will never come to know or even understand what kind of man Mahon is if you do not speak with him. If it will help ease your worries, ask him of his sister and all she has done for this village and of *her* marriage to one of the Milidh."

"Kieran?"

Glancing up, he found Daire approaching him from the Banqueting House with a cup in hand.

"Ah, forgive me, Lord Kieran," said Aislinn suddenly. "I shall trouble you no longer." She glanced at Daire and offered him a nod. "Lord Daire."

Daire nodded in turn before taking a drink from his cup.

Turning, the woman walked along the path back toward the village walls.

"Mahon's marriage with Aislinn worries me," Daire stated abruptly.

Kieran nodded. "She is a frightened child. Let us give her time to see if she is capable of proving herself."

* ~ * ~ * ~ * ~ *

Night had come to Caher Dearg once more and Shiovra's restlessness grew. Although her desire to return to Tara was great, Ceallach and Odhrán had commanded one day to rest was in order. The priestess found more than once that her thoughts drifted to her cousin Daire, worried about how he was handling the death of his wife Úna. He had greatly regretted his actions with the Neimidh woman and Shiovra fear that he would continue to blame himself for Úna's death.

Leaving the lone standing cottage, Shiovra walked the moonlit remains of Caher Dearg. The breeze was cool and an earthy dampness lingered in the air from an earlier rainfall.

"Though Caher Dearg has fallen and Méav's power bound, you should not wander late into the night."

Shiovra paused, looking up at the moon. "I am safe," she responded. "There are eyes upon me, watching."

Caillte moved to stand beside her.

Silence fell heavily over them, leaving for a small bit, the only the sound the rustle of leaves in the wind and occasional chirp of the night birds.

"You are anxious to return home," Caillte said abruptly.

Shiovra only spared him a slight glance from the corner of her eye. "Of course," she replied. "I have been away too long. I am the High Priestess of Tara. What use am I if I am not there to defend her and her people?"

The Fomorii man nodded. He was quiet a moment and then said, "My brother looks upon me with the eyes filled with anger and hatred, and justly so. I fear that although I have pledged my sword in your service, he will not accept me."

"Can you expect any less, Caillte of the Fomorii?" Shiovra asked in a firm voice. "You have done much to warrant his distrust and abhorrence. The blood of many stains your hands as surely as Saibh's blood stained Ailill's. While it holds true that your actions were out of revenge for her death, and though you may have been manipulated, one moment of clarity does not condone the previous years of carnage. If you truly wish to prove your desire to atone, then you must show so in your actions, not just your words."

"You scold me as if I were a child," countered Caillte. "Do you not fear me in the slightest?"

She looked over at him, brow raised. "Should I?" questioned Shiovra. "You are a man who sought to capture me, a man who sent Morgan to study me, it *would* be expected that I should fear you. However, if I was to fear you, then in turn I should fear my own husband, a Milidh man who bears the marking of a druid and has threatened me more than once. I should fear Morgan, whom you sent to study me. Fear is a weakness and a priestess must be strong for her people."

The ghost of a smile crossed Caillte's lips. "And should my promise be naught but a ruse? How can you be sure that you will not find my sword through your back?"

"Your eyes speak otherwise, Caillte of the Fomorii," she replied simply, "as do previous actions. You could have commanded Morgan to capture me or even kill me; instead you had him watch over me for little over a year. You could have taken Ceallach's life when you captured him, yet you stayed your hand and allowed him to walk away. Darkness may taint your heart, Caillte, but a flicker of light remains within." Shiovra paused, offering him a tight smile. "However, bear in mind that *should* you betray me, should this be all a ruse, you will quickly find your blood spilled by the hands of my warriors if Ceallach does not get to you first. I accept your sword for battle, but my trust will need to be earned."

Caillte nodded. "I understand."

Sighing, Shiovra turned. "We still have a small journey ahead of us," she told him. "You should rest. We leave at dawn."

* ~ * ~ * ~ * ~ *

Aislinn stood in the cottage doorway, looking down at Tara with a frown marring her brow. The day was laden with heavy rainfall and had set her into a dour mood. A lingering feeling of dampness clung to her clothing, only fueling the feeling. Aislinn had greatly begun to miss Úna's smiling face and gently scolding words. She regretted having not taken any notice of the Neimidh woman's illness. Perhaps if she had seen some hint to it, Úna would still live and her children would have their mother.

Sighing, Aislinn turned away from the door and let it fall shut behind her as she walked over to the hearth fire to warm herself. Mahon sat beside the fire, scrutinizing the length of a sword he had recently forged. While he was indeed a good man, Aislinn found it difficult to forget the warning given by her mother: to bear a child quickly lest he break the alliance and send her home.

"Do not look so melancholy," he said abruptly, glancing up at her briefly before turning his attention back to the blade. "The rain shall pass in due time."

She sat down across from him, prodding lazily at the fire. "I am afraid," admitted Aislinn quietly.

Her words garnered Mahon's full attention. Setting the sword aside, he leaned forward on his knees. "Afraid of what?"

Aislinn did not meet his gaze. "Of failing you as your wife," she told him. "Three moons have passed since we were wed and I have yet to come with child."

"You have not failed me by any means, Aislinn," he assured her gently. "I may have wed you for the sake of alliance, but do not think that I do not care for you. Child or not, you are my wife and will remain so until the day you tire of me." Mahon offered her a mischievous grin. "Till then, have patience with me."

She could not help the smile that tugged the corners of her lips. "Aye."

* ~ * ~ * ~ * ~ *

The heavy clouds which had lingered stubbornly finally parted as they approached Tara, covering the village a warm glow as it came into sight. Shiovra paused, hand resting upon the cloth hiding her honor marks as a High Priestess, as she looked over the familiar green hills. A light wind rustled past her, stirring her hair and clothing. For all her anxiousness to return to her home, she felt mild unease looking upon it once again.

"You were so fervent in your desire to return and now it seems like you are apprehensive," said Meara from her right.

She turned to look at the Neimidh woman. "No, not fear," Shiovra replied honestly, "only concern. I was born in Tara, and though I spent ten years training on Rúnda, it will always be my home. However, I feel that I am away far too often."

Meara nodded, smiling. "I understand how you feel. I have a home as well although I have not been there in nearly two years now."

"Where at?"

"Inishmore."

Mild surprise crossed the priestess' face. Inishmore was one of the islands to the west of Éire, a good distance from Tara which held place on the eastern edges. "You are far from your home."

Meara nodded. "Aye, however it does not trouble me too greatly," she replied. "I have good companions to keep me company." Grinning, she glanced back at the others. "They may be an odd assortment, but to me, they are my real home."

Shiovra's gaze drifted over the faces of those she called friend. Each stood beside her for their own reasons, and each held a place within her heart: Odhrán, though Milidh, fought not only to protect her, but the lives of his own village and kin; Eiladyr was a stranger to Éire yet considered it home with ferocity equal to that of those born there; Ceallach Neáll of the Fomorii had abandoned his own clan dwelling within the churning seas and found solace with the Túath; Meara was a strong Neimidh woman who raised arms in defense of those she cared about.

She turned her attention to Caillte. He was a man who had served as an enemy of the Túath clan for several years, their blood stained his hands. Nevertheless, he stood looking upon Tara with great unease written clearly across his face; he was afraid. The former Fomorii war lord to Ailill was *afraid* of setting foot in Tara. Of what the man feared, Shiovra could not be certain, be it the retribution that may be delivered or the mere knowledge he would be standing face to face with those he had betrayed all those years ago. Regardless, the man was fearfully anticipating their arrival.

"You will not walk freely in Tara," ordered Ceallach suddenly, setting a stern gaze upon his brother. "Until we deem you will hold true to your words, you must remain in the presence of a guard at all times. Is that understood?"

The Fomorii man remained silent and simply nodded in response.

* ~ * ~ * ~ * ~ *

Mahon sat by the hearth, sharpening the blade of a newly forged sword. His gaze drifted to his wife occasionally, studying her as she longingly watched Eithne care for Daire's children. He could see it on her face: the need to conceive. Although he had tried his best to assure the woman that he would not cast her aside, he could clearly see that their lack of a child continued to trouble her.

The cottage door clattered open noisily, causing Mahon to startle and his finger to slip along the sharpened edge of the blade.

Naal rushed breathlessly into the cottage. "Mahon!"

Hissing and muttering a curse under his breath, he glanced up at the man. "Aye?"

"Your sister has returned from Dún Fiáin."

Mahon found his mood lightening instantly. "Then we should greet her properly, should we not?"

Naal nodded and quickly left.

Sitting the sword aside, Mahon stood and walked quickly over to his wife. "Come, Aislinn," he told her. "You must meet my sister, Shiovra." Glancing over his shoulder, he found Kieran was already setting aside the herbs he had been preparing and was rising to his feet. Offering his hand to Aislinn, Mahon continued, "Her husband is Odhrán, a Milidh man from Dún Fiáin."

Nodding, Aislinn accepted his hand and walked with him from the cottage.

Mahon waited with his wife for Shiovra to make her way up the hill. He joy at her returned was marred slightly by the presence of another Fomorii man in their group. It had been many years since he had set eyes on Caillte; however it was a face he would never forget. Regardless, as they neared, he offered his sister was warm smile followed by an embrace. "Welcome home."

Shiovra returned his greeting without a moment of hesitation. "It is good to be home."

Mahon spared Odhrán a small glance and told him, "I thank you for upholding your word and keeping my sister safe. You continue to prove that my trust in you is indeed well placed." Turning back to Shiovra, he gestured for Aislinn to step forward. "Sister, this is my wife, Aislinn."

The priestess greeted his wife with equal warmth. "Welcome to the clan of Tara, Aislinn." Placing a hand on Odhrán's arm, Shiovra told the woman, "This is my husband, Odhrán of Dún Fiáin. The rest of my companions you may not know so well, but you will soon enough."

Aislinn, cheeks flushed lightly, nodded with a small smile.

"Shiovra!" Daire's voice interrupted their greetings as he ran up the path toward the main cottage. Seizing the priestess, he pulled her into a tight embrace. "I am glad to see you have safely returned home. I have been worried."

"You often worry too much, cousin," scolded Shiovra gently.

"Rightly so, for the most part," Daire replied with a touch of bitterness to his voice.

Mahon was keen to notice his cousin's gaze was set on Caillte when he spoke those words.

"My lady priestess," said Kieran, stepping forward. "Might we speak later after you have had a moment to rest?"

Shiovra nodded. "Aye, Kieran. We shall hold council and discuss what you have discovered involving Gráinne," she told the man. "I am glad to see you are unharmed."

Kieran nodded. "As you, my lady."

Aislinn leaned toward Mahon, a confused frown crossing her brow.

"Your sister is a priestess as well?"

Mahon nodded. "Aye, the High Priestess of Tara," he explained. "It is a heavy burden or her to bear, but she carried it with great strength and defiance…"

12. TRUTH NEVER LIES

Fall came upon Tara quietly as the winds gradually grew colder and the rains more frequent. Days grew colder and grains were harvested to be stored away, ready to last the winter. Gray clouds drifted over the village, blotting out most of the sunlight and warning of colder months to come.

Shiovra stood in the fields near the village, sword in hand with the blade angled and ready to block the blow. The attack came as expected, what was not was the strength behind it. Stumbling back, she quickly regained her footing, and twisted her blade up in a follow-up strike against Kieran. She tried to not think about the misty rain or the wet ground beneath her feet.

Kieran effortlessly countered each and every one of her attacks.

Her thoughts turned to everything she had seen in battle, each attack and defense that had been employed by her warriors. In her years on Rúnda, Shiovra had been trained in the use a sword for defense, yet she realized the need for further training. Gráinne not only sought to control Tara, she sought her death. Shiovra wanted to be able to hold her own, no matter the situation, without having to face the feeling of vulnerability again.

Shifting her stance, she turned her blade and waited patiently for Kieran's next attack. The Neimidh man circled her slowly for a moment, looking her up and down. Shiovra watched his movements carefully and when he thrust his sword, she pushed it to the side and spun, hitting him with the flat of her blade across his back.

He stumbled and turned quickly, a stunned look crossing his face. The Neimidh man obviously had not expected her attack strategy and now the growing welt on his back was proof. "That," he began, lowering his blade and grinning, "was very unexpected and good."

Shiovra allowed a satisfied grin to cross her lips.

Kieran rubbed his back with his free hand. "Now that will leave a mark…" Exhaling loudly, he brought his blade up. "Shall we continue?"

She tried to peer at his back, only to have the man turn it from her. Frowning, she sheathed her sword and told him, "Perhaps I should take a look at your back first."

"I will be fine."

Arching a brow, Shiovra crossed her arms. "Let me see, you stubborn lout," she told him sternly. "I need to make sure no skin was broken."

Exhaling in defeat, Kieran turned his back to her.

Shiovra's eyes narrowed on the red welt which had already begun to form on his back. "Hmm…looks painful," she said, prodding it roughly with a finger as a wicked grin crossed her face.

Kieran flinched and pulled away. "Aye, that it does, especially so when you touch it, my lady," he chided. Shifting into a defensive stance, he brought his sword up and pointed the tip at her. "As we stand, I am your enemy. Do not show me mercy. Draw your sword, Shiovra Ní Coughlin."

Taking a deep breath, she did as ordered and drew her blade. Slowly releasing it, Shiovra studied Kieran. The Neimidh man remained completely still, his hands firm upon the hilt of his sword. She knew he would not attack first, that he waited for her to move. Licking her lips, Shiovra considered her options for a moment then charged him.

Swinging her blade, her attack was quickly blocked. Frowning, Shiovra moved to strike from the back only to have Kieran spin and block once more. It was then that she took note of how intently he watched her movements. The ghost of a smile crossed her lips.

Feigning an attack high to the right, she swiftly changed her stance when he fell for her ruse and moved to block. Twisting her arm and wrist, she followed through and struck the flat of her blade across his arm.

Cursing loudly, Kieran dropped his sword and rubbed his arm.

It was then that Shiovra heard a clap of approval. Turning, she found Odhrán and Mahon standing on the nearby path, watching. "How long have to two of you been there?" she asked.

"A bit before stubborn lout," replied Odhrán simply.

Groaning, Kieran retrieved his dropped sword. "It would seem my lady is quite capable with a sword," he said, glancing at Odhrán, "although I do believe that continued training would be highly beneficial. Whether we like it or not, war is approaching and times will come when my lady may find herself without guardians to stand at her side." Sheathing his blade, the Neimidh man grabbed his tunic from the ground and turned his attention to Mahon. "We cannot be sure when Gráinne will make her move against Tara and as thus we must be prepared to defend at all costs. Most likely, with the loss of Deasún and Aichlinn, she will delay till after winter."

"I have already increased the watch along the village borders," Odhrán told him. "All able men and women have been armed. When Gráinne makes her move, we will be prepared."

* ～ * ～ * ～ * ～ *

Caillte stood in the doorway, watching as his brother spoke with Earnán and Mahon down the hill. Since his arrival to Tara a fortnight prior, he had followed orders without a single protest. He kept to himself, remained within constant sight of his guard, and did not leave the cottage for the most part, only when necessary. The Fomorii man had not failed to notice the distrustful looks cast in his way from the villagers. Such was to be expected such after all he had done. Trust would not come easily for a tainted man like him.

From his place in the doorway, Caillte studied the villagers, watching them as they lived their lives down the hill. He had spent many years blinded by his hatred, believing Saibh had died by Túath hands when it had been none other than Ailill himself. In his grief over his sister's death, he could not see the truth. Glancing down at his hands, Caillte felt a shudder creep through his spine. He had shed Túath blood wantonly, and now he stood among them, seeking their trust and offering himself in their defense.

"Caillte of the Fomorii."

Turning at the voice, he found a woman with long mahogany hair approached up the hill to his left. The woman was familiar to Caillte and it was not until his met her unusual gaze that he realized who she was. The years had been kind to her; however he noted a heavy weariness lingering behind her gaze. "Réalta Dubh," he said, nodding.

"Many years have passed since we last met," remarked Réalta.

Caillte nodded and studied the woman with a guarded gaze. "Aye," he replied. "I am afraid, though, that my presence is greatly unwelcomed and such is understandable with the past which follows in my wake." His eyes drifted to return watch on his brother.

"Your past does not define who you are," Réalta told him, "it shapes you, strengthens you. What defines you is how you act in the months to come. The Morrigú and Shiovra could see as much, perhaps you should try to as well."

He remained silent.

Tilting her head back, she looked up at the sky and sighed. "Kin betray kin while those who were once called enemy are now allies." She glanced at him from the corner of her eye. "More than anger over that you have done, Ceallach feels betrayed. Words alone will not return trust long lost."

Caillte said nothing. There was great truth behind the woman's words. He feared, though, that no amount of proven loyalty would gain back his brother's trust. Too much blood had been spilled by his hand.

~~*~*~*

Heavy gray clouds filled the sky, blotting out the sun before dumping a torrent of rain upon Tara. Drawing the hood of her cloak up, Aislinn slipped from the main cottage and made her way down the muddy path and into the village, a small nearby cottage within her sight. Approaching the cottage she hesitated, hand raised to knock upon the wicker-work door. She knew Eithne would be inside with Daire's children while the man was at council.

Taking a deep breath, Aislinn tapped lightly upon the door. At first only silence greeted her and she feared that perhaps Eithne had gone to sleep already, but then there was some noise from within and the door opened. The warmth and brightness of the hearth fire poured from the doorway as Eithne looked out.

A surprised expression crossed the woman's face and she ushered Aislinn quickly into the cottage. "Lady Aislinn, why are you out in such dreadful weather?" she asked in a hushed tone.

"I wished to speak with you," replied Aislinn, removing her sopping cloak and setting it on a bench beside the fire to dry. Glancing around the cottage, she found that save for Daire's young children sleeping soundly on one of the beds, they were alone.

Adding wood to the fire and stirring up the embers, Eithne asked, "What would you like to speak of, my lady?"

Aislinn's gaze drifted once more to Daire's children and a sigh escaped her lips. "I long for a child," she admitted quietly. "I understand that it may take time, nevertheless I had hoped that after coupling with Mahon nearly every night I would carry his child by now. I fear the problem may lie with me." She slowly met the woman's gaze, fighting back tears. "I come to you with the hopes that there may be some herbs that could perhaps help?"

Eithne nodded, however her hesitation did not go unnoticed.

"Lady Eithne?" questioned Aislinn.

"There are herbs that have been known to help," the Túath woman explained. "Yet, they can be *very* dangerous and will not assure that a child will come. They are only meant to help aid in conceiving."

Aislinn offered the woman a tight smile. "I would like to try, for the sake of my clan's alliance."

Eithne sighed and shook her head. "Mahon will not send you home if you do not come with child, Lady Aislinn," she scolded firmly. "The alliance your clan forged with our will hold strong, even if you remain childless the rest of your days. Mahon will not cast you aside. There is no need to risk dangerous herbs only for the hope of conceiving."

"I fear the disappointment I can see in his eyes. Will you not help me?" pleaded Aislinn.

Eithne held her gaze for a long while before turning away and approaching a table covered in herbs. "I shall do as you wish," she told her, selecting a few herbs and placing them in the mortar, "however heed my warnings: take no more than I tell you lest it harm you greatly, and remember, this will *not* ensure a child will come."

Aislinn nodded. "I understand."

Exhaling, the Túath woman began grinding the herbs with the pestle. Once they were finely ground, Eithne poured them into a water skin and sealed it closed before shaking it vigorously. "Allow this to seep for the rest of the day," she told Aislinn, handing her the water skin. "Take one sip come morning, and another sip before bed. Do this for the next five days. No more, no longer."

"Aye," replied Aislinn, taking the water skin and clutching it tightly to her chest and smiling brightly at the woman. "I thank you very much, Lady Eithne."

"Luck be with you, Lady Aislinn."

Excusing herself, Aislinn grabbed her cloak and threw it over her shoulders before returning to the downpour of rain. After a quick glance around, she made her way back along the path to the main cottage. Although the rain pattered heavily on the hood of her cloak, Aislinn heard his voice clearly.

"Such horrible weather to be wandering about the village in, Lady Aislinn."

She stopped suddenly, glancing to her right to find Kieran approaching her. Pulling her cloak shut against a particularly strong gust of wind, she greeted him with a small laugh. "Aye, very true," Aislinn told him, taking a few steps forward.

The Neimidh man nodded, falling in step beside her as she continued along the path. "Please forgive my bluntness, my lady, but it would appear to me that you remain uncomfortable here within the village," he said after a moment of silence.

Aislinn's hand tightened on her cloak as she walked along, her eyes drifting to Kieran. Even though she had not known him long, she had learned quickly that the man resembled her late brother in more than just appearance. Kieran was a man she felt at ease around, a man she could confide her worries to. "It is not the village to which I feel uncomfortable," confessed Aislinn, "but the disappointed look my lord husband casts my way."

Kieran came to an abrupt halt and turned to face her. "Lady Aislinn, I have known Mahon since childhood and I can assure you there is no disappointment in his eyes, only worry," he said firmly, a deep frown crossing his brow. "For the sake of his clan and this village, Mahon sought to take a wife in the hopes of forging a strong alliance between Túath and Milidh, just as his sister has. While *you* fret over being unable to conceive, *he* fears for your health. Perhaps instead of worrying over the lack of a child, you should find means to strengthen this union."

She flinched at the harshness of his words.

"If you are unable to do such, perhaps it would be best for you to return to your clan. Do not hurt Lord Mahon any further than you already have," Kieran continued bluntly. "Also, Lady Aislinn, it would be best if you do not mistake me for a companion. I have long served the Túath clan of Tara and I will *not* allow any harm to come to it, even by the hands of a frightened child." Giving her a short bow, he turned and left.

Aislinn stood in the rain for a long while, watching as the Túath man walked away until she could no longer see him. Kieran's words not only spoke the truth but also cruelly reminded her that, though the resemblance was strong, he was *not* her brother. His words, spoken cold and hard, held a dangerous air to them; a stern warning that left her a bit shaken.

Her eyes shifted down to the water skin in her hand. Eithne had warned that the herbs were dangerous, yet she had pressed the woman into making it for her despite noticing her obvious unease with it. The truth in Kieran's words filled Aislinn with regret. Hand clenching, she gave the water skin one last look before casting it violently aside. While she acted very much the frightened child, fretting over being unable to conceive, she had neglected what held the most importance: strengthening the alliance.

Taking a deep breath, Aislinn tried to calm the heavy beating of her heart. She could not return to Mahon in such a shaken state, it would only worry him more. Biting her lip, she spun on her heels and walked back down the hill and into the village.

* ~ * ~ * ~ * ~ *

Shiovra watched as Eiladyr circled her. She noticed his eyes remained focused on her face and the stance in which she stood. Her eyes in turn followed his every movement down to even his simplest step. Shiovra's gaze lingered on Eiladyr hand as he flexed it while slowly passing her once more. Stiffening, she shifted her weight slightly to her other foot; she knew what his next move would be.

As Eiladyr came up behind her, Shiovra spun quickly to face him. Grabbing his wrist, she ran her hip into him while seizing his arm with her freehand and flipping him onto his back. Her victory was short-lived, however, as he grabbed her ankle and she subsequently fell roughly to the ground.

"You are getting better," he told her, standing up and running a hand through his hair. "You actually managed to catch me off guard." Grinning, Eiladyr offered her a hand up.

Taking his hand, Shiovra allowed him pull her to her feet before dusting off her clothing.

"Now, if you would like to do that again," he instructed, "you will want to throw your opponent much harder. The desired objective is to knock the wind out of them so they cannot react as I did." He clapped his hands together and began circling her once more. "Again."

Shiovra watched him carefully, her eyes narrowed upon his movement. Each footstep he took was carefully placed and she knew he would not fall for the same trick. Closing her eyes, she slowed her breathing and focused only on what she could hear. She could just barely hear each intake of air he took and listened intently for any change in the pattern. Shiovra could only guess Eiladyr intended to take her off guard just as she had done to him.

Then it came, his breathing changed and his footfalls altered slightly when he was to her left.

Opening her eyes, she turned and took a hasty step back. As she moved to knock his balance off, he ducked and tackled her.

Together they fell roughly to the ground. Shiovra fell on her back and, as she did so, brought her foot up to propel Eiladyr over her head and into the grass behind her. Climbing quickly to her feet, she turned to find him lying sprawled on the ground.

"Better..." he groaned through heavy breaths.

Shiovra cocked her head to the side. "Are you all right?"

"If all wrong is all right..."

Crouching down by his head, Shiovra leaned over him.

Eiladyr looked up at her, arching a brow.

She poked him on the nose with a finger and chided, "I only did as you instructed. I would assume that my attack was adequate, then?"

Chuckling painfully, the man sat up. "Aye, aye, very much so," he told her, standing with a grunt. "I think that will be all for today. Odhrán will have my head if I hurt you while we spar." Eiladyr stretched out his arms and back, but not without a grimace of pain. "I believe a good meal is in order," he said with a grin. "Come, let us find some food."

Shiovra laughed softly and began to follow the man back to the village. Unfortunately, with all the rain Éire had suffered, the ground remained heavily sodden and her foot slipped. She barely managed to catch herself yet her stumble was not without consequence as a sharp pain raced up her leg from her ankle. Hissing in pain, Shiovra dropped down to a knee. It was the same ankle she had injured previously after falling from her horse on her journey to Dún Fiáin.

Eiladyr turned at her hiss and quickly returned to her side. "Shiovra?"

She looked up at him. "My ankle…" she muttered in irritation.

He frowned, crouching down beside her. "Can you stand?"

Placing a hand on his shoulder for support, she tried to stand but the pain was too great and she shook her head. "No, it hurts too much."

"I will carry you then." Eiladyr shifted so that his back faced her. Glancing over his shoulder, he held his arms back toward her and ordered, "Climb on my back."

Without hesitation, Shiovra climbed onto the man's back, trying her best to keep as much weight as possible off her injured ankle. Wrapping her arms around his neck, she leaned against his back.

Eiladyr looped her arms around her legs and, with a grunt, stood and balanced himself. Without another word, he walked through the fields and toward Tara.

As they neared the village, it became apparent that a crowd had gathered at the gates.

"Did something happen while we trained?" asked Eiladyr, shifting her weight. "I heard no sound of warning…"

"I am not sure," she replied, frowning. Indeed, to have nearly the entire village gathered at the gates was unusual. If a guest had arrived, a horn would have been sounded to announce it.

Approaching the commotion, they found Mahon and Aislinn standing at the head of it all.

Shiovra studied her brother and his wife carefully. The Milidh woman sat upon a horse with Meara and Ainnle close at hand, her eyes lowered and focused on her hands as they clenched the reins tightly. Mahon stood not far away from the woman, speaking with Ceallach and Réalta.

"What has happened?" Shiovra asked Odhrán quietly as Eiladyr moved to stand beside the man.

"Aislinn has appealed to be returned to her kin at Traigh Lí for a short time and Mahon has permitted it," explained Odhrán, turning. If he was surprised to their situation, he gave no notice of it, only looked them over in turn before demanding of Eiladyr, "What happened?"

"It is of no fault of his," Shiovra told him, holding her injured foot out. "I slipped and aggravated an old injury to my ankle."

Odhrán took her foot in his hand and looked it over carefully, gently running his fingers over the slightly swollen skin. "Have Kieran tend to it later," he said.

Shiovra nodded. "You can set me down now, Eiladyr."

Without question, Eiladyr carefully crouched down and released her legs.

Taking Odhrán's offered hand, Shiovra balanced against him as she stood, careful to keep weight off her ankle.

Wrapping an arm around her waist, Odhrán brought his mouth to her ear, his voice low as he told her, "Kieran spoke with Aislinn the other day. He offered her a choice: to forget about conceiving and strengthen the alliance, or return to her kin. She has chosen to return home."

Shiovra turning her attention back to Aislinn, looking the Milidh woman over more carefully.

Aislinn sat rigidly upon her horse, her hands gripping the reins so tightly that her knuckles were white. Her face was pale, the skin carrying a sickly undertone to it. The dark circles beneath the woman's eyes spoke of her lack of sleep.

Leaving Ceallach and Réalta, Mahon stepped up to Aislinn and touched her hands.

The woman flinched in return, hesitantly bringing her eyes up to meet Mahon's.

"We shall all await your return," he told the woman gently. "Please give my tidings to your kin and assure them that the alliance holds true." Mahon paused for a moment, staring at the woman before continuing. "Meara and Ainnle shall guard you well. May your journey go without hindrance."

Aislinn nodded, her lips trembling slightly as she tried to smile.

Releasing her hands, Mahon took a step back.

The woman visibly blanched, her hand suddenly moving to rest on her abdomen. It was not pain that crossed her face, but a bout of illness.

Noticeable concern crossed Mahon's face and he grabbed her arm. "You are obviously too unwell to travel, Aislinn," he said in a firm tone. "Returning to your kin can wait for another day."

Aislinn shook her head hastily. "As I told you earlier, I am fine," she reassured him. "I am only uneasy from the lack of rest, nothing more." Tugging her arm free, she nodded to Meara. Giving her steed a swift kick, Aislinn followed the Neimidh woman's lead through the gates, Ainnle taking up the rear.

The woman's actions carried a strong note of familiarity to Shiovra. The paleness, the mood changes, and the brief bout of illness: it all reminded her greatly of Úna. The signs were subtle, easily brushed aside and ignored yet completely apparent.

"Are you so sure Aislinn remains childless?" questioned Shiovra as Ceallach approached. "It would seem to me that she carries Mahon's child within her already."

"Why do you believe so?" asked Ceallach.

She turned to meet his gaze. "I have seen such before while Úna carried Daire's children," replied Shiovra. "Her anxiousness to conceive Mahon's child has blinded her to the fact that she may already carry one within her. I believe that Aislinn should be followed to prevent the possibility of her loosing the child she so desperately sought."

The Fomorii man nodded. "I shall inform Réalta and we shall depart immediately," stated Ceallach, turning to leave.

"Ceallach."

He paused, glancing back at her.

"Allow Aislinn time to reflect on what has been said or done," Shiovra told him. "She must return to Tara of her own accord and prove herself worthy of not only this alliance, but Mahon."

* ~ * ~ * ~ * ~ *

Stepping into the main cottage, Odhrán helped Shiovra to a bench. Once the priestess was situated, he gestured for Kieran to tend to her wound. Leaning against a support post with his arms crossed, he spared Eiladyr a side glance before turning his attention back to Shiovra and Kieran. "I trust her training goes well?" he asked.

"Aye," replied Eiladyr as he moved to stand beside him. "While there is much room for improvement, she is quickly learning tricks of her own. I believe that, should she be faced with an enemy and have no weapon readily at hand, she will be capable of defending herself."

Nodding, Odhrán watched as Kieran lifted the hem of Shiovra's skirts and took hold of her foot, removing her shoe before carefully running his deft fingers over her ankle as he probed the swollen areas. The priestess' flinch did not go unnoticed by Odhrán, his eyes narrowing on the bruise which had already begun to form.

"It would be best if the priestess was not faced with a circumstance similar to that of Cúmhéa again," stated Odhrán in a low voice. "Although the man no longer poses a threat, many more dangers lie ahead."

Eiladyr nodded silently.

"Regardless, I want the careful watch on the village borders maintained. When Kieran finishes with tending the priestess' wounds, I would like you to join him in a patrol of the borders," he continued. "Gráinne is not the only threat Tara faces."

"Aye."

"You will need to keep your ankle bound fairly tight during the day, but not at night. Try to keep off it as much as possible," Kieran instructed the priestess as he reached for a strip of cloth and began wrapping her ankle. "It will heal more quickly that way."

"Aye," replied Shiovra.

Kieran straightened and turned to Odhrán. "If Lady Shiovra takes care, her wound should heal quickly," he said. Looking at Eiladyr, he gestured for the man to follow.

Exhaling, Odhrán sat down beside the priestess. He was silent for a long while as he poked at the hearth fire, stirring the embers. "Morgan has made it clear that he intends to hold his own watch over Tara's borders," said Odhrán after a moment. "In Caher Dearg, I asked of him if he would join us, however he was resolute in maintaining a distance. If we are to have his sword steadily on our side, *you* will have to be the one to sway him." He paused, thinking over how to word it. "From what I have seen, you are more than just a priestess to him, but a woman who greatly holds his interest. Do not deny him what he seeks and he shall come to us. All we will need to do is wait."

Shiovra hesitated a moment and then nodded. "I understand."

Tossing a piece of wood into the fire, Odhrán exhaled and leaned forward to rest his elbows on his knees. From the corner of his eye, he could see the priestess was tense. "Winter will be quiet," he continued. "It will be when warmer winds begin to blow that the threat to Tara will become greater. Till then, be sure to continue your training."

"Aye."

The long, low note of a horn sounded, muffled through the cottage walls and thatch roof.

Frowning, Odhrán rose to his feet and touched Shiovra's shoulder gently. "Stay here," he ordered. Without another word, he flung the cottage door open and stepped out into the cold air.

The horn sounded warning once more, carrying a note of urgency to it. As the gates were opened, a man on horseback rode into the village.

Odhrán waited patiently with a hand resting upon the pommel of his sword. Although the horn had not brought warning of attack upon Tara, the urgency of it did not sit well with him. He watched carefully as the man spoke briefly continuing along the path toward the main cottage. As the horseman neared, Odhrán's eyes narrowed on the face of Bradan, warrior of Dún Fiáin.

Quickly pulling his steed to a halt, the man dismounted and gave a short bow. "My lord, I must speak with you."

Nodding, Odhrán gestured for the man to follow. Slipping into the cottage, he met Shiovra's questioning gaze briefly before turning his attention back to Bradan and demanding, "What happened?"

"Dún Fiáin was attacked by a host of Fomorii," Bradan explained as he circled the fire. "Many villagers were injured and unfortunately one life was lost. The outer wall sustained some severe damage while the gates and several cottages were set on fire."

"How many warriors were injured?" he asked.

"Twelve," replied Bradan.

Odhrán's jaw tensed. Twelve men was a substantial blow to Dún Fiáin's defenses. "What of the Fomorii?" he pressed. "Were there any survivors?"

"Aye," the man answered. "A small band of about twenty survived. They headed eastward, but I cannot be sure they will not turn north."

Odhrán ran a hand through his hair. "Rebuilding the outer wall is of the most importance," he stated, crossing his arms. "Dún Fiáin's defenses cannot remain so greatly weakened while her warriors are injured." Rubbing the back of his neck, he paced beside the fire. He could not risk having warriors that Tara desperately needed return to Dún Fiáin. "I will go."

"As will I." Naal stepped into the cottage, followed by Mahon. "If Dún Fiáin is in need of aid, I would like to lend my assistance."

Nodding, Odhrán glanced at Mahon. "When Eiladyr returns from his rounds, tell him to journey to Ráth Faolchú and see how many men Artis can lend," he ordered. "Kieran is to remain here and continue strict watch over Tara's borders. I would suggest having Caillte join the patrols to prove his worth. We can only hope the Fomorii will not be foolish enough to trespass the village bounds."

"Aye," answered Mahon.

He turned to Shiovra as she rose slowly to her feet. Odhrán regarded her quietly a moment, then said, "Keep a wary eye out," he told her. "Should you feel even the slightest touch of Fomorii power in the air, be sure to have the gates sealed tightly shut and all warriors posted on alert." Stepping closer to the priestess, he reached a hand out and caught a lock of her hair in his hand. "Do not leave this village without proper guard," Odhrán instructed, letting the strands slip through his fingers as he leaned towards her, bring his mouth close to her ear. "Keep my words in mind."

Shiovra nodded silently.

Stepping away from the priestess, he quickly filled his pack and tossed it over his shoulder. "Naal, gather your weapons and ready the horses. We leave immediately."

~~*~*~*

From his perch in the tree, Morgan had a clear view of Tara. After the swift departure of the priestess' Milidh husband, as well as his own brother, Morgan moved his watch closer to the village. In the three days that followed, he noted an increase of guards at Tara's gates as well as more frequent patrols of the borders. More than once he was forced to abandon his position and find a new one as Tara's warriors crossed his path. For the time being, he preferred watching from the shadows, away from the eyes of others.

The snap of a branch drew his attention.

Pressing back against the tree trunk, Morgan readied his bow and waited.

The woods were quiet around him, leaving only the slightest rustle of the wind through fading leaves. The Neimidh man's approach was silent as he came into view, walking slowly through the trees before pausing beneath Morgan's perch.

He had seen the man more than once at the priestess' side and knew him as an ally. Lowering his bow, Morgan returned the arrow to his quiver.

Below, the Neimidh man leaned against the tree and crossed his arms. At first he remained completely still as he looked off toward Tara. "Dún Fiáin suffered an attack by Fomorii," he said abruptly, titling his head back slightly however still not looking up into the tree. "Although their numbers were greatly diminished, we cannot be certain they will not turn their attention upon Tara."

Shifting quietly on the branch, Morgan said nothing in response, only leaned forward and looked down at the man. While he was able to conceal his presence from the village warriors, the Neimidh man had found him quite as easily as the priestess' Milidh husband.

"I trust you will keep a close watch?" questioned the man. "Uphold your promise to Lady Shiovra?"

Amused, Morgan gave a short laugh. "Of course."

"Good." Dropping his arms, the Neimidh man walked away.

Exhaling, Morgan rubbed the back of his neck. He had learned much about Fomorii tricks and strategies while serving Caillte and did not doubt his skill in dealing with them. If they were to try and attack Tara, he would be more than ready for them.

* ~ * ~ * ~ * ~ *

A fortnight's time had passed since Odhrán's departure for Dún Fiáin and dark clouds had begun to gather over Tara. Thrice a day Shiovra would walk to the village gates and stand watch alongside the warriors, her eyes searching each field and hill carefully for unusual movement. Drawing the hood of her cloak up to ward of the chill carried by the wind, she closed her eyes and took a deep breath. The scent of rain hung heavily in the air. Sighing, she opened her eyes. A rainstorm would make their watch far more difficult.

"Do you see anything?"

Shiovra glanced at Mahon as he came to stand beside her. "No," she replied. "All is quiet—for the time being."

"I will be more at ease once Odhrán returns," stated Mahon as he rubbed his wrist restlessly.

She could understand her brother's concerns. Even though Mahon served as Tara's acting chieftain, he was not well suited for the title and, as such, left many decisions involving the village up to Odhrán. "A storm approaches," Shiovra told him. "I fear the rain will be heavy and hinder the warriors watch. We should add men to the walls and bar the gates shut till it passes; a necessary precaution should Fomorii indeed linger close."

Mahon nodded. "Aye."

A movement in the corner of Shiovra's eye caught her attention. Looking closer, she found Kieran rushing after a cloaked figure leading a horse down into the Sloping Trenches.

Mahon brought his hands down hard on the wall. "Who—"

As the cloaked figure disappeared from her sight with Kieran quickly following, an apprehensive feeling filled her. Without another word, Shiovra grabbed the lengths of her skirts and climbed down the ladder.

"Shiovra!" Mahon called after her.

Tearing her sword from its sheath, she hastened through the gates and ran down the path toward the Sloping Trenches. The hood of her cloak fell from her head, but she cared little. It was not long before she heard the sound of angry voices speaking in hushed tones. Slowing her pace, her hand tightened on the hilt of her sword. As Shiovra rounded the path, she found Daire with his horse, bow and quiver in hand.

Kieran blocked Daire's path, a deep frown marring his brow as he spoke in a low, stern tone. Noticing Shiovra's approach, the Neimidh man suddenly fell quiet and met her gaze.

Shiovra watched as Daire stiffened before slowly turning. Her eyes flickered to his bow before returning to his face. There was no doubt in her mind that her cousin was being foolish. Taking a slow breath, she released it and sheathed her sword, asking in an even tone, "Where are you going? Your rounds are not till much later."

He did not answer.

"Shiovra!" Mahon shouted, running up behind her.

She brought her arm up quickly, bringing her brother's approach to an abrupt halt. Eyes narrowing on her Daire, Shiovra took a step closer to him. "I asked you a question, Daire. Where are you going?" Shiovra demanded.

Daire glanced away. "To keep an eye on Caillte."

Dropping her arm, Shiovra's irritation grew. "Leave him be," she told him. "If Caillte is to prove his value as an ally, he must walk Tara's borders and keep watch, just as the other warriors do."

"He is not worth the risk," countered Daire, without meeting her eyes. "I will not be at ease unless I watch him. Move aside."

Kieran took a step forward, hand resting on the pommel of his sword. "Are you going to disregard your priestess' orders?" he questioned coldly.

Daire ignored the Neimidh man, slowly meeting Shiovra's gaze. "Move aside, cousin."

Raising her chin defiantly, Shiovra replied with a simple, yet firm, "No."

Exhaling in exasperation, Daire made to step around her.

Shiovra quickly blocked his path. "Caillte needs to prove his worth. Do not interfere," she told him sternly.

"It is my *duty* to protect this village, even if means following around the likes of Caillte to ensure we remain safe!" snapped Daire. "You may have accepted the promise of his sword, but I have not!"

She rubbed her temples in frustration. "Caillte is of no threat to Tara."

"Can you be so sure, after all that he has done?" scoffed Daire. "It is my duty—"

"Your duty is to *me*," Shiovra hissed.

"Then allow me to do my duty and keep watch on him until he has fully proven he can be trusted!" shouted Daire in return. "Too much has already been risked by welcoming him so easily into the village. It matters not what promises he has offered you. What matters is that Caillte remains a very dangerous man!"

"Cousin or no, Daire, I remain your priestess and you shall abide by my orders," she stated harshly. "Return to the village until the time comes for your rounds."

"I cannot do that, cousin," replied Daire, hand tightening on the reins as he took a step to the side.

Shiovra moved once more to block his path.

Grabbing her arm roughly, Daire pulled her aside.

Wrenching her arm free, Shiovra struck him hard across the face. "Do not *touch* me," she snapped.

Drawing his blade, Kieran pointed the tip at Daire's throat, his voice dangerous when he spoke, "You shall not lay a single harmful finger upon Lady Shiovra. Return to the village, Daire."

Daire's gaze drifted slowly down to the blade as it pressed against his skin before meeting Shiovra's yet again. "I will do as you order."

Kieran nodded his head toward Mahon. "Accompany Lord Mahon back to Tara," he said, hand steady upon the hilt.

Without a further word spoken, Daire turned and walked away, his steed and Mahon following.

"Forgive me, my lady, for turning my blade upon your lord cousin," apologized Kieran, returning his sword to its sheath.

Shiovra shook her head. "No need to seek forgiveness, Kieran," she reassured him as she watched Daire's retreat. "Daire has made many a foolish choice. Sometimes severe actions are the best to make him realize his recklessness." Taking a deep breath, she released it with a frustrated sigh.

"My Lady?" questioned Kieran.

"Aye?"

"Forgive me, but being as there are watchful eyes nearby who can guard you well, might I return to Tara so that I may speak further with Lord Daire?" he asked.

Shiovra did not question the meaning behind Kieran's words, only nodded her consent.

Offering her a small respectful bow, Kieran turned and made his way back toward Tara.

Shiovra remained still for a long while. She knew that Daire worried for her safety foremost, but in order to fully gain Caillte's trust, they needed to give some of their own. She was pulled from her thoughts as something wet and cold fell upon her cheek, quickly followed by another. Tilting her head back, Shiovra realized it had begun to rain and pulled the hood of her cloak up.

"Lovely weather, aye?"

Shiovra turned to find Morgan stepping out from the thicket.

The man grinned mischievously and offered his hand to her. "Shall we go for a walk?"

She had not expected to see the man so soon after what had happened in Caher Dearg. Allowing a small smile to cross her lips, she took his hand and nodded.

* ~ * ~ * ~ * ~ *

The rain grew heavier as Kieran set foot through the village gates. His cloak and garments were thoroughly soaked by the time he reached the main cottage. Nodding to the guards posted, he opened the door and ducked inside. Mahon glanced up as he entered, but Kieran raised his hand and stayed the man's movement. He turned his attention to Daire, who stood beside the fire with his back to him. Kieran quietly stepped up behind him and waited for a moment before saying, "Daire."

As the man turned, Kieran's fist flew up and struck him full in the face.

Daire stumbled back a step, eyes widening with surprise.

"How dare you argue with your priestess' order!" growled Kieran, fist clenched. "It is your duty as a guardian to trust in her decisions."

"It is also my duty to *protect* her!" snapped Daire as he rubbed his jaw, cursing. He spared Mahon a quick glance before turning his attention back to Kieran. "Caillte has well proven in the past what his is capable of. I do not believe he is a risk worth taking. I fear, in the end, that Shiovra will be *hurt*."

Kieran's eyes narrowed in anger. "You just hurt her."

Daire said nothing, only turned back to the fire.

"Words can cut more cruelly than any blade," continued Kieran, crossing his arms. "Your adamant disregard of her orders is alike to thrusting a blade through her back. You essentially told her that you do not trust her decisions as High Priestess. For once, think of the possible consequences before you speak of act!"

"Do you honestly tell me that you trust Caillte completely?" asked Daire without moving.

"He must be allowed to prove himself before I can answer," Kieran told him calmly. "Treaties are forged on the basis that an enemy can prove themselves to be a capable ally. In order for Caillte to prove he is worthy of our trust, we must first place some in him. The same was done with Ceallach in the past and even Odhrán. Both were considered hated enemies, yet both proved themselves capable allies."

Daire remained quiet as he stared into the fire.

Kieran exhaled and admitted, "Do not assume that am pleased with

Caillte's presence within the village. The Fomorii man has done much to warrant my hatred, but if he is indeed the one of whom the Morrigú spoke to Shiovra, then I shall welcome his blade."

A bitter laugh passed Daire's lips. "How can you say that so calmly?" he questioned.

"I am *not* calm, Daire, I am far from it," Kieran explained, voice hard and dangerous. "I am never calm when threats remain close to my priestess. However, there is a terrible storm brewing, Daire. We cannot be sure when the sons of Míl will act and as such, we need to be prepared with every sword we can get. Caillte's knowledge and skill can be put to good use and Shiovra has seen that. She does all within her power to protect Tara, even if it brings risk of danger to herself." He ran his hands through his damp hair in frustration. "You should apologize to Shiovra."

"I agree with Kieran," added Mahon, rising from the table. "While I take no pleasure from the thought of calling Caillte and ally, we need every sword we can get."

Rubbing his bruising jaw, Daire glanced between the men before muttering a dejected, "Aye."

13. FROZEN FIRE

Dusting his hands off, Odhrán crossed his arms and looked up at the stone wall surrounding Dún Fiáin. The outer wall had suffered sufficient damage and repairs were nearly completed. He had wanted to return to Tara before the coming of Samhain, but he feared it would be well after the fall equinox before he deemed the repairs on Dún Fiáin adequate enough.

Beside him, Eiladyr sat down as stack of stones and rubbed his back with a groan. Giving he wall a brief glance, he turned to Odhrán. "This is the last of them," he said. "Bradan said he will send men to the river come morning to search for some more."

Odhrán nodded. "This will do for now," he replied, grabbing a leather tie from his belt pouch and pulling his hair back. "Once Dún Fiáin's wall has returned to its former strength, then we can rest easier." Bending, he grabbed one of the stones and worked it into a gap in the wall. Placing his hands against the stone, he focused upon it, melding energies together and tightening the bond between the rocks. Exhaling, he repeated the process on a stone Eiladyr had placed. Using his abilities as the earth guardian was tiring, but necessary in protecting his village.

Naal approached and handed him a water skin. "The evening meal is nearly completed," he stated. "You should rest."

Stretching his back, Odhrán shook his head. "Not until the gates are completed," he said after taking a long drink of water. "The repairs are nearly done. By nightfall we should be able to seal them shut. I will rest then." Glancing at Eiladyr, he continued, "Tell Bradan to join me by the gates then eat and rest."

"Aye," replied Eiladyr with a nod.

As the men walked away, Odhrán made his way slowly along the village wall. He had used his power to strengthen many parts of the village wall. Once the gates were secure, he would focus his attention on strengthening the rest of it. Only then would he return to Tara.

* ~ * ~ * ~ * ~ *

Shiovra woke to her name gently being called. She remained still for a moment, listening to the soft pattering of rain upon leaves overhead. She had remembered taking shelter beneath a thick cluster of trees when the rains became far too great to return to Tara, yet after that, she could not remember much. Opening her eyes, she found she lay within Morgan's arms as he leaned against a tree. Shifting in his hold, Shiovra pressed her ear closer to his chest and listened to the steady rhythm of his heartbeat. She felt his arms tighten around her.

"We should not tarry long," he told her in a low voice. "Morning has come upon us and though I am quite enjoying the moment, I fear your kin and guardians may differ."

Sitting up, she met his gaze and said, "I thank you for watching over me, Morgan."

A playful grin crossed his lips. "Have I not told you before that my place is by your side?" Morgan questioned before pausing for a moment, his eyes drifting slowly over her face. "May I touch you?"

Shiovra did not hesitate to nod.

Reaching his hand up, Morgan tucked a lock of her damp hair behind her ear before moving his fingers to her face, tracing the blue woad spiral curling beside her eye.

He had done such once before, following the lines marking her skin. She watched his face carefully as his focus remained completely on his ministrations. However, when her lips parted and his gaze quickly shifted to them, Shiovra was reminded of Odhrán's words: *You are more than a priestess to him, but a woman who greatly holds his interest. Do not deny him what he seeks and he will come to us.* As Morgan brought his fingers to her lips, caressing the soft skin, the hidden meaning behind Odhrán's words came to light.

Shiovra fell completely still, her heart quickening. She had never before been touched so gently by another man other than her husband. The feeling of Morgan's fingers across her skin filled was like a path of fire that filled her body with a surge of warmth.

Morgan's fingers slipped beneath her chin, tilting her head up slightly.

Her eyes drifted shut as he leaned closer and placed a gentle kiss upon her lips, lingering. A moment of disappointment filled her, however, when Morgan pulled away. Opening her eyes, Shiovra met his gaze with slight hesitation, unsure of how to react.

Morgan offered her a small grin. "Your face is red," he told her with a slight chuckle.

Although his comment was lighthearted, Shiovra noticed he rubbed the back of his neck in a nervous manner and looked away. She watched him as he rose to his feet, checking to make sure his sword was secure, before offering his hand. Accepting it, Shiovra allowed Morgan to pull her to her feet. She wanted to say something, but words would not come.

"Lady Shiovra."

Following the voice, she found Kieran approaching them.

"Forgive me for before," apologized the Neimidh man, "but I could not ignore Daire's blatant disregard of your orders. Although I trust Morgan's capabilities in protecting you, I believe it would be best to return to the village, my lady. To have been outside the protection of Tara's walls all night has left Lord Mahon a bit…apprehensive…to say the least."

Shiovra glanced at Morgan.

He nodded for her to go with Kieran. "Now is not the time for me to enter Tara," he told her with a grin. "We shall meet again, Shiovra, you can be assured."

She watched as he turned and disappeared around a hill, her hands clenching the folds of her skirts.

"My lady?"

Kieran's voice startled her and she turned sharply.

"We should return to the village," he stated.

Nodding silently, she followed the Neimidh man from the Sloping Trenches, Odhrán's words and Morgan's kiss lingering in her thoughts.

* ~ * ~ * ~ * ~ *

The coming of early morning brought a thick, heavy frost to coat the ground with a glistening sheen while a bitter wind swirled a milky fog about. Crowded around the morning fire, a small group of travelers ate their meal. Each breath taken puffed out before them, mingling with the fog. From his place beside the fire, Odhrán watched carefully as the horses snorted and pawed anxiously at the hard, frozen earth.

Reaching into his pack, he pulled out his water skin, only to find it frozen solid. Such extreme cold was highly unusual for Éire, even with the steady approach of midwinter, and Odhrán had the irking feeling that perhaps Fomorii were playing part. Tossing the water skin back into his pack, he skimmed over the woods surrounding them. The intense fog made it greatly difficult to discern any movement. Enemies could easily surround them and they would not be the wiser. With Artis' men having returned to Ráth Faolchú, it was but Eiladyr, Naal, and him.

Rising abruptly to his feet, Odhrán ordered, "Pack up, we move out." Hearing no protests, he quickly smothered their camp fire with dirt.

The steeds were quickly prepared and everything gathered up, leaving hardly a trace of their camp.

Without a single word spoken, Odhrán climbed upon his horse and gave it a swift kick, starting off in a steady canter. He knew if they kept pace, they would be able to reach the outskirts of the village but a little past midday.

As they neared the river, however, Odhrán noticed thick black smoke rising above the trees to the west, stretching in a long line. Jaw tensing, a deep frown crossed his face. From the concentration and darkness, it was no campfire smoke they say, but something that offered a threatening feeling.

Holding his reins tight, Odhrán gave his steed a swift kick and headed off quickly toward the smoke. Leaning forward on his horse, he urged it into a gallop, weaving around trees and ducking away from branches. Breaking through the lines of trees, he abruptly jerked on the reins, brining his steed to a halt.

Before him, the entire river, as far as he could see, burned with great intensity.

Eiladyr and Naal were quick to join him

"What the—!" began Eiladyr, voice trailing off as he tried to calm his panic stricken steed.

The wave of heat coming from the river kept them from getting too close.

Odhrán turned to Naal. "Ride off that way and see how far it reaches," he ordered. "Eiladyr, you take the other direction."

The men nodded and rode off without question.

Dismounting, Odhrán grabbed the largest rock he could find and neared the river as close as he dared before hurling the rock at the fire. It landed with a resounding thud. His frown deepened. It would seem that the river remained somehow frozen beneath the consuming fire. Grabbing another rock, he repeated the process only to garner a fierce cracking sound which filled the air.

The attacks had caused the melting ice to crack and fairly soon after the hissing of flames being quenched could be heard, rising in intensity. Yet the fire had become too high to become altogether extinguished and continued to rage fiercely. The ice groaned in defeat, collapsing into the frigid waters and taking the fire with it.

Odhrán stepped up to the edge of the river, watching charred branches bobbing alongside ice in the churning water. Although Fomorii were the first to come to mind, he was nearly certain he knew who truly lay behind it; a thought which by no means sat well with him.

After some time, Eiladyr's shout reached his ears.

"Odhrán!"

"How far?" questioned Odhrán without turning.

The man pulled his horse to an abrupt halt and replied, "It appears to follow the river all the way to Tara."

Odhrán's jaw tensed.

Not long after, Naal came galloping around the bend and stopped beside Eiladyr. "I believe it may reach beyond the Boyne, perhaps even to the sea," he told Odhrán breathlessly.

"Fomorii?" asked Eiladyr.

Odhrán shook his head. "No, this is beyond their abilities," he told them, crossing his arms as his eyes narrowed on the waters. "It has to be Amhergin, son of Míl. This part river is a branch off the Boyne. These waters not only flow past Tara but Brú na Bóinne as well. This is a warning to the High Chieftains: a warning of war." Turning away from the river, Odhrán mounted his steed. "We return to Tara with haste."

~~*~*~*

The quiet peacefulness which Tara had come to enjoy was quickly shattered by the sight of heavy black smoke in the distance. Battle horns sounded warning and as a precaution, the village gates were pulled shut and barred. As midday drew near, Shiovra took her place on Tara's wall, despite the protests voiced by her brother and cousin. She stared at the smoke for a long while, watching as it shifted in the wind. From her vantage point, it appeared to stretch far, as if it followed the river.

"The river burns with frozen fire," she said in thought, rubbing her arms in a futile attempt to ward off the cold which seeped through her clothing. "Fomorii?"

"No," came Caillte's deep voice from her left. "That is not of Fomorii creation."

Resting her hands on the edge of the wall, Shiovra tensed. The more she watched the smoke, the more an unsettling feeling crept through her. However, of one thing she was absolutely clear. "A warning."

Caillte nodded in agreement. "Aye," replied the man. "It would appear that way. The question is, for whom?"

Shiovra thought a moment. While the smoke from the fires could clearly be seen from Tara, she had a feeling the warning was not meant for them, at least not entirely. The words fell from her lips before she even realized she was speaking. "The High Chieftains."

The Fomorii man glanced at her.

"The river Boyne stretches far, reaching beyond even Brú na Bóinne where the High Chieftains currently reside," explained Shiovra. "This warning, more than us, is meant for *them*." Her fists clenched on the wall as anger mounted within her.

The sudden call of a bird filled the air, loud and clear. It was quickly followed by another, slightly different one from behind her.

Glancing over her shoulder, she found Kieran lowering his hand from his lips. Shiovra had heard similar whistles before, when Odhrán and Eiladyr would signal to one another. Swiftly turning back to the fields, she searched the hills carefully for any movement. At first she saw nothing, but as another bird call reached her ears, three men on horseback rode into view.

"Open the gates!" she shouted as she rushed to the ladder, Kieran and Caillte following closely behind. Climbing down, Shiovra stood along the path and waited.

Odhrán was the first to dismount, handing his steed's reins off to one the village guards. "Tend to the horses and bring our packs later," he ordered. Without waiting for the man to respond, he turned to Shiovra. "Where is Mahon?"

"In the main cottage," she replied.

Nodding, he took her hand firmly within his own and pulled her along with him as he made his way along the path.

"You have seen the smoke?" His question was hardly above a whisper.

"Aye." Shiovra glanced at Odhrán from the corner of her eye as they walked along. His jaw was tense and his eyes were focused solely on the main cottage. "A warning of frozen fire."

"Indeed," he replied, his hand tightening upon hers.

Cresting the hill, the guards posted nodded to them before stepping aside and allowing passage.

Entering the cottage, Shiovra found that brother sat with Earnán and Daire at the table, enjoying a meal. Nodding to them, she took a seat on a bench beside the fire before turning her attention back to Odhrán.

"You have returned," Mahon said, rising to his feet. The smile faded from his lips as he looked Odhrán, Eiladyr, and Naal over. "Is all well in Dún Fiáin?"

The concerned tone to Mahon's voice did not go unnoticed by Shiovra.

"Repairs have been made," stated Odhrán, removing his cloak and setting it aside. "However, that is of little importance. From what we could see, fires have been built all along the river Boyne and her branches."

Mahon nodded and admitted, "We have seen the smoke, although we have been unsure of the cause."

"It is a warning to the High Chieftains," explained Odhrán. He brought his left hand and pushed his sleeve down, revealing the blue woad marking his wrist. "Long have I served as a druid for the sake of my village and people. By acting as council to the sons of Míl, I was privy to knowledge otherwise unobtainable. There is but one man with the capability of such: Amhergin, son of Míl. While I am sure word has already reached Brú na Bóinne, I believe the High Chieftains should be informed that the fire have reached down this far," continued Odhrán. "More than that, they should be made aware of recent Fomorii attacks."

"Allow me to go," suggested Kieran from his position near the door. "It is important that they also learn of Gráinne's betrayal as well as Caillte's promise of alliance."

Odhrán thought a moment and then nodded. "Aye."

"I shall depart in a few days then, as soon as I am assured that Tara remains safe from attack," stated the Neimidh man.

Removing his sword, Odhrán sat down beside Shiovra. "It would be best if we spend these cold moths preparing for war," he said. "Tara is no longer safe."

* ~ * ~ * ~ * ~ *

The first graying of dawn began to tinge the sky as Kieran secured his pack to the horse. He carefully checked the straps, making sure they were secure. His journey to Brú na Bóinne would take him but a few days if he pressed his steed hard. Nonetheless, he fully intended on keeping close watch over the river along his way to the High Chieftains.

"Leaving?"

Nodding, Kieran turned to face Odhrán. "I have lingered long enough," he said. "Between Gráinne's betrayal, the recent Fomorii attack upon Dún Fiáin, and the fires on the Boyne, I fear Tara will not remain safe much longer."

The Milidh man nodded, crossing his arms. "Keep a watchful eye out," Odhrán told him. "We have many enemies now."

"Is that any different from before?" Kieran asked with a lighthearted chuckle. Exhaling, he watched his breath in the cold, morning air. "I shall take my leave for Brú na Bóinne now," he continued, pulling the hood of his cloak up as he climbed astride his horse. "Keep an eye on Daire. He has been rather *disobedient* of his priestess' orders of late."

Odhrán raised a brow. "Disobedient?"

"Aye," replied Kieran. "Merry part until we meet again." Giving his steed a swift kick, he rode through the gates and away from Tara.

* ~ * ~ * ~ * ~ *

Shiovra cursed under her breath when Eiladyr blocked her attack and shifted his stance, swinging his arm at her. Dodging, she stepped back quickly. She could feel his eyes following her every movement. Shiovra hesitated in her defense, unsure of what tactic the man possibly considered employing. However, as her guard was lowered, Eiladyr rushed forward suddenly.

At the last moment he crouched down and kicked his foot out, knocking her legs out from beneath her.

Taken by surprise, Shiovra fell roughly to the ground.

He laughed heartily as he looked down at her. "You need to focus more," he told her. "While knowing the enemies tactics may come in handy, once in a while it is good to improvise."

She remained still upon the cold, hard ground as she looked up at the cloud filled sky. "That was a cheap shot," Shiovra told him.

Eiladyr chuckled harder, scolding, "Nothing in fair in battle."

"Aye, you are entirely correct." Bringing her arms up quickly, she wrapped them around his ankles and brought her feet up to kick him in the abdomen. Shiovra's attack proved effective as he topped and fell back into the grass.

He landed with a grunt that was quickly followed by a string of curses in his native language. "Better..." he muttered.

Allowing a smirk to cross her lips, Shiovra moved to sit beside him.

Eiladyr put his hands behind his head. "You need to keep focused on what you are doing and not let your enemies movements distract you," he instructed. "There may come a time when a cunning trick such as that just may save your life. Also, never look where you plan to attack, it gives your enemy enough warning to avoid your attack or deflect it."

Shiovra nodded and fell quiet for a moment, pulling her knees to her chest as she listened to the creaking of the trees in the wind. The winter months were drawing steadily closer.

Her gaze shifted to Eiladyr. The man greatly resembled his brother in looks and their personalities were similar. Thinking for a moment, Shiovra asked, "What was your life like before you came to Éire?"

He did not answer at first, his eyes remaining on the sky. "I am the youngest of five sons," replied Eiladyr. "My father was the chieftain of a small village and my mother—well she was a kind and gentle woman. Being the youngest, I did not have much in the manner of authority or wealth. As much as I hated being called that man's son, I could not turn my back on my mother. Nearly four years ago no she died of an illness. With her gone, I no longer had any reason to stay." A short laugh passed his lips. "I never thought Morgan would follow me here."

A blush unconsciously rose to Shiovra cheeks and she hastily pushed aside the memory of Morgan's lips upon hers.

Eiladyr sat up abruptly, cocking his head to the side as a frown crossed his face. "Do you hear that?" he whispered.

Listening carefully she heard it: shouts in the distance mingled with the undeniable clash of weapons which came from the Sloping Trenches. It was then that she felt it, an all too familiar lingering chill that crept through her body. She knew all too well what lurked within the trenches.

The man stood swiftly and retrieved his sword from its resting place in the grass. "Return to Tara," he ordered, drawing his blade.

"No." Standing quickly, Shiovra shook her head and turned to retrieve her bow and quiver.

Eiladyr exhaled in frustration and grabbed her arm. "Shiovra—"

"Warnings have not been sounded, which means none of the warriors have been alerted of this threat, nor are they in it," she said, tugging her arm free. "I will not allow Fomorii to sneak upon Tara's grounds." Turning away from him, she grabbed her bow and quiver before making her way toward the Sloping Trenches.

Eiladyr seized her arm once more. "Fomorii?!"

Shiovra's gaze snapped to meet his.

Even though the man said nothing more, his eyes pleaded silently with her.

"Either help me or leave me be," she commanded coldly, freeing herself from his grasp once more. Gathering up her skirts, she ran down the path and into the Sloping Trenches. As Shiovra made to break through the thick brush, she paused and quickly crouched down.

Caillte was surrounded by a group of misshapen Fomorii. The creatures appeared to have the advantage as a large, bloody gash was visible on Caillte's back. Despite his wound and heavy, ragged breathing, the man held his sword steady as he blocked each attack thrown at him.

A hand came down firmly on Shiovra's shoulder.

"We cannot take them alone," Eiladyr whispered in her ear.

"No, but we can *upset* them long enough to retrieve Caillte," she told him quietly.

He hesitated and then nodded.

Stringing her bow, Shiovra pulled an arrow from her quiver. Finding a Fomorii with a spear in hand, she aimed her arrow at it before glancing at Eiladyr.

The man brought a hand up, one finger raised as he signaled for her to hold position. Taking careful steps, he began to make a wide arch around the battle, creeping his way to the back. Shifting his hold upon his sword, Eiladyr gestured toward her left.

Frowning, she followed his signal and found Morgan creeping up behind the Fomorii from the other side, blade drawn and ready. Looking back at Eiladyr, he nodded. Checking her aim, she knocked the arrow free and it landed soundly within the arm of the creature, forcing it to drop the spear.

Hissing in rage, the misshapen Fomorii turned its attention to her hiding place.

Shiovra moved back as the pale eyes searched the brush she hid within.

Shouting, Eiladyr burst into the open and lunged at another creature, Morgan quickly following to flank. "Take him and go!" Eiladyr shouted without looking her way as he dodged an attack whilst throwing one of his own.

The long, low note of a battle horn sounded suddenly. The attack had been noticed by Tara's warriors.

Readying another arrow, Shiovra slipped out from her cover and slowly approached Caillte. Her eyes never left the Fomorii, taking caution not to draw their attention while Eiladyr and Morgan served as a distraction. "Come," she said in a low voice, returning her arrow to the quiver. Grabbing the man's arm, she slung it over her shoulder.

Caillte made no word of protest as she led him away from the battle, his hand still tightly gripping his sword.

It was not long before several warriors rushed past them and into the Sloping Trenches with weapons ready. Odhrán quickly followed the men, pausing beside Shiovra to take Caillte from her.

"Where you injured in any way?" questioned the Milidh man in an urgent tone as he led them into the village and toward the main cottage.

"No," Shiovra replied. "I am fine."

As they neared the cottage, the men posted hastily opened the door and stepped aside.

Once inside, Shiovra gestured one of the benches. "Sit him there and remove his tunic," she ordered before turning to a table along the far wall.

"What happened?" asked Mahon in concern.

Without looking at her brother, Shiovra replied, "Misshapen Fomorii attack, but they are being dealt with." Searching over the numerous clay jars and herbs, she looked for the ones needed for such a great wound. Glancing over her shoulder, she found Daire staring in stunned silence. "Daire, pour me a bowl of water and grab all the clean bandages you can find."

Nodding, her cousin did as told.

Gathering what she needed, Shiovra returned to Caillte's side.

The Fomorii man sat slumped over on the bench, his sword lying on the ground by his feet. His breathing remained ragged, almost as if breathing itself was cumbersome.

As soon as Daire sat the basin of water down, she took a piece of cloth and began cleaning the blood from the wound. The sheer amount of blood left Shiovra wondering if the obvious gash on his back was his only wound. Rinsing the cloth off, she continued the tedious task of removing all the blood before finally finding the full extent of his injury.

A deep frown crossed her brow as the more blood she removed the more an old scar became apparent, running parallel beside the fresh one.

The scar was long, stretching across his back and marring his pale skin.

Shiovra paused a moment to run her fingers along the raised, poorly healed wound. "There is such sadness and anger behind this," she stated quietly.

Caillte remained silent for a long moment, staring down at blood covered hands that continued to remain steady despite the trembling of the rest of his body. "It is because of that wound that I was unable to protect her," he said after a long while, voice laden heavily with grief. "Because of it I had to watch her die before my very eyes. Now it serves as a reminder of my failure."

"And now you will surely have another," she told him as she dipped her fingers into a jar and began rubbing an ointment into his wound.

His reply was simple and blunt. "I am weak when attacked from behind."

Shiovra made to speak again yet another, deep voice drew her attention.

"Is that what happened with Saibh?"

Glancing over her shoulder, she found Ceallach Neáll stepping out from the shadows near the table where Mahon and Earnán sat. She had not even seen the man when they had entered the cottage. His arrival must have come during her training with Eiladyr.

Ceallach moved to stand in front of his brother. "Is it?"

"I never saw the attack coming," admitted Caillte. "She was smiling at me only a moment before I saw the man behind her, only a moment before I helplessly watched the sword pierce her heart." The man hesitated, his hands clenching. "I reached out for her as her smile began to fade, only the have a sword taken to my back," he continued. "I tried to take my vengeance, nevertheless wounded as I was and being outnumbered, I nearly lost my own life. I never questioned why Ailill was there, or how he managed to fend off my attacks. And for that, I failed not only Saibh, but you as well."

Shiovra remained silent as she finished applying the ointment and began wrapping the wound.

Ceallach merely looked down at his brother with arms crossed. "Is that the truth to what happened?" he questioned.

As Caillte's body stiffened beneath her fingers, Shiovra hesitated.

"Aye," came the man's simple reply.

Ceallach watched his brother with a narrowed gaze.

"What more do you want?" asked Caillte impatiently. "Shall I fall to my knees and beg forgiveness for failing our sister? Shall I throw myself upon my own blade, or would you prefer to strike me down yourself? Tell me what to do so I can stop suffering!"

Ceallach dropped his arms and turned away. "Nothing," he answered in a hard tone. "You have suffered enough."

Standing, Shiovra cleaned her hands off and said, "Ceallach."

He glanced at her.

"The past is what makes us who we are," she continued, her gaze drifting back to Caillte. "At times it can be painful, far more for some than others. In facing our past, facing the anguish, we prove ourselves to be better." Walking around Caillte, she touched Ceallach's arm. "This is a man who has suffered far greater than anyone. Saibh's death and the blood staining his hands will haunt him till the end of his days. Allow him some relief from the torment by offering your trust."

Ceallach remained silent and merely nodded.

The cottage door opened suddenly and a raven hair woman with flushed cheeks stepped inside.

Shiovra's hand dropped from the Fomorii man's arms as her eyes met those of a familiar face. "Aislinn."

14. TRANQUIL MOMENTS

Winter came upon Tara quietly as heavy clouds began to linger in the sky, bringing on crisp, frosty mornings. The thick smoke of warm hearth fires rose from the circular cottages. When the first light dusting of snow graced the ground, giggling children ran outside to play in it. With the Fomorii attack quelled and Caillte's wound healing, a small sense of security had returned to the village. The whispers of the frozen fire and the warning in which it brought were, for a time, forgotten as the midwinter celebrations were planned.

Tensions between Ceallach and Caillte were slowly beginning to ease. After helping fend off the Fomorii attack, Morgan returned to his watch of Tara's borders, maintaining some distance between him and Shiovra. Mahon, relieved to have his wife back, became both anxious and excited about the child Aislinn carried. Daire and Eithne became steadfast companions while the woman continued to care for his children just as Úna would have.

Smiling at her family, Shiovra wrapped a warm cloak around her shoulders and stepped out into the cold. Although a new year was coming upon them, it did little to ease her own fears. She knew the wheel of time was turning and that war was eminent, the frozen fire was warning enough. False pretenses of peace were already beginning to crumble. All that remained was to wait for the Milidh to make their next move.

A crow called out suddenly, dipping down to circle Shiovra before disappearing behind the cottage. Glancing at the men guarding the door, she ducked around the cottage to find a woman waiting for her with pale skin and a cloak of black feathers.

The woman's clothing was a deep hue of crimson. Her long ebony hair was embellished with thin braids and feathers while an intricate blue woad design ran from her right temple and down to her jawbone.

"Macha of the Morrigú," Shiovra said.

Macha nodded, slowly walking further away from the cottage. Her feathered cloak shifted in the wind, like great wings.

Following, Shiovra asked, "What tidings do you bring?"

"Míl seeks blood in payment for Ith's life," replied the woman. "It was as you said many moons ago: pleasant smiles hide hidden daggers. The oncoming storm gathers immense strength. When the cold breaks, the battle for control of Éire will begin."

Her words did not come as a surprise to Shiovra; she could see as much easily. Nevertheless, there was one questioned she wanted answered. "I have done all I can to protect Tara," she told Macha, taking a step forward. "I welcomed enemies as allies. I risked my own life more than once. Yet nightmares of Tara's fall continue to linger. Has our time in Éire, the time of the Túath clan, come to an end?"

Macha said nothing at first, standing with her back to Shiovra. "I am unable to say," she replied simply. Turning, her feather cloak swirled with the movement and her body shifted till it became that of a crow. Circling Shiovra, Macha's voice spoke in the priestess' mind. *"Be prepared."*

Shiovra watched as the crow disappeared over the village wall. She remained there for a long while. She would continue to do everything within her power to protect Tara and her people. However, if the Milidh were meant to reign, she would only be able to stall the inevitable, not stop it. Sighing, she tilted her head back and looked up.

Snowflakes began to lightly fall from the sky to dance upon the breeze.

She knew she would not be alone when the time of battle came. Turning, Shiovra found Odhrán standing near the cottage waiting for her. Pulling the hood of her cloak up, she smiled lightly and walked toward him. Together they would all face a battle which would deem the fate of Éire. Together they would survive.

Pronunciation Guide

Ailill: *all-yill*
Ainmire: *AE-NMih-r*
Aislinn: *ash-lin*
Artis: *AR-tis*
Caher Dearg: *KAW-heer JAR-ug*
Caillte: *Cahl-tyih*
Caoilin: *KEE-lin*
Ceallach Neáll: *KELL-ach nye-al*
Culann: *KOO-lun*
Cúmhéa: *kovay*
Daire: *di-re*
Deasún: *DYA-soon*
Dubheasa: *duv-essa*
Dún Fiáin: *dun fee-aw-in*
Dún Scáth: *dun skaw*
Éire: *air'a (Ireland)*
Fir Bolg: *fir bull-ug*
Fomorii: *foe-vor-ee*
Gráinne: *graw-nya*
Kieran: *KEE-ran*
Mahon: *ma-hoon*
Meara: *meer-a*
Méav: *may-v*
Milidh: *mile-iv*
Neimidh: *nev-eh*
Odhrán: *oh-ran*
Ráth Duibh: *rath DUV*
Ráth Faolchú: *rath FWEEL-khoo*
Réalta Dubh: *RALE-tah DUV*
Shiovra Ni Coughlin: *SHE-vra Nee Cough-lin*
Tara: *tEH-ruh*
Tréigthe: *trayk-huh*
Túath: *too-ha*
Túatha Dé Danann: *too-ha day dahnon*
Úna: *OO-na*

Melissa Sasina

Coming Soon:

An all new short story by

Melissa Sasina

Follow Melissa on Facebook

for release dates and more!

ABOUT THE AUTHOR

Born in 1982 in Cleveland, Ohio, Melissa has always been an avid lover of fantasy. In her youth she would write short stories and add artwork to them. While in high school, she decided to change her career path from graphic art to writing, though she still enjoys drawing up a random picture or two, usually of her characters. During her younger school years, she won a Young Authors Honorable Mention for a short story she had written. She has also won a few Visual Arts awards during her school years and upon graduation from High School, she was given a President's award for Outstanding Academic Achievement.

The first book she began to write seriously for publication was *The Priestess*. Completed in 2008, the book was separated into a trilogy and published in 2010. After undergoing reediting, it was re-released as both the individual books and as a one book collection, *The Priestess: A Complete Collection*.

Her current book series is *The Chronicles of Midgard*, which will be a five book collection once completed.

Made in the USA
Charleston, SC
05 June 2015